I0549318

Black Dog Magic

Book Three of
IT ALL STARTED WITH A DOG

By

Leigh Somerville

Perseverance Books
Published by Indigo Sea Press
Winston-Salem

Perseverance Books
Indigo Sea Press
302 Ricks Drive
Winston-Salem, NC 27103

First Perseverance Books edition published
January, 2016
Perseverance Books, Moon Sailor and all production design are trademarks of Indigo Sea Press, used under license.

For information regarding bulk purchases of this book, digital purchase and special discounts, please contact the publisher at
indigoseapress.com

Cover design by Stacy Castanedo

Manufactured in the United States of America
ISBN 978-1-63066-336-0

This book is dedicated to Mercy,
the little black dog who started it all.

Chapter One

Belle clutched Rachel's bridal bouquet to her heart like a drowning woman latches on to a life preserver. She buried her nose in the white roses, inhaled the perfume and sighed from her belly—deep, long and loud.

"That must have felt good," George whispered in her ear. The wiry whiskers on his chin tickled the tenderness of her neck. She giggled as she watched her daughter run from the stairs where the women had waited for the bride to toss the flowers.

Mary's lower lip stuck out. "No flowers," the child pouted and stamped her feet, one after the other. Her little black patent leather shoes beat out a staccato temper tantrum George had never heard before.

"It's her nap time," Belle explained. "She's tired and all wound up from the excitement."

George knelt beside Mary and reached out to smooth a loose curl from one eye. His finger came back wet with hot tears. "I bet your Mommy will share those nice flowers with you," he said. "You've been such a pretty little flower girl. Don't go ruining your beautiful dress with those soggy old tears."

Mary looked down at the frilly blue taffeta skirt that stuck out around her, propped up with two stiff petticoats. She had insisted on two—one pink and one purple. The effect had been a magic rainbow of color as she walked down the steps in front of the bride.

The small group of friends gathered in the living room to witness Rachel's long-awaited wedding to John Turner had tittered with delight as they watched the little girl carefully descend the stairs.

Ben, John's grandson, dressed in a tiny tuxedo, marched stoically behind her like a soldier going off to battle.

And behind them, the show-stopper—Rachel, an old-fashioned bride in her grandmother's wedding dress. The satin, lovingly restored to its original pure ivory, glowed in the soft light of the chandelier. Beside her, Ralph pranced proudly, wearing the blue ribbon Ben had recently won in a spelling bee.

The small procession paraded to the fireplace where the groom waited. A smile erased all the wrinkles that had creased his brow during Ben's hospital visit a few weeks before. John's face lit up as he forgot the meningitis scare and beheld the only reality in his life at the moment. His bride. His family. His friends.

George and Belle looked at the newlyweds surrounded by so much love and then turned their eyes to each other. George spoke first and broke the spell. "The saying goes that the lucky lady who catches the bride's bouquet is the next one to get married."

"Do you believe that?" Belle whispered.

George stood silently for a few minutes and then reached over for another peck on Belle's cheek. "I sure do. Question is, who will the lucky man be?"

Belle ducked her head, thoughts of Ricky as he battled his addiction in a treatment center competed with memories of the peace she had found on the farm with George. "I think right now I'd better get this little lady downstairs for a nap," she said.

"Want me to go down with you?"

"No. You stay here and enjoy the party. I'm sure Rachel wouldn't want you to miss out on all the fun. You've been such a big help."

For the most the morning, George set up folding chairs and helped the florist and caterer haul their deliveries into the house.

"George! George!" Mary squealed as she threw her arms around his knees and almost knocked him off-balance.

"Hey, there, little one. Don't forget you're tackling a one-legged

2

cowboy here. Careful you don't land us both on the floor and ruin your pretty wedding dress."

Mary let go of her death grip and smoothed out her petticoats. She looked up at her mother and smiled. "George nap," she pronounced with a huge grin.

"Guess somebody wants me downstairs," George said as he took Mary's hand and led the way through the crowd toward Belle's basement apartment.

"I'll tell Rachel we're leaving and be right with you," Belle called after him. As she passed through the folding chairs to the dining room where the wedding party gathered, she noticed a single rose perched in a crystal vase near the front door. A florist's card sat propped on a plastic stick, the writing exposed. Belle stooped to read the message. Her breath caught at the familiar scrawl.

"Best wishes on your wedding day. Thanks for what you're doing for my family. Ricky."

Tears filled Belle's eyes as she leaned over to smell the rose, a perfect yellow that stood out like a beacon among all the masses of pink and white petals Susan chose to decorate the house. Belle stood for a moment and thought of Ricky and all they had been through since the day they met under a cloudless blue sky at the Washington Monument. She had gone to the hill to fly a kite. He sat in the shade of a tree and strummed a guitar. Both young. Both vulnerable to love on a sunny day.

Neither felt the cares of the world. Neither knew the horrors that lay ahead of them along the path of addiction. A path that led to Belle's pregnancy and Ricky's music career. A path that ended with them living on the streets.

A path that one day merged with the path on which Rachel Springer walked.

The two women—one young and down on her luck and the other a seasoned lawyer wise to the ways of the world—found an unlikely friendship together. Against the advice of well-meaning neighbors, Rachel offered John's vacated apartment to Belle and Mary. In that basement, the mother and her child found healing.

As she thought of Rachel's kindness, Belle felt tears begin to spill onto her cheeks. As she reached up to wipe them, she felt a warm tongue lick her fingers. "It all started with a dog, didn't it," she whispered to the animal at her feet. "Come on, Ralph, let's go check on the bride. She may need you. If not, I sure do."

* * *

Downstairs, George held Mary on his lap. He rocked in the old wooden chair Belle rescued from the street, discarded by a neighbor who failed to see the magic in rocking. Mary's little body quickly grew limp in the arms of the man she fell in love with at first sight.

If only her mother were this trusting, George thought. His own tension released as he responded to the soft breathing and warm little body nestled in his arms. Mary slept soundly, oblivious to the happy sounds that drifted down from upstairs. Ah, the sleep of the innocent, George mused. If I could only keep her this way. Safe from all the monsters under the bed.

George faced his own monsters in Vietnam. In that faraway war-torn country, photography offered some small protection. He hid behind the camera lens and focused on the inward lives of the victims of war rather than the damage the war did to his own soul. Years later, on a farm in Virginia, he began to heal as he turned the camera toward cows and captured the quiet acceptance in their eyes.

He found that same quiet acceptance from Rachel's cousins, Nancy and Simon, the couple who hired him to manage their dairy operation. He knew he could do nothing about his missing leg—destroyed by a land mine—but slowly he began to embrace life again. On one of her recent visits to the farm, he described the process to Rachel as "magic."

4

Magic, he thought as he rocked Mary. It's going to take a lot of magic to break through the walls Belle built up during her life on the streets of DC. Rachel started her on the road to recovery when she gave her a home in the basement apartment. She felt another boost to her self-esteem when John trusted her to care for Ben. But to love a man in the way George hoped she would allow herself to love him would require even more healing.

He knew that truth in a deep place of knowledge.

George witnessed Ricky's latest drunken visit, and his pickup truck still bore the scars. Enraged that Belle appeared to be interested in life with another man, Ricky showed up with a golf club and bashed in windows and mirrors in a jealous rage. After a few days in jail, he admitted himself into a 28-day treatment facility. George knew enough about addiction to understand that Ricky faced a long road ahead of him. And since Mary was Ricky's daughter, he also knew that Belle would most likely suffer some of the bumps and pitfalls along that road with him.

But the dangers of loving a woman with so much baggage paled by comparison to battle in a foreign land. At least with Belle, he knew where the bombs were hidden.

George looked up as Belle tiptoed into the apartment. She smiled at the rugged farmer who gently cradled her little girl. George saw the look of tenderness and felt hope.

"Why don't you go back upstairs and enjoy the party," Belle suggested. "Rachel and John are getting ready to leave soon."

"I'd rather stay here with you."

Belle gathered Mary up in her arms and headed for the bedroom. "Go. It will mean a lot to Rachel."

George closed the door quietly behind him and limped up the back stairs and through the kitchen. He stopped in the hall where he, too, noticed the single yellow rose. When he bent to read Ricky's simple note, some of the hope he felt, only minutes before, changed to fear. Just as he turned to head back downstairs, Ralph leaped around the corner and wagged his tail.

"Okay, Ralph. I get the message," George laughed and turned his back on the rose and walked away.

* * *

Carrie Johnson saw George as he stood by himself and waited for his turn to hug the couple before they drove to the airport. "I know Rachel was glad you could be here for her big day," the young woman said. "She speaks of you often."

"Likewise," George said. "Sounds like she was able to get things sorted out for you at The Gilbert Companies. Not that she betrayed any confidences, mind you, but she did say you'd had some difficulties after Horace's death and that she was so glad they had been resolved before she left for her honeymoon in Taos."

Carrie smiled and held up her left hand to show him the engagement ring, returned to the finger from which it had disappeared. After the reading of the will—in which Carrie had been left in charge of his father's business—Horace Junior, in a fit of rage, abandoned the company and his relationship with Carrie.

"Congratulations," George said. "So glad that young man came to his senses. Will you be working together?"

"No, he's decided to go into business for himself. Do something he's always wanted to do—landscaping. For years, he took the easier path and followed in his father's footsteps, but property development was never his passion."

"So, in the end, his father did him a favor, I guess."

"He sure did," Horace said as he stepped forward and draped his arm around Carrie's shoulders. "And Carrie did me an even bigger favor by accepting the challenge and sticking to her guns through my childish temper tantrums."

"Takes a big man to admit something like what you just did,"

6

George said. "Best of luck to both of you. Hope I'll get an invitation to the wedding."

"Actually, we've decided to elope. Keep it simple," Carrie said. "What with the funeral and all the upheaval at The Gilbert Companies, we just want to escape for a few days and then come home and get on with our lives together."

"Sounds like a good plan," George said as he shook hands with Horace and hugged Carrie. The sound of applause refocused their attention to the stairs where Rachel and John stood. Ralph ran to them for one final good-bye, Ben a few steps behind him. Susan snapped pictures beside the wedding photographer.

Rachel wore white cotton pants and her favorite black hemp top, despite Susan's admonition that she needed a special "going away outfit." Rachel stood her ground and insisted on the comfort of the familiar for the flight to Albuquerque. John relaxed in faded jeans and a navy blazer. Ben wrapped his arms around John's knees, as Ralph rubbed up against Rachel.

"We'll call you as soon as we land in New Mexico," John whispered to Ben. "And you can tell us all about what we missed here, okay? You're in charge now, remember? You and Ralph."

Ben wiped tears from his eyes in an attempt to hide his disappointment that he had not been invited to join the honeymoon couple. "Yeah, me and Ralph will take care of each other," he said.

Susan stepped forward. "We've got all kinds of fun things planned. Time will fly by, and everybody will be back together before you know it."

Rachel leaned down for one last hug and a kiss. Ben buried his face in her neck and grabbed her braid and the beads at the end of it. "I love you, Rachel."

"I love you, too, Ben. Take care of Ralph for me."

Ben grinned at the reminder of his big job. "Don't worry, Rachel. Ralph's safe with me."

At the sound of the taxi's horn toot, Rachel and John left the house on O Street and headed for the honeymoon Rachel had never believed would be part of her story.

Until the day she found a stray dog in an alley in Georgetown, and her life turned upside down.

Chapter Two

S usan and Jim sat in their breakfast nook early in the morning after the wedding. They sipped coffee and listened to the sounds of another day. Down the street, a taxi driver leaned on his horn. Across the street, the Moser's front door slammed shut as Mr. Moser stepped outside to pick up the newspaper. The woodpecker that had been hard at work in the cherry tree at the corner of their backyard for the past week began to bat for bugs.

"I guess today's the day," Susan said in her usual get-right-to-the-point approach to life.

Jim looked at his wife over the top of the sports section. He didn't speak. After many years of marriage, he knew he didn't need to ask any questions. Susan would fill in the blanks without any help from him. He smiled at the sight of his wife, wrapped in her favorite ratty robe. She owned several. This morning, she wore the pink bunny robe with matching bunny slippers. For a few weeks after her scare that her husband was enjoying an affair with his new secretary, Susan attempted a sexier morning look with several purchases from Victoria's Secret, but—assured that her marriage was secure and that the affair had only been the product of her overly-active imagination—she returned to comfort.

"Today's the day the realtor is putting the "For Sale" sign in the yard, right?" she asked.

Jim nodded and disappeared back behind his newspaper.

"I don't understand why we need a sign in the yard when we've already got a buyer," Susan whined. "What's the point?"

Jim lowered the *Washington Post* again and sipped his coffee.

9

They'd had this discussion several times, and he knew Susan understood the reasoning. The sign served as an advertisement for the realtor—a friend of theirs—and also attracted other potential buyers in the event the sale fell through. Because he realized that Susan's question was more about her reluctance to move than it was about the sign, he humored her.

"Susan, we'll still see a lot of Rachel, I'm sure. She's going to be retiring soon. Slowing down. She loves the beach, and she'll visit often. Who knows, maybe we can even convince her to move with us."

"It won't be the same," Susan said. "I see her every day. It's an everyday friendship. It's not a weekend friendship."

"Well, weekend friendships have their advantages, too, Susan. It'll be different, but different isn't always worse."

Susan didn't look convinced. She rose from the table and shuffled over to the sink where she rinsed her coffee cup. Jim looked at her slumped shoulders and noticed the aging effect of heartbreak and disappointment. One more time, he questioned his decision to sell the house—but for only a minute. He set his jaw and did what he did best—avoided conflict.

"Why don't you get dressed and wake Ben up and take him to the Mall. Visit the Air & Space Museum. He probably needs a distraction as much as you do today."

The night had been long. Ben had been up and down several times, to ask for water, to go to the bathroom, to tell them he'd heard a noise.

Rachel and John called as soon as they got to their room at the Mabel Dodge Luhan House in Taos, but Ben still worried about them throughout the night. His therapist warned John that the child would suffer from separation anxiety for some time after his parents' death in a car wreck the year before. The night before provided his first opportunity to deal with his biggest fear—that someone else he loved would die.

Ralph slept in the bed with him. And each time Ben padded down the hall to wake Susan and Jim, the dog plodded along beside him.

"What do you think?" Jim asked when Susan met his suggestion with silence. Susan nodded but didn't express the truth she knew. The sign would still be in the yard when they returned from the Mall. "Great. Then it's a deal. You and Ben go out and have fun at the museum, and I'll stay here and wait for the realtor. She's got some names and numbers of movers she wants to give me so we can get some quotes. Start packing. Go through stuff to get rid of."

Susan stopped on her way out the kitchen door and wheeled around to face her husband. She threw the towel she used to wipe the counter tops to the floor and stomped one bunny slipper. "Listen to me, Jim," she yelled. "I will move. I will live with a realtor's sign in my yard, but I will not get rid of stuff. No stuff."

Jim saw the fire in his wife's eyes and knew not to argue. He'd seen that look before and knew the battle would be a losing one, with him as the loser. He grabbed the sports section and hid behind it as Susan stomped up the stairs to wake Ben.

* * *

Across the street, things hadn't gone any smoother the night before.

When Rachel invited Belle and Mary to move upstairs while she and John honeymooned in New Mexico, Belle felt tempted by the idea of more room. On their first night in strange surroundings, however, Mary reacted fiercely to the strange room. "My room. My floor. My bathtub," she insisted.

"Doesn't look like this is making Mary as happy as it is me," George said, as he poked his head out of his bedroom door. He planned to return to the farm in a couple of days, but the thought of sharing the upstairs of the house with Belle, even such a short time, made him feel like a young man. Still, he realized that if Mary wasn't comfortable in a strange bed, the night would be very long for everyone. "Do you need help carrying your stuff back downstairs?" he asked.

"Do you mind?" Belle looked as disappointed as George felt.

"Do I mind carrying? No. Do I mind that you won't be sleeping across the hall from me? Yes." George grabbed an armload of stuffed animals and led the way down the stairs and out of the house. As he turned to see how Belle managed the suitcase she packed for the short trip upstairs, he noticed the blush on her cheeks. He smiled. "You can call me after she's gone to sleep, and I'll come down so we can debrief the wedding. How's that sound?"

Belle nodded. "That will be nice. I'll make tea. Jasmine."

"Sounds like Rachel has influenced you in more ways than one."

"In many more ways than one. I owe her my life, you know. And more. She's given me a belief that my life can actually be good. Seeing her open her heart to John has been like watching a miracle."

George nodded as he remembered Rachel's effect on him when they first met. He also remembered the disappointment he suffered when he realized she had fallen in love with John. But then he looked at Belle and recalled something his staff sergeant had said so often. "Things have a way of working out, boy. Just keep marching." George never believed him, especially after the man had been killed by the same land mine that had cost George his leg.

But now, as he looked at Belle and dared to dream that their feelings for each other could grow into something deep enough on which to build a life together, he felt the stirrings of a belief in "things working out."

"I'll wait for your call," he said. "No need to rush."

Belle opened the door to the basement apartment, and Mary rushed in and squealed, "Ralph?"

"Ralph is across the street with Ben, remember? You and I have

12

each other, and Ben needed Ralph with him."

"George needs Ralph?"

"No, George is a grown-up, and he doesn't need anybody."

"Well, that's not exactly true," George said as he picked Mary up. "Right now, I need a big good-night hug." Mary wrapped her little arms around his weathered neck and squeezed with all her might.

"Don't choke the poor man to death," Belle laughed. "Give him some air. He needs a hug, not a death grip."

Mary patted George on the cheek and whispered, "Mommy hug." George held out his arms, and Belle allowed herself to be folded into a group hug. Mary burrowed in between them and giggled.

"Call me," George said as he closed the door behind him.

* * *

Several blocks away at the Brickskeller, Carrie and Horace sipped wine as they discussed Rachel's wedding. "I never in a million years would have pictured Rachel on her way to Taos to honeymoon," Horace said. "Sure wish Dad could have seen it. Course, that might have given him a heart attack, for sure."

Carrie laughed and signaled the waiter for another glass of wine. After the young man walked away, she reached across the table and took Horace's hand in hers. "I'm so relieved we've decided to elope.'"

"Keeping it simple. When we get back from our elopement trip, we'll have a party so our friends can celebrate with us. After we get settled in our house. How does that sound?"

"Perfect. Work is hectic, and the last thing I need right now is to have to deal with caterers and florists."

"Can you ever forgive me for putting you through such hell? I was such an asshole, Carrie. Thanks for putting up with me."

"I understand what a shock it was for you to learn that your father left the company to me. You must have felt so betrayed. I wish I could have spared you that hurt."

"Life with Dad was never easy," Horace said and gulped a big swig of wine. "I don't know how Mother put up with him all those years." He looked at Carrie and hesitated before he continued. "There were other women, you know." Carrie nodded. "I suspected."

Horace looked across the room at a young couple as they entered the restaurant. They hardly looked old enough to be out without their parents, but they bellied up to the bar and ordered beer from the extensive list that made the Brickskeller famous.

"They were about that age when they got married. Too young. Mom grew up, but I don't think Dad ever did. Continued sowing his wild oats till the day he died."

"Well, I'm glad you didn't take after your father. Except in the positive ways. He did have many of those, you know."

"No. I saw the pain he caused and swore never to be like him. You'll never have to worry about me being a skirt-chaser. But let's change the subject. Enough about old Horace Gilbert, God rest his soul. How are things going at work for you? Calmed down, I hope."

Carrie skimmed over the events of the past week since she weeded out the dead wood in the company—the few people loyal to Horace Junior who had objected to her at the helm of the company. She quickly posted the positions and moved forward to fill them.

"I'll start interviews Monday," she said. "I'm meeting with a young man Rachel recommended I talk to about your job, in fact." Carrie glanced out of the corner of her eye to gauge her fiancé's reaction to the news. She was relieved to see a smile. "You'll be missed. But I'm sure you know that."

He nodded and looked Carrie in the eye. "I know. I also know I'm doing the right thing. Landscaping has always been my dream. I can't wait to get started. And speaking of yards, when are we going to start looking for our house?"

"Let's give The Gilbert Companies time to stabilize, and you need to get your business up and running. I don't want too many things on our plates. I can't handle too many changes. Let's stick with our original plan for you to move into my condo after we get back from our trip."

"Okay, but I want us to have a house. I want to create a yard that will knock your socks off every time you come home. I've already designed it." Carrie smiled as Horace —like a little boy with a new toy—began to sketch on his cocktail napkin.

* * *

George had finished reading the front section of the paper when the phone rang. He realized he had dozed off briefly. The ring startled him, and he jerked upright on the sofa.

"She's finally asleep," Belle said. "Come on down. The tea is ready."

George smiled. What a comforting image—tea. What an inviting phrase, "The tea is ready." So was he. Ready. He wasn't so sure about Belle, but he told her he'd be right down.

"Big day for a little girl," Belle said as she opened the door for him.

"Big day for all of us. A perfect day, I'd say." George walked over to the sofa where Belle had laid out the tea set. "Let me pour," he said as he pointed to the cast iron tea pot cozied under the crocheted cover that kept the tea warm.

"Thanks," Belle said and knelt in front of the low table as George poured the steaming Jasmine tea into two cups.

"Honey?" she asked.

"No. I'll take mine straight up. You're all the sweetness I need."

When Belle didn't respond, he feared he might have gone too far, even as a joke. "What's wrong, Belle? You don't like to hear how I feel about you? Surely, you know."

15

Belle stood and retreated to a chair across from the sofa where George sat. "We need to move slowly, George. For Mary's sake. She's had so much drama in her short life."

"I don't think Mary would agree with you. She seems to like my attentions. Why don't you?"

"I do, George."

"I know. You're the adult. You're the one who has to watch for danger. The protective mother hen. Well, can you drop the armor just a little. Just for tonight and come sit on the sofa with me? Please."

Eyes downcast, Belle sipped her tea to buy some time, but when she looked up at George's kind face, at his gentle eyes, she laughed. George walked over to her chair and smothered her laughter with kisses. "Don't want to wake Mary, silly girl. Not for a while, at least," he said as he picked her up and carried her to the sofa.

Chapter Three

From her living room window, Susan watched George walk downstairs to Belle's apartment. She smiled when she saw the lights dim a few minutes later.

• "What you grinning about?" Jim asked, as he entered the living room and wrapped his arms around his wife.

"I think George and Belle are making progress in their relationship."

"Quite the romantic, aren't you. First Rachel and John and now George and Belle. Who's next? Looks like you've run out of women to use all your *Bride* magazine inventory on."

Susan's brow furrowed.

"Hey, I'm just joking," Jim said. "I'm sure someone will turn up who needs your expertise."

"It's not that."

"Well, then what is it?"

"It's that you think that's all I'm good for. Meddling in other people's lives. Living vicariously through other people's stories."

"Hey, slow down a minute, sugar plum."

"And I'm not a sugar plum," Susan spat out at her husband and stormed into the kitchen. Jim followed her. He realized that similar scenes seemed to happen more frequently than they ever had during the course of their long marriage.

"Susan, talk to me. What's troubling you?"

"I want a job."

Jim sank down on one of the kitchen chairs and carefully set his beer bottle down on the table. "Susan, your timing is a little off, don't you think? I'm getting ready to retire. We're selling the house. And we're moving to the beach. Why now? You haven't worked a day in your life."

"I know. That's the problem. I look around me, and, even Belle—a young woman who's been homeless—is going to school to do something with her life. Everybody has accomplished something important except me. And I want my own money."

"You sell poems. Poetry on demand. People love them, and they buy them every time you go out to sell them. You're a huge success. Unique."

"That's not a real job. I want a real job. I want to draw social security."

Jim laughed out loud but stopped himself when he realized his wife was not amused. The swinging door to the kitchen opened, and Ben padded into the brightly lit room. Ralph trailed along behind him.

"Ralph and me need a drink," the child said as he rubbed his eyes. Then he noticed Susan's hands on her hips and Jim's arms crossed over his chest. "What's wrong? Is Granddad okay? Did he and Rachel have a wreck?" Ralph leaped into action and licked the boy's hands.

"No, sweetie," Susan said and rushed to his side. "They're safe in their bed right now. Dreaming about you, I bet."

"That's good. Now they can sleep together cause they got married. Now Granddad's not lonely anymore."

"That's right," Jim said. "Everybody's got somebody. And Ralph's lucky to have you to take care of him when he needs a drink." He refilled Ralph's water bowl and poured Ben a small glass of milk.

"Can I have some chocolate in it?"

"Not this late at night, sweetie. But how about let me warm it up for you a little. That'll make it special and help you go back to

18

sleep." Ben insisted on wearing his tuxedo shirt to bed, and it was twisted almost backward after several hours as he tossed and turned. "Sure you don't want to change into your pajama top now?" Susan asked.

Ben hesitated just a minute and then smiled. "Yeah, I guess so. These buttons kinda poke. And Ralph wants to take his blue ribbon off, too, don't you, boy?" He leaned down and whispered in the dog's ear. "He said, 'yes.'"

Susan set the warmed milk on the table and helped Ben with the buttons on his shirt.

"How many days now until Granddad and Rachel get back?"

Susan and Jim looked at each other and shared the same thought. If the first night proved to be any indication of how the next fourteen would pass, they had a long two weeks ahead of them.

* * *

Belle smiled as she locked the door behind George and watched him walk by the little window at street level and then disappear up the steps. Tomorrow she would try again to persuade Mary to move upstairs for the two weeks Rachel and John planned to honeymoon in New Mexico.

George would return to the farm in a couple of days. Rachel's cousins had grown to depend on him, and he took his job there seriously. Belle realized that was one of his traits she admired the most. And yet, she knew she would miss him after he left the city. The house would seem huge without him there. *Maybe I should stay down here,* she thought. Then she remembered that Ben and Ralph would make the trip back across the street the next day.

Belle enjoyed a warm shower. She lingered under the fine spray and ran her hands over her arms. She remembered George's strong touch on her back. His caress. An arousal she had never felt with Ricky. As she turned her face up toward the water, she realized the

19

danger that dogged her life with Ricky had created a shield around her senses. A necessary but numbing protection.

With George, she sensed the walls begin to tumble down to reveal a pleasure she had never known.

As she dried herself with a fresh, sweet-smelling towel, she recognized her tendency to do what Rachel cautioned her not to do—get out of the moment. Fear began to set in. The "what ifs" started to attack.

She wrapped herself in the heavy plush robe Rachel gave her and breathed deeply. "All is well today," she whispered. "All is well."

As she walked past the little cot where Mary slept the sleep of the innocent, she smiled to herself. No fear there, she thought. She adores George. Trusts him with every fiber of her little body. Why can't I?

Belle knew the answer to that question even though she struggled with the effort to dig through the layers of doubt to see it. "Progress, not perfection," she told herself, in Rachel's words. Tomorrow night I'll be upstairs with George, she thought. Mary will have her own room. We'll have privacy. Stop. It's too soon. If I cross that line with him, there's no turning back.

"Mommy, where's George?"

Startled, Belle turned and saw her daughter seated on the cot. She rubbed her eyes with her both little fists.

"He's gone upstairs to his bed, honey. To go to sleep. He's tired. It's been a long day."

"Ben? Where's Ben? Where's Ralph?"

"They're across the street with Susan, remember?"

"Just me and Mommy."

"That's right. You and Mommy."

"Good," Mary said as she lay her head back down on her pillow and promptly fell back to sleep.

Oh, dear, Belle thought. What was that all about?

* * *

Upstairs, George poured himself a glass of water and stood at the kitchen sink. He stared out at the moonlit courtyard. Not bad, he admitted reluctantly. The stars in the city aren't as bright as the country stars, but the moon still looks pretty damn good, even here in DC. A slight smog film over it but the same perfect roundness. The same mystery that always fills me with awe. With a sense of power. Even in Vietnam, that moon was a beacon of hope.

George stopped himself as he started to enter the enemy territory where he could still sometimes get lost in the clutches of demons he worked so hard to put behind him. He rinsed out the glass and laid it on the drain board. He smiled as he looked around the kitchen. So different from the kitchen he visited before John and Ben moved upstairs. The once spartan refrigerator door was now plastered with Ben's crayon drawings. His eyes focused on the picture of four stick figures—one with a tail, obviously a drawing of Ralph. They all wore smiles and held hands.

How quickly life can change, he thought. He rubbed his chin and nibbled at a cuticle as he thought about his own life and the possibilities he faced as he allowed himself to picture Belle and Mary in it. I'm too old to feel this way. Rachel was a whole different thing. An older woman. A woman my age. But Belle is young enough to be my daughter. I'll never be able to meet her needs. And, my god. I'll have to hobble down the aisle on a walker on Mary's wedding day.

George caught himself. Slow down, man. Take it easy. Belle may not even feel a thing for you. She may be the kind to toy with your emotions. Women can do that, if you let them. Gotta go slow, old man.

He felt the familiar fear and loneliness creep up his spine. He confessed the emptiness of his life to Rachel on her last visit to the farm. He told her how desperately he wanted someone to share his

21

days and how few and far between were the opportunities to meet a woman out in the country. He hoped Rachel might fill the hole in his life and still remembered the disappointment when she told him of her decision to marry John.

He felt surprise at how quickly his heart lifted when she brought Belle and Mary to visit. He wasn't blind to the challenges Ricky presented—even after the young man's drunken golf club assault on his truck—but he wasn't ready to give up yet.

Chapter Four

The message she found on the answering machine when she arrived at the office Monday morning did not surprise Georgia. It was simple and short. "Call me."

Georgia smiled as she punched in the phone number Rachel left. She hesitated when she remembered the three-hour time difference. Serve her right if I woke her up. Imagine calling work on the first few days of your honeymoon, she muttered to herself.

Rachel answered on the first ring. She spoke in a whisper, "John's still asleep. Wait a minute while I walk out to the balcony."

As Georgia waited, she watered the African violets with one hand while she held her phone with the other. Finally, Rachel continued the conversation. "What's going on there? How are things? Any messages? Anything important come in the mail?"

"Well, I'm watering the plants right now. How's the honeymoon?"

"But were there any messages other than mine?"

"Rachel, relax. You're on your honeymoon. You're supposed to be focused on John. Lolling in bed, sleeping late, doing cuddles."

"Georgia, I'm sixty-two. You can't teach old dogs new tricks."

When her outburst met silence, Rachel realized she had acted like a child and promptly apologized. "Sorry, Georgia. This is just harder than I thought it would be."

"What's wrong? Bad flight? Food disagree with you? Didn't get the room you requested? Does John snore?"

Rachel laughed at the last question and Georgia's thorough run-down of all the possible problems. Knowing her, she's probably got a solution to all of them, Rachel thought. "No, everything's fine. Going according to plan. But surely you didn't expect me—a workaholic—not to think about the office just because I got married."

"Some people do."

"Well, I'm not 'some people.' Give me a few days, and maybe I'll let go a little, but, please, humor me this morning."

"Okay," Georgia sighed. "Carrie called early today and left a message that she can't find her copy of the will. I've taken care of that. A couple of potential new clients called for appointments. I'll call them back later and schedule them to come in after you've had a few days to settle in."

"Thanks. You're a dear. Settling in is going to be harder than ever, I'm afraid."

"Even for a workaholic?" Georgia teased.

"Anything else?" Rachel asked as she ignored the jab.

"Yes. You got a call from Ricky's counselor at the treatment center. Said it was critical that you call back immediately. Want me to let him know you're out of town?"

"Call and see if you can find out what he needs. Maybe it's just some paperwork from the temporary restraining order we filed. If so, you can take care of that."

"I know. And if not, you'll call him."

"Well, do I have a choice?"

"Most people, yes. You, probably not."

"I won't even ask what you mean by that. Talk to you later."

"Yes, boss lady." Georgia disconnected from her conversation with Rachel and immediately called the treatment center and asked to speak to Fred Hampton. The receptionist put her through when she identified herself as Rachel Springer's assistant.

"Thanks for calling, Mrs. Payne," answered a gravelly voice. "I appreciate your prompt response. Is Ms. Springer available?"

"She's Mrs. Turner now, and she's on her honeymoon. Anything I can do to help?"

Mr. Hampton hesitated. "Well, I suppose I can trust you to keep this confidential."

"Yes, of course."

"It's very important that I speak to Mrs. Turner about Ricky as soon as possible. To get her insight into his relationship with Belle. To get her perspective. To get a different picture maybe."

"Why? Has something happened?"

"Of course, this must be strictly between you and me. You may, of course, share the information with Mrs. Turner so she will understand how important it is she call me."

"Yes, of course."

Georgia waited for what seemed like an eternity for the man to continue. "Ricky tried to hang himself last night. We're thinking about transferring him to another facility."

Georgia dropped into the chair behind her desk and inhaled several deep breaths to calm herself. "Is he alright?"

"Physically, yes. Emotionally, definitely not. And we're just not equipped to deal with someone with a problem as serious as Ricky's. We think he needs to be in a hospital with round-the-clock observation for a few weeks."

"And why did you call us?"

"Well, he left a note."

"Yes, go on."

"It was fairly rambling but directed to Belle Mason, the mother of his child."

"Yes, I know who Belle Mason is," Georgia said, surprised by her impatience. "Surely, you already knew about Belle and Mary. This couldn't have come as a surprise."

"No, Mrs. Payne, we weren't surprised."

"Well, I don't see how Rachel can do anything that you haven't been able to. My goodness, the woman's on her honeymoon. Surely, she deserves some privacy."

"Our first duty is to our patients, Mrs. Payne. Please ask her to call me when she can. The sooner the better. We'll be transferring Ricky to the state mental hospital, but, obviously, we'll continue to be part of his care plan."

"Does Belle know?"

"As next of kin, we were obligated to inform her. And for her safety."

"Her safety? He'll be locked up. How could she be in any danger?"

"Things happen, Mrs. Payne," the counselor said and then ended the call.

"'Things happen, indeed,'" Georgia huffed. She hesitated over the choice of which to do first—call Rachel back or rush over to check on Belle. Thank goodness, George is still in town, she thought as she reached for her cellphone.

Rachel took the news better than Georgia had. Years of experience with her own clients and daily courtroom drama gave her a toughness that Georgia's life of chocolate chip cookies in the office had not. Rachel said very matter-of-factly that she'd call the treatment center and offer whatever help she could.

"I'm headed over to check on Belle," Georgia told her. "Any advice?"

"Just tell her that the restraining order is still in effect and to keep the door locked."

"Lot of good that's going to do," Georgia said. "Maybe she and Mary should go back to the farm with George. At least until they get Ricky stabilized."

"He'll be in a lock-down ward, Georgia. Locked down."

"Still, things happen."

"I don't know. Why don't we let Belle make that decision. Call me after you've seen her. In fact, tell her to call me."

"Don't you and John have some kind of plans for the day? Something fun?"

"We're heading to Ghost Ranch at some point, but I'll have my phone with me. Tell her to call."

"I don't know, Rachel, if I should do that."

"Thanks, Georgia," Rachel said and ended the call. When she stepped away from the balcony and back into the bedroom, John still slept, burrowed under the thick duvet. She snuggled in beside him and fitted her body against his back.

John moaned with pleasure. Rachel wiggled closer, and he turned over to take her in his arms. "Where have you been all my life, Rachel Turner? Where have you been?" Before she could answer, he covered her mouth with his and kissed her deeply and longingly. All the years of waiting—for a woman and a love he found in Rachel—poured out in the kiss and in every inch of the rest of his body. And were returned with equal passion by his bride.

* * *

"I've got a question," Rachel said when she finally broke away from her new husband.

"What, my lovely wife? Ask me. Ask me anything."

"How did we get so lucky?"

"Has nothing to do with luck. I've paid my dues. I deserve this. And so do you."

Rachel thought about her life before John and compared it to what she enjoyed now. Her solitary existence had been one of peace and contentment. Friends to fill the occasional loneliness, but, in general, she had been a woman happy to live life alone. Hard to consider anything about her life that might compare to John's marriage to an alcoholic and his son's recent death.

"Not sure I've paid dues," she finally said, "but maybe I've saved myself all these years for the best."

"That works."

"Sure is nice sharing."

"That works."

"Sure is nice being here in Taos with the man I love—even if you do snore."

"That's why God made earplugs. Did you bring some? I thought you bought a box at the airport."

"I did. Just kidding you. I slept fine."

"What is it?" John asked as he propped himself up on his elbow to look down at his wife, her hair unbraided and spread out across the pillow in a pool of silver.

"It's Ricky. I talked to Georgia this morning. I got a call from his treatment center. He tried to hang himself. I'm worried about Belle. I'll need to call his counselor before we head out for the day. I don't want them dragging her in on his treatment plan."

John knew Rachel well enough not to try to discourage her as she made as many calls as she felt necessary to put her mind at ease. He also knew any chance for more morning lovemaking had been blown. But the thought of the rest of his life making love to Rachel comforted him. The benefits of growing older, he thought. Patience.

Rachel gently kissed John's cheek, crawled out of bed and reached for her cellphone on the bedside table. "Why don't you jump in the shower while I make this call," she said. "Won't take a minute, I promise. I doubt I'll even get through to Ricky's counselor, but at least I can leave a message and let him know I've gotten the news. Get the ball rolling in the direction I want it to go—away from Belle."

* * *

As Georgia slid her car beside the curb in front of Rachel's house, she looked across the street and saw Ben outside with Ralph. The boy sat dejectedly on the front porch steps while the dog sniffed at the boxwood bushes. The animal never strayed far from the child who looked like he'd lost more than his best friend.

Georgia crossed the street to speak to him before she continued with her mission to tell Belle the news about Ricky. "Morning, big boy. Why the long face?" she asked.

Ben refused to look at her, and Georgia realized he was in no mood to be teased. He needed a mother at the moment and not a buddy. She put her arm around his frail shoulders and pulled him close. "You miss your grandfather, don't you?"

Ben nodded.

"And Rachel," she added.

He nodded again. Ralph trotted over to join the pair on the top porch step. He first licked Ben's knees and then Georgia's hand.

"How lucky you are to have Ralph. And pretty soon, Mary will be awake, and I bet you'll do something fun together today, won't you?"

Ben's face brightened as he remembered the plan for a trip with Mary and Belle to a movie that afternoon. "And maybe George will go with us," he said. "He's going to try to get all his chores done so he can go. Men do chores, you know."

"Yes, I know," Georgia agreed with a smile. She hoped her news about Ricky didn't put a damper on things. The little boy had enough disappointments to last a lifetime. He didn't need one more. "Tell you what," Georgia said. "I need to go across the street to talk to Belle for a minute. Why don't you go on inside and see who's up, and I'll tell Belle you'll be ready to go to the movies whenever they are. Okay?"

"I've got a better idea," Ben shouted as he jumped off the steps. "I'll go with you!"

"No, Ben. I need to talk grown-up talk with Belle. You stay here. I'll come over and say good-bye before I leave."

Ben hung his head and looked about to throw one of the temper tantrums she heard Rachel describe. Ralph nudged the boy's bottom with his nose and broke the mood. Ben giggled and knelt down to hug the dog. Georgia saw her chance and made a quick escape across the street. Before she walked down the steps to Belle's apartment, she looked back over her shoulder and was relieved to see Ben and Ralph disappear into Susan's house.

* * *

Mary yanked the door to the basement apartment open minutes before Georgia lifted her hand to knock. The little girl jumped up and down and squealed.

"Wow, I wish everyone was this excited to see me," Georgia laughed as Belle walked toward her.

"Mary, I've told you not to open the door like that. That's my job, remember? We don't know who's on the other side, and we don't want strangers in our house, do we?"

"No! Georgia!" Mary shouted as she stomped her little foot.

"I think she must have heard me say 'good-bye' to Ben," Georgia said in the child's defense. She leaned over and picked Mary up in her arms. As she turned back to Belle, she told her she needed to speak to her alone. She asked if George were awake and able to occupy Mary's time while they talked.

Belle—always prepared for dramas that made "speaking alone" necessary—made a quick phone call and, within a few minutes, George appeared at the door. "Everything okay?" he asked as he removed Mary from Georgia's arms.

"Sure. We'll call you in a little bit, and Belle can fill you in after I leave."

With a puzzled look, George closed the door behind him. The two women listened to his uneven footfalls and Mary's happy giggles grow fainter. They stood in a silence like the eye of a hurricane.

"It's Ricky, isn't it?" Belle asked. "It's always Ricky."

Georgia sat on the sofa and patted the place beside her. She told Belle the story as calmly as she could. She stuck to the facts and

Rachel's reminder that the restraining order was still in effect. "But, you do need to be careful," she said. "He's being transferred to the state mental hospital for observation, and he may be there for a few weeks."

"Yes, I know, but things happen," Belle said. Tears dripped from her chin to the afghan she pulled around her like a cocoon.

Georgia handed her a Kleenex from the box Belle kept on the coffee table. She looked at the vase of wilting roses left over from the wedding and thought about how quickly scenes could change. Damn, Ricky, she fumed and then felt guilty for her lack of compassion.

"I don't understand," Belle finally said. "He was doing so well. Sober. Working."

Georgia sat silently. Both women knew the answer to the question. Jealousy wasn't called the "green-eyed monster" for no reason. The knowledge that the only two people he loved had begun to develop a life with another man proved more than Ricky could handle. It had been a tough test of his new sobriety, and he had failed.

Georgia moved closer to Belle, put her arm around her and patted the young woman's back as she wept from a deep well of sorrow. Slowly, the tears subsided, and Belle straightened her shoulders and moved back to her role of mother. "Thanks for coming, Georgia," she said. "I guess I need to go get Mary. And tell George. That man's gonna want to head back to his farm even quicker now. Get away from this crazy city and never come back."

Georgia shook her head. "I don't think that will happen. George cares very much for you and Mary. He's not the type to abandon you."

Belle looked doubtful.

"I've got to get back to the office. Call me if you need anything. You're moving upstairs today, right?"

"That's been the plan. Ben's coming back to his room this

evening. I'm not sure now, though."

"No reason to change your plans. Nothing's changed here. Just be aware." Georgia rooted around in her purse and pulled out a plastic bag of chocolate chip cookies. "Here. I brought these for you."

Belle smiled. "Thanks. Chocolate. Like George says, 'It's magic.'"

I hope so, Georgia thought as she watched Belle head upstairs to face George. "Wait a minute," she called out. "Why don't you bring Mary back down here, and let me watch her while you tell George. She doesn't need to hear about this."

Belle nodded and, within a very short time, returned with the little girl in tow. Mouth full of cookie, she gave Georgia a big grin and leaped down the few steps into the basement apartment.

"I'll be right back," Belle said with a weak smile of appreciation.

Georgia nodded and prayed silently for a miracle. For magic. For some happy ending for the young woman. And the man who suffered so horribly that he would want to end his life.

Chapter Five

George listened. He didn't interrupt while Belle shared the latest Ricky chapter. The story of the attempted suicide. The story of the transfer to the state mental hospital. The story he found hard to swallow was the one in which Rachel told Belle and Mary they could feel safe because of the restraining order.

George snorted. "Sure. Lot of good that will do. No, Belle, I think you and Mary need to drive back to the farm with me. At least until Rachel returns home from her honeymoon. The man's nuts. You're not safe here."

"But what about Ben? Susan's planning to bring him over here today. They're already looking at a full plate with getting the house ready to sell."

George grabbed her hands and held them firmly in his. "You let me take care of that. I'll walk across the street and talk to Susan right now while you run downstairs and send Georgia on her way. And tell her you and Mary will stay at the farm with me."

"But, George, I don't know."

George stopped her stuttering with a long and loving kiss that worked its magic. Belle felt safe.

When Rachel called later that afternoon and heard that George planned to take mother and child back to Virginia with him, she didn't feel even a moment's surprise. Belle told her Susan had insisted that Ben and Ralph were welcome across the street and that she would have plenty of help from Mrs. Moser next door. "In fact, she made it seem like I was doing her a favor by leaving. She said she needed the distraction of house guests to get her through the move."

Rachel laughed. "I hope you didn't try to argue with her. When that woman sinks her teeth into a mission, there's no changing her mind."

"She seemed pretty determined," Belle agreed. "I just feel so bad about the whole thing."

"Well, don't. This isn't your fault, and it will pass. You and Mary will love being at the farm. John and I will be home before you know it, and everything will get back to normal. When are you leaving?"

"Early in the morning. Real early. George wants to beat the rush hour traffic."

"Will you stay upstairs tonight?"

Belle said they would and felt butterflies in her stomach at the thought. Her lips still tingled from his kiss.

"Belle, are you still there?"

"Yes. Just thinking of all I need to do to get ready to go. And about Ricky."

"Don't think about Ricky. Pray for Ricky. He needs it."

Belle said "goodbye," with a farewell promise to take care of herself. Think I'll start with a nap, she decided, as she lay down on the bed next to an already dozing Mary. The sleep of the innocent, she thought. Will I ever be able to sleep like that again? Will things ever "get back to normal again," like Rachel promised?

But Belle did fall asleep and rested for about an hour. She woke when Mary shook her arm. "Mommy, door."

Belle heard the knock then, and her thoughts raced immediately to Ricky. He's here. He's here already. We didn't even make it to the farm.

But when she looked through the peephole, she saw Ben and Ralph in the stairwell. When she opened the door, Ben launched immediately into an invitation to supper across the street. "Susan's making sagetti and garlicky bread. And I'm going to help," the little

34

boy pronounced proudly. "I get to hold the cobbender when she plops the sagetti out. It's a very portant job." Then Ben's smile disappeared. "Susan says it's a going-away party. That you're going away. That Ralph and I aren't coming over here back to my room after all."

Belle stooped to the child's level and looked him in the eye. She smiled and tousled his hair. "Ralph loves Susan's big back yard. He'll have so much fun rolling around in the grass, won't he?"

Ben's face lit up. "Yeah, and I'll play on the swing set. But when is Granddad coming home? And Rachel?"

"Just thirteen more days. Not long."

Ben looked at his fingers and a frown clouded his face.

"Time will fly by because you'll have so much fun."

Mary ran into the room, grabbed Ben around the waist and squeezed him in a hug that almost toppled them both.

"Hey, watch out there, Missy. You'll hurt someone with all that lovin'." And as she got the words out of her mouth, she thought of Ricky. So many times, some well-meaning counselor warned her that what she thought was love was enabling. The money she loaned him to buy guitar strings. Giving up all her own interests to follow his lifestyle. As a groupie, she had very little time to spend with friends she knew before she met him. Not once did she fly a kite after she met Ricky at the Washington Monument. Finally, during the days they lived on the street, she had no money to lend nor friends to neglect. And the love turned to a resentment so deep she couldn't even see it.

"Mommy, let's go," Mary shouted and pulled Belle's hand. The three walked around the side of the house and up to Rachel's front door. Ben lifted Mary up so she could ring the doorbell. Belle's heart skipped a beat when she heard George walk down the hall toward them. I wonder how long it will take before I stop feeling excited when I see his face, she thought and then chided herself for her cynicism.

George greeted them with his crooked smile and opened the door wide. "Why the doorbell? You know you can walk in here any time," he said. "You've been here a lot longer than I have."

Ben and Mary raced to the end of the hall. The two adults stood alone in the foyer. Belle shared Susan's dinner invitation, and George grinned. "I'm really enjoying having friends," he said. "Life on the farm is pretty isolated."

"But you have Nancy and Simon. I thought you were like part of their family. They sure do appreciate what you do for them."

George took Belle's hand and lifted it to his lips for a gentle kiss as he struggled with a response.

"What's wrong?" Belle asked.

"Not sure you'll understand."

"Try me," Belle said and squeezed his hand.

"Do you always feel comfortable with Rachel and John?"

"Sure. I'm so grateful for what they've done for me and Mary. Every time I'm with them is like a day in heaven for me. Course, I don't know what heaven is like, but if it's any better than sitting at the dinner table up here with people who love me, I sure do want to be there."

George led Belle down the hall to the den where the children played a video game. Still, he said nothing.

"What is it, George? Tell me."

George looked at the two children as they sat on the floor at his feet. He smiled wistfully. "I don't know if I can explain it," he said. "If you've never felt it, I'm sure you won't understand."

"Try me," Belle said.

"I hate to express myself with an overused cliché, but when I'm with Nancy and Simon, I feel like a fifth wheel. Like I'm intruding. Like I don't belong."

"But they love having you there. They'd be lost without you."

George's face hardened. "Yeah, they need me to mend fences and help with the milking. Sharing dinner is a different story."

Instinctively, Belle stepped back to put some distance between her and George's bitterness. "Well, that may be the way you feel," she said, "but Rachel tells me feelings aren't always fact, and I think this may be true with your story."

"Let's change the subject, shall we," George said as he forced a smile. "What time's dinner?"

"Good question. Let me call Susan and find out." Belle walked to the kitchen and over to the wall phone. She smiled at all the little notes Rachel had stuck around the room to remind George of when the garbage was collected, where Ralph's food was stored and how often the fern needed to be watered.

Belle was about to hang up the phone when Susan finally answered it, breathlessly.

"Sorry," Belle said. "Did I catch you at a bad time?"

"No, not at all. But the most horrible thing has happened, and I was trying to shake myself out of my funk before I answered the phone. Guess I wasn't very successful."

"What's happened? Is Rachel alright?"

"Are you sitting down?" Susan gasped.

"No, but go ahead. I can take it. Is it Ricky? Have you heard from Ricky? Is he out?"

"No, it's nothing like that, Belle. It's our house. The buyers don't want it. They've backed out."

* * *

As George eased the truck away from the curb and into the still quiet of O Street, Belle settled in her seat. Mary had fallen back to sleep behind them. Belle thought about her conversation with Susan the night before and about how quickly life could change. She smiled as she remembered the phone call. Susan had gone from what sounded like devastation to relief in less than sixty seconds.

Belle sighed.

"The city sure feels a lot more civil at this hour of the day," George whispered. "No screaming sirens. No cursing cab drivers. I can actually hear birds singing."

"You really love country life, don't you," Belle said.

George nodded and reached over to touch her knee. "Think you could get used to it?"

When Belle didn't answer and turned her head to look out the window, George feared he had rushed her with the question. He remembered her smooth young skin in his arms the night before and the sensations he hadn't felt in a long time. He wanted more of her, and he wanted her for the rest of his life. But he hadn't pushed then, and he knew not to push now.

"Hey, don't worry. I'm not kidnapping you," he laughed. "I'll bring you right back here as soon as Rachel gets home. As soon as I know you're safe."

Belle turned her face away from the scene at the Circle where Deejee set up her hotdog cart. Two old men sat on a bench and tossed breadcrumbs to the pigeons. She looked at George and smiled. "You're a good man, George. It's been a long time since I've had a man take care of me."

"So, how does it feel?"

Belle thought for a minute. "Good. It feels good."

George resisted the urge to suggest that she could enjoy his care for her a lot more if she wanted it. Instead, he focused on the traffic in the circle. Already, early morning buses crawled around it and veered off to one street or another. George found the street he looked for and headed toward Key Bridge and across the Potomac River toward Virginia.

When he had safely dodged several near misses with more street-savvy commuters, he relaxed his grip on the steering wheel and took a sip of the coffee Belle poured him from the thermos she packed.

"I'm so glad I was able to reach my teachers and make arrangements to get my assignments for the next couple of weeks," she said. "I don't want to let anything interfere with my plans to finish my education. I've waited too long as it is."

"I'm proud of you, Belle. I really am. You're setting a fine example for that little girl back there."

"I hate what I've put her through. I'm hoping she'll forget all the other stuff. The living in a shelter and begging on the streets. I hope that all she will remember is the mother who got her life together again."

"I have no doubt about it. You're giving her a wonderful life now. She's certainly surrounded by a lot of people who love her. And love heals, you know."

Belle laughed. "Susan says 'art heals.'"

"Well, aren't they one and the same? Or at least kissin' cousins?"

Belle turned around to look at Mary, her little arms tightly wrapped around the Pooh Bear Ben had again loaned her for the trip. Her heart ached when she left Ben behind. She worried that her own escape at the same time Rachel and John were away on their honeymoon would be too much for the little boy to handle. He still attended regular therapy sessions to process the trauma of his parents' deaths. When Belle called the therapist to ask for her advice, she had been assured that his close relationship with Susan would give him the anchor he needed during the brief separation from the others.

The fact that he had been willing to part with Pooh—to share him with the little girl he adopted as his sister—provided further proof that his healing had progressed well. Maybe better than mine, Belle thought.

Chapter Six

The drive to the farm lasted a little longer than George anticipated the night before, when he called Nancy to let her know about the house guests who would travel back with him. Mary demanded two potty stops along the way. When they drove up in front of the "Big House," as George referred to it, Nancy ran out to greet them.

"I was getting worried," she shouted. She ran to the car and unfastened Mary's restraining belts. The child held out her arms to be picked up.

"Chickens?" she squealed. "Cows?"

The three adults all laughed. "Yes, we've got plenty of chickens and cows. But what took you so long?"

"When was the last time you traveled with a little girl?" George laughed.

"Too long. Come on in the house. I've got a little brunch ready for you. If you're like me, riding in the car is hungry work."

George saw Belle's look of discomfort and immediately understood. "That's mighty kind of you, but do you mind if we get the truck unpacked first and unwind a little. Maybe call the meal 'lunch' and see you in about an hour?"

Nancy looked at Belle's weariness and took the bait. "Sounds good. You all take your time, and I'll stick this casserole in the oven so it will stay warm. Come on back down when you're ready."

Mary whined that she didn't want to climb back in the truck.

"Tell you what," Nancy said. "Why doesn't Miss Mary stay here with me while you two unpack and freshen up."

Mary ran up the porch steps, turned and waved good-bye to her mother.

"Obviously, the child does not suffer from separation anxiety," George laughed. He grabbed Belle's hand and led her back to the truck. As he drove to the farmhouse, Belle felt as if she'd been transported into another world. When she stepped out of the truck and reached for her bags in the back, she felt her muscles relax and the load on her back lift.

"Thanks for this," she said.

"For what?"

"For knowing what I needed. A little time to unwind. How do you do it?"

"Do what?"

"Read my mind so well."

"I think it's more a matter of the heart than the mind," George said. "Mine's pretty open, and you, my dear, are an easy read."

* * *

Both hands full of mail, Georgia heard the phone ring—both lines, loudly and insistently. She dropped the envelopes and fliers on her desk and punched the button that connected her to Rachel's private line. Stan Berninger's gruff voice greeted her at the other end.

"Rachel?"

"Stan?"

"Yeah. Where's Rachel?"

"You know she's on her honeymoon, Stan Berninger. My goodness, don't tell me your memory is that short. She just got married Saturday."

Silence at Stan's end of the line. Georgia paused to wait for his comeback and then grew concerned when she heard none. Maybe he is losing his memory, she worried. So many of her friends had family members who suffered some form of dementia. Why not Stan?

41

Georgia sat down heavily behind her desk, as images of jovial, fun-loving, wise-cracking, doting grandfather Stan disappeared into a fog of confusion. Her brow furrowed.

"So, when's she due back?" Stan barked in an interruption of Georgia's free-fall into worry.

"A couple of weeks. What's up? Anything I can do in the meantime?"

"I saw Deejee the other day, and she told me about Ricky's transfer to the state mental hospital. Just checking to make sure Belle and Mary are okay. Wanted to see if Rachel needs me to keep an eye on things."

Georgia assured the private eye that his services weren't needed and that Belle and Mary were safely at the farm until Rachel returned.

"And when's that, you say?"

"A couple of weeks. I'm sure she'll give you a call when she gets back, Stan."

"Sure. Tell her to give me a call. Business is a little slow right now. I could use some work." The conversation ended with a Lily story. Stan's granddaughter remained his greatest love, and even her simplest accomplishment provided fodder for an exciting story told from Stan's perspective. After Georgia hung up, she sat and pondered Stan's abrupt decline. Or had she not been very observant? He had seemed fine at the wedding. Or had she not paid attention?

When she checked the message left on the main line and heard Susan's voice, she called her back immediately. After Susan assured her that she had called "just to check on things," Georgia took the opportunity to share her concern. "Did you notice anything strange about Stan at the wedding?" she asked.

"Other than his Scooby Doo tie, you mean? That's just old Stan, Georgia. Wanted to make Lily happy. She gave him that tie for his birthday."

"No, not the tie. Did he seem confused at all? Forgetful? Disoriented?"

"No, but I was spinning in circles, myself, if you'll recall."

Georgia stopped herself before she agreed that Susan was perhaps the last person who would notice anyone else's confusion. Susan stayed in a state of dizziness most of the time. But her confusion qualified as endearing, Georgia thought. For a private investigator, the same characteristic could be debilitating.

"What's wrong?" Susan demanded. "Something wrong with Stan? Should we call Rachel? Should we call his children?"

"Slow down, Susan. We're not doing anything," Georgia said as she ended the call as quickly as she could without rudeness.

But she wondered.

As she began to sort the mail into piles for Rachel to go through when she returned, the phone rang again.

"I forgot to tell you something," Susan announced. Georgia waited patiently. She continued to slit open envelopes. "Guess who's interested in buying the house?" Before Georgia had a chance to ask "Who?" Susan squealed, "Carrie and Horace Junior! Can you believe it? Rachel will be so excited. I just can't believe it, can you? Should I call Rachel or wait?"

Georgia insisted that, even though the news was indeed very exciting, perhaps the honeymooners should be left alone to focus on each other, uninterrupted. "After all," Georgia reminded her, "I've already called them once about Ricky."

"But maybe this good news would balance out the bad news."

"Let's wait a few days, at least. Suppose Carrie and Horace change their minds. Then we'd have to call again."

"Oh, they won't change their minds. They've put down a huge earnest money deposit. They're in love with the house. Horace Junior has big plans for the yard, and Carrie is thrilled that she can walk to work. Wow! She can walk to work with Rachel!"

The other line rang, and Georgia stopped Susan from going any further into her fantasy about Carrie's new life in the Dupont Circle neighborhood. After a quick "good-bye," she punched the button to connect the other call.

Belle's voice sounded clear and strong as she left the message for Rachel that they had arrived at the farm, and all was well. "Just in case she calls in for messages," Belle said.

"Oh, she will," Georgia laughed. "If I know my boss, she will."

* * *

Dupont Circle bustled in the late afternoon as Susan made Ralph's rounds. She and Jim had met for lunch at her favorite place, the Mayflower Hotel, and her mind still raced with their plans for the move. Not focused on the animal at the other end of the leash, she almost tripped when he suddenly dragged her across the courtyard toward Deejee's hotdog stand. Breathless, Susan watched her friend. Deejee stooped to feed Ralph his daily treat. The two laughed as the dog sniffed at the hotdog tentatively, as though he had never seen one before, and then gobbled it down in two bites.

"Aren't you feeding this animal?" Deejee joked, as she scratched Ralph behind his ears.

"Actually, he's not eating very well. Guess he misses Rachel and John. Ben's worried and thinks it's all his fault because he suggested they get married. Poor little guy. Children do take a lot of responsibility on their small shoulders when they've had tragedies early in life. Wish I could wave a magic wand and make all his worries go away. He asks me at least once an hour if Rachel and John are okay."

"Is he still seeing a therapist?"

Susan nodded and said they had an appointment later the next day with the same psychiatrist who treated Lily after her dog bite. The two watched Ralph as he rambled around the Circle and sniffed the regulars seated at benches along his path. He stopped as if to pay homage at the spot beside the top of the metro stairs where he had last seen Chelsea before her death on the tracks below.

"That's some dog," Deejee said.

"Yeah. In some ways, I think he's the best therapy Ben has. He's good for all of us, really. Don't know what we'd do if anything happened to him."

"Don't even go there, woman," Deejee said and made the sign of the cross as if to ward off evil spirits. "Those days when he went missing were the blackest days I can remember here on the Circle. Blackest days, bar none."

"Yes, they were black. And the happiest day was the one when that van pulled up in front of Rachel's house and out jumped our Ralph."

When he heard his name, the dog ran back to Deejee and sat as if he thought he might take advantage of the moment's sentiment and get another hotdog. "No more today, smarty," Deejee laughed. "Don't want you to get in the habit of expecting more."

"Speaking of wanting more, heard any news about Ricky?"

Deejee said she talked to the treatment center counselor earlier in the day. He told her that Ricky made the trip to Staunton uneventfully. She didn't know how long he'd be there, but she suspected he'd charm his way out and be back at the Circle sooner than later. "He's a good boy, but right now he's eat up with resentment. He's hurtin' bad."

"Well, I just hope they keep him until after Rachel and John get back. I'd worry about Belle and Mary downstairs alone."

"Maybe Belle and Mary won't come back. Maybe you'll be planning another wedding."

Susan giggled. "You sound just like me, Deejee."

"The girl did catch the bridal bouquet, didn't she?"

"Yeah, but maybe it's not George she'll marry."

The two women looked at each other. Neither wanted to voice the fear they shared.

* * *

Nancy centered a huge pot of impatiens saved from the summer on the dining room table. When Mary saw the plant, she ran to it and shouted, "Rachel! Rachel!"

"You'd better keep an eye on that one," Nancy said. "She's smart. Not every little girl identifies plant types at her age. They just see a plant. I'm impressed."

"Yeah, sometimes she's too smart for her own good," Belle laughed. "I think we've got a wild ride ahead of us."

"Well, hold on tight and enjoy it, honey. I'll be right here to catch you both any time you jump the track," George said as he limped into the room. He sniffed the tempting aroma of fresh biscuits and country fried ham and let out a long sigh of satisfaction.

"Sorry Simon can't join us," Nancy said. "He's out in the fields this morning checking on a cow that wandered off. He said to tell you he's looking forward to seeing you tonight."

"Me, too," Belle said, surprised that she sincerely meant those words. She felt grateful for her time with Rachel's "country cousins," as they jokingly referred to themselves. Their dining room table held more than hearty food, she realized. It held lots of love as they sat around it and held hands to say a blessing over the food.

"And bless the hands that prepared it," George added after the "Amen." He squeezed Belle's hand.

"Yes, thank you so much—not only for the food, but for giving us safe haven," Belle said. "I promise we won't stay beyond our welcome. I'm sure we'll be able to get back to the city soon."

Nancy interrupted her. "You stay as long as you want, young lady. Any friend of George's is family to us. And having a little girl around the place is a gift from God. Simon and I never had a daughter. Feels like we've got not only a daughter but a granddaughter now. We should thank you."

Tears welled up in Belle's eyes as she recognized the sincerity of Nancy's words. Even after several months spent surrounded by Rachel's kindness, Belle still sometimes felt off-balance when she experienced such expressions of love. She glanced across the table at George and smiled at his wink. When Mary tried to copy the wink but ended up batting both eyes, the adults all laughed.

What a glorious day, Belle thought. To laugh. To laugh deeply from the pit of my stomach. She looked around the dining room. The large mahogany buffet still sat laden with breakfast food, even after everyone had served themselves. The large and lush Boston ferns brought in from the wraparound porch for the winter. The immense rag rug that almost touched the four corners of the room. Everything she saw spoke to her heart of plenty. Of more than enough. Of comfort. She let her mind wrap itself in the bountiful surroundings and remembered Rachel's words, "All good things come to those who wait."

Five years with Ricky felt like several lifetimes as they plummeted together from the heights of a nightlife full of drugs and jazz clubs down to the depths of life on the street. A very long wait it had been until the day she met Rachel and Ralph at the Circle. She remembered Rachel's gift of a night's stay in a hotel where she and Mary soaked so long in their first bath in months. Their first bath since they moved into the homeless shelter. She could still feel the joy of that moment when she wrapped herself and her child in the plush bath towel and cocooned them in its sweet-smelling whiteness.

The next day, Rachel invited them to move to her basement apartment, and John asked her to work as Ben's nanny. The wait had been long, but the "good things" far exceeded her wildest dreams.

George interrupted her memories to ask what she wanted to do with the rest of the day. Without a moment's hesitation, Belle said she'd like to see George's photographs. "Rachel says they're wonderful," she said.

"I'm afraid little Miss Mary will be pretty bored looking at walls full of pictures," George balked.

"Why don't I take Mary with me," Nancy offered. "We'll ride out into the fields and see if Simon has found his lost cow."

Mary clapped her hands. "Cow! Cow!"

"Thanks," Belle said, "but let me help you clean up here first."

While the women cleared the table of dishes and carried the leftovers into the kitchen, George chased Mary out into the yard to the tire swing. Belle smiled as she watched the man tie her daughter's hood tightly under her chin to protect her ears from the chill.

"That's a good man, you know," Nancy said behind her. "Treat him well, and you won't be sorry. He's been through a heap of pain, and he's still got some ragged edges, but he's solid under it all. And he seems to be very fond of you and that little girl. Never seen him like this before."

"What about Rachel?"

"What do you mean?"

"I mean, didn't they have a thing for each other just a little while ago?"

Nancy walked to the window and looked out at George as he carefully pushed the swing. Not too high, even though Mary kicked her little feet and tried to soar higher. When Nancy turned back to face the younger woman, her eyes focused intensely somewhere in the distance.

"Belle, let me tell you something about men. Been married to one for umpteen years and fed a bunch of them around my table. They've talked around this table, not knowing I was listening, but I was. There's two kinds of lovin' in a man. The hot intense kind that flares up and fades fast. And that's what I think George felt for

Rachel. It was magic, and it did what it was meant to do—opened his heart. But then there's the slow steady burn that lasts a lifetime."

Nancy hesitated. She walked over to Belle where she stood at the window. She grasped her by the shoulders and turned her so they stood face-to-face. Belle waited. "That's the kind of love I think George needs now. That's what I see in his eyes when he looks at you. And at Mary."

"I'm not sure I understand."

"All you need to understand is don't play with that fire, sweetheart. I don't want to see either one of you get burned."

Chapter Seven

As soon as Belle entered the first room where George's photographs hung, he felt the difference. As the young woman circled the room, she glanced quickly from one child's face to the next—without even a minute's pause to read the names written neatly on the cards tacked beneath the frames.

George remembered his other visitor, not too long ago.

Rachel stood on the threshold of the room, frozen. Slowly, she entered. Reverently, she approached the first face, and not until she lingered in front of six or seven portraits did she finally find her voice. The experience felt spiritual, and George hadn't realized exactly how deeply he felt the spirit until he observed Belle's very different reaction.

Maybe she's distracted, he thought as he made excuses for her shallow approach to his shrine. Maybe the timing is wrong. But when Belle turned to him shortly after she entered his gallery and pronounced the collection "pretty," he knew the problem was more than distraction or timing. He didn't offer to show her the room dedicated to the black and white study of cow faces. No way that could be called "pretty," he thought. Not sure I could restrain myself if she used that word again to describe the art form with which he expressed something so much deeper than the word "pretty" could begin to touch.

"Glad you like them," George muttered as he ushered Belle out of the room and toward the stairs.

"What's the matter? Did I say something wrong? Isn't there another room? Aren't there more pictures?"

"Not finished," George mumbled. He roughly pushed Belle forward. Her foot caught on the edge of the top step, and he caught her as she began to fall. When she turned back to grab the handrail to steady herself, he saw the horror in her eyes. "I'm sorry, Belle."

"You pushed me, George. You tried to push me down the stairs."

"No, Belle, I didn't try to do anything like that. I'm sorry that scared you. Falling is a terrible feeling, but trust me, I would never do anything to hurt you. Here, let me hold you," he said and patted her back. "Shh. It will pass."

The two stepped back into the hall, away from the stairs, and stood in a loose embrace. George felt Belle's breath slow. She waited for his kiss. The grandfather clock at the bottom of the stairs struck noon. Twelve brassy gongs echoed up the stairs in what sounded to George like a death knell. I wonder if she hears what I hear, he asked himself. But he knew she probably didn't and that he should disentangle himself from the vulnerable young woman in his arms— and from her even more fragile child.

And he knew that to disentangle himself might be more crucial to his survival than when he dodged the landmines in Vietnam.

"Come on," he whispered into her sweet-smelling hair. "Let's go downstairs. I'll fix us something to drink."

"Tea?"

"I think what I'd like right now is a sip of scotch. How about you?"

Belle's eyes widened with surprise but, despite the early hour, she agreed to join him in the parlor where he pulled out a dust-covered bottle of Dewar's and poured them both a splash of the amber liquid. As they raised their glasses in a toast, George stopped.

"Sorry. I forgot. Forgot about Ricky."

"No big deal. Just because Ricky's got an alcohol problem doesn't mean the rest of us can't enjoy a drink now and then. Cheers!"

George watched as Belle drained her glass before he even raised his to his lips. "More?" he offered as he took a sip and felt the welcome warmth.

Belle shook her head. "No, thanks. If it's okay with you, I think I'll walk back down to the main house and check on Mary." She looked at George, her usually clear eyes clouded.

She knows, George thought. She knows.

* * *

Rachel leaned over to hang up the phone beside the bed when Georgia finally answered. "I was almost ready to give up," she said. Georgia laughed.

"You? Give up? So, let's see. This is day number two of your honeymoon, and you've only called twice. I guess that's not too bad. And this time I've got some very good—very exciting—news to tell you, so I'm actually glad you called."

Georgia paused and waited for Rachel's response. When she couldn't wait any longer, she prompted her friend with, "Guess who's moving into Susan's house."

"Come on, Georgia. Don't play games with me. Who?"

Rachel welcomed the news that Carrie and Horace would be her new neighbors. Since the sale would be a cash deal, they expected to close within a month and move in plenty of time for Horace to do his spring planting.

"What about Susan?" Rachel asked. "Have they found a place at the beach yet?"

"Susan says they're going to store all their stuff and rent a furnished condo. Sounds like she's still not real sure she wants to relocate. Probably a good idea to move slow. You know Susan."

Rachel smiled. Yes, she knew Susan and all her flights of fancy, but the move to the beach had been Jim's idea. Strong, steady, always-knew-what-he-wanted Jim. Rachel knew the move was a done deal, and she hated the thought of going home to find her best friend surrounded by packing boxes. The fact that Carrie would be her new neighbor softened the blow—but only a little.

"So, what's on your agenda for today, Mrs. Turner?"

"We're signed up for a canoe trip down the Rio Grande."

"Isn't it a little cold for that at this time of year? I know you're in the heat of passion, but surely you've got some sense at your age. That water must be freezing right now."

"That's why we're planning to stay in the canoe. Any phone messages I need to know about? New clients?"

"All's well here, boss. Have fun. I'll call if I need you," Georgia said and hung up before Rachel had a chance to spend any more honeymoon time with shop talk.

"That was a quick conversation," John said as he walked out of the bathroom, a towel wrapped around his waist. His chest hairs still glistened from the shower, and he stood in front of the kiva to warm himself at the fire.

"Susan and Jim have already found new buyers for their house. Carrie and Horace will be moving in just a few weeks after we get home. I can't believe it. Wouldn't old Horace Gilbert be tickled to know I'll be able to keep an eye on his son's every move. Not that I want that responsibility."

"I've got some ideas about your responsibilities, Mrs. Turner," John said. He dropped the towel and walked toward the bed where Rachel lay burrowed under the duvet.

"What time do we need to be at the river?" she whispered in mild protest as he covered her body with his.

"You let me worry about the canoe trip, my lovely bride. You just enjoy the ride I'm about to take you on right here."

And she did.

* * *

Rachel and John called the inn's front office and asked for a to-go breakfast of fruit and freshly baked muffins. They found them packed in a hand-woven basket outside their door when they opened it to leave.

"This is what I call 'service'," Rachel said as she tucked the basket under her arm and turned to lock the door.

"No, what you just enjoyed in that bed, Mrs. Turner, was 'service,'" John said, nodding his head toward the rumpled sheets. He laughed at Rachel when she insisted that the sheets be straightened into some semblance of what she called "decency" before they left the room. "For an old woman, you sure know how to make a man feel like he's sixteen again."

Rachel smacked her husband playfully on his rugged jaw. "Careful who you're calling 'old woman.' I bet you'll have trouble keeping up with me today. When was the last time you were in a canoe?"

"Hey, this was my idea, remember. I didn't spend all my time in New York City. I know my way around a canoe. Just like a woman's body, in fact."

"Morning," Rachel interrupted him to speak to Maria. The innkeeper laid more wood on the living room fire. "Thanks for the picnic breakfast. We're getting a late start. I'll miss your fruit compote. It's always such a delicious start to the day."

Maria smiled knowingly and asked if they planned to be back in time for supper. When John mentioned their plans for dinner at Doc Martins, Rachel thought she noticed a darkness pass over the other woman's eyes. She knew how private the locals were, and how Maria, in particular, seemed to keep a shell around herself. She didn't probe, but as they drove out of the parking lot, she asked John if he had seen Maria's troubled look.

"Relax, Rachel. You're on your honeymoon." He reached over and stroked her left hand. He rubbed the wedding band on her ring finger, as if for good luck. "No solving other people's problems here. You can pray for them, if you must. You can mention them in your meta practice, if that's what you do." He turned to look at her, his eyebrows raised.

"Yes, that's what I do."

"Okay, but you will not do anything else that even remotely smacks of helping the folks in Taos who may be in some kind of trouble. Got it?"

Rachel smiled sweetly and squeezed her husband's hand. "You're sounding mighty bossy, John Turner. Don't think that just because I married you, I'm taking orders from you."

John laughed. As they stopped at a traffic light, the couple who waited at the corner to cross the street looked at them.

"Stop all that noise, John. Those people will think you've lost your mind."

"I have lost my mind. Lost my mind over you," John said as he reached across the seat and tickled Rachel so that she joined him in her own fit of laughter until the driver behind them honked his horn. They looked up to see that the light had turned green. John waved an apology and slowly drove forward, headed out toward the point on the river where they arranged to rent two canoes for the day. Rachel insisted on her own. She reminded John that she paddled alone for many years and warned him not to rush her surrender of independence. John knew not to argue.

She unwrapped the muffins and handed one to her husband. The smell of cinnamon and apples filled the car. Rachel inhaled with a deep sigh of satisfaction. She bit into the warm muffin and smiled, all thoughts of Maria and any problems at Doc Martins disappeared in the pure taste of pleasure.

John parked their rental Jeep in an empty lot. Neither was surprised to have the river to themselves on such a cold day.

"Sure this is a good idea, city girl?" John asked as he gestured toward the desolate stretch of water in front of them. Rachel snorted but didn't bother to answer. In their short past, they enjoyed many discussions about the fact that life in the city did not make her a "city girl." Her roots developed on the farm where she grew up, and they had not been totally uprooted when she began her life in DC. The deepest parts of Rachel still resonated most strongly when she spent time in nature. And for some reason she never could explain, New Mexico stirred feelings in her that were as heady as the finest wine.

John looked down at the two canoes tethered to the dock, and, as Rachel began to drop her backpack into one of them, he stopped her. "Please, Rachel. Let's just take one. I promise to let you steer the boat. I promise."

"Why? What's the problem with taking two?"

"How are we going to talk? I don't want to have to yell across the water to the back of your head all day. Does that sound like fun to you?"

"Talk?" At the pained look on Rachel's face, John realized that conversation hadn't been part of her vision for the day.

"Not lots of talking but maybe a very occasional word or two," he said. "Nothing obnoxious."

Rachel looked at the water, barely rippled by a gentle breeze. She looked down at the two canoes as they bounced gently beside the dock. And then she looked up at her new husband and smiled. "Okay, John Turner, but I sit in the back."

Without a word, John dropped his own backpack into the front of the canoe closest to him and stepped down into it. He reached for Rachel's hand before she could change her mind. The young dock attendant ran over to them and waved his arms. "Hey, I thought you reserved two canoes. What's going on?" he shouted.

"Lady changed her mind. We'll only take one."

"I don't know, sir. May have to charge you for two. I mean, you know, you did reserve two."

"Sure, we'll pay for two," John said as he pulled out his wallet.

"I don't think so," Rachel said as she pushed John's wallet away. "Young man, obviously you don't have a huge line of people waiting for canoes today, and I doubt you had to turn anyone away this morning for lack of one canoe. We haven't signed anything saying we'll take two. We'll take one, and we'll probably be back another few times to take it again—unless you push us with this ridiculous demand that we pay for what we have no intention of using." She pulled out her credit card and held it out to him as she stepped into the back of the boat. "Paddles, please."

John followed her meekly. He settled himself on the wooden seat, his backpack at his feet. He pulled his wool scarf tighter around his neck and turned his jacket collar up.

"Need a headband? I brought one for you," Rachel said behind him.

John smiled as he enjoyed the new gift of a partner who wanted to take care of him. Someone in his life who thought about things like his cold ears. He turned around to smile at her. Rachel had already put on her own headband—a bright orange strip that seemed to create a halo around her silver hair. "Yes, I'll take one, as long as it's not orange," he said.

Rachel pulled a modest black band out of her left pocket and passed it to her husband. While he adjusted it around his ears, she pushed off from the dock with her paddle. As the canoe glided away from land, Rachel looked up at the hillside that towered above them, rocky and covered with pinion trees. From a distance, the ground appeared to be sprinkled with polka dots. The clear blue New Mexico sky contrasted with the many shades of brown below.

Suddenly, a huge hawk soared across the ridge ahead of them, and Rachel gasped. "It's her," she whispered as she reached forward to grasp John's shoulder. "It's her."

John waited for her to say more. He knew she would. He knew

his wife would share the story when she was ready. Finally, as the bird disappeared behind the ridge, she spoke.

"The day we buried my mother was the first day I saw the bird. As we walked away from that horrible gaping hole in the ground where they had dropped her coffin, I walked off, my head buried in my father's raincoat sleeve. I felt someone—something—staring at me, and when I finally looked up, there she was. The hawk, sitting on a fencepost at the edge of the little cemetery. Every time I've come here, I've seen her again. Here in Taos. The only other place I've seen her since that day."

John knew better than to ask why she thought it was the same hawk fifty years later.

"My mother grew up here. I think her heart never left. She talked about it often, and when I finally visited for the first time, I understood why. I felt the freedom, too. What I never understood was how she ever left. Until now," Rachel said. "Until I met you."

Chapter Eight

R icky sat ramrod straight in the gray metal folding chair. The seat lay cold beneath him. His cotton pajama bottoms didn't provide much insulation between his skin and the hard steel. His throat still throbbed in a circle of pain where the sheet had choked him. As he sat, head down, hands gripped together in front of him, dangling between his knees, he whispered the Serenity Prayer over and over. "God grant me the serenity to accept the things I cannot change, the courage to change the things I can and the wisdom to know the difference."

He sat in the day room, alone except for the attendant who crouched in a corner and stared at the television. The volume, turned down to a low hum, sounded like a bumblebee. Ricky couldn't make out any of the words, but he could feel the attendant glance at him during the commercials. The soft sound of the television, and the mere presence of someone awake, helped ease the loneliness.

Nights hurt the most. The darkness provided a perfect backdrop for the maddening images of Belle and Mary with George. While Ricky didn't know for sure, he suspected they had escaped to the farm after his failed suicide attempt. He knew Rachel well enough to figure she would suggest that move for their safety.

George would jump at the chance, Ricky thought and clenched his teeth. He began the Serenity Prayer again. The drugs didn't help. Maybe I need to ask for another sleeping pill, he thought. No, the doctor will interpret that as a sign I'm getting worse rather than better. I need to get out of here and not wind up staying another month because I asked for an extra sleeping pill.

"God, grant me the serenity."

Ricky raised himself from the chair and began the slow walking meditation Belle showed him. Rachel taught it as a good alternative for someone who couldn't sit still for long periods. Ricky felt the big black man on the other side of the room stare at him as he walked slowly around the periphery of the room. I hope he knows I'm meditating and doesn't think this is some symptom of my insanity, Ricky worried. He tried to refocus from that fear to his footsteps. After several laps around the room, he felt calmer and nodded to the attendant.

"Having trouble sleeping, Ricky?"

"Not a problem. Just wanted a little space."

"Need anything?"

"No, I'm fine. Back to bed now. Enjoy your show."

Ricky shuffled quickly out of the day room and down the hall. His slippers slapped along the slick linoleum floor. Soon after he lay back down on his narrow bed, he felt himself drift toward a less troubled sleep. Images of Belle and a kite soothed the rough edges and eased the pain around his throat. He prayed that he could lose consciousness before that peaceful picture could be destroyed by demons of fear. Demons with George's face. The face that haunted so much of Ricky's waking and sleeping hours.

"God grant me the serenity," he repeated one last time.

* * *

On the farm, Mary's magic hour of the day struck at four o'clock in the afternoon. Although she didn't know how to tell time yet, George taught her where the hands on the clock needed to be when they should trudge to the barn to milk.

The little girl sat patiently and watched the minute hand creep toward the twelve. When Belle walked into the kitchen, she knew the story. She smiled and patted the child's shoulder. Mary's eyes never left the clock.

"Are you going to help George milk?"

Mary nodded. Belle's heart warmed at the sight of the ear-to-ear grin. "I hear a new cat has come to live at the barn. Have you seen her yet? Does she have any kittens?"

Mary shook her head from side to side but still wouldn't take her eyes off the clock. She already wore her coat, hat and mittens, and her boots sat beside her chair, ready for George to help her put them on. When George walked into the kitchen five minutes before four, Mary finally allowed her attention to be diverted from the clock above the refrigerator. She jumped down from the chair, grabbed her boots and held them out to George.

"Thanks for not keeping her waiting," Belle said. "I don't know what I'd do if that hand moved past twelve, and you weren't here. She's obsessed. Got a real thing about milking. I don't understand it."

"I'm not in the habit of disappointing my women," George said as he knelt beside Mary and helped her step into her boots.

Belle blushed, but George didn't look up at her as she expected. Something's changed, she thought with a sinking feeling.

"Ready to go, Missy? Those cows have been watching the clock, too, you know. We don't want them to bust."

Mary laughed and ran out the door. George looked back at Belle with a smile. "See you at supper."

"Need any help? I could go with you."

"No. I think Mary and I have things covered. You catch up on your studies. How's that going, by the way?"Good. Real good."

"I'm glad. You keep your eye on that goal, girl. Don't let anything get you off course again. You deserve the best, and that degree may be the key to your best."

As George turned his back and followed her daughter into the dusk, Belle stood quietly. She knew George was right. She and Rachel had repeated the same conversation many times. The story in which she finished school, found a career she enjoyed and became self-sufficient. Made a good life for herself and Mary. A life that didn't depend on a man to provide for them. Or leave them in the lurch like Ricky had.

Belle realized she had allowed herself to indulge in fantasies about George and life as a farmer's wife.

After she moved into the room across the hall from his, she felt a country comfort settle around her—a feeling in sharp contrast to the city energy that created such damage. She wrapped herself in the quiet, but now she felt it slip away from her.

"Has the milking shift begun?" Nancy asked as she noticed the lost look on Belle's face.

Belle nodded but didn't turn from the window where she watched George disappear into the barn. The sound of cows happily greeting the pair echoed down the hill toward the house. Belle turned toward Nancy. "Something's changed with George," she said. "I'm not sure what, but he's acting strangely."

"George is a moody man, dear. Don't take it personally."

"But it happened so suddenly. He took me to see his pictures, and then it was like a light switched off."

Nancy hesitated and then asked the question that to her was always the answer. "Did he show you the cows?"

"No. I asked him if there were more pictures after he showed me the kids, but he said the rest weren't finished."

Nancy nodded her head. She had witnessed this scene before. She knew that, other than herself, George had shown his most recent exhibit—the collection of cow portraits that represented his transformation—to only one other person. Rachel.

The second collection symbolized the turning point in his life. The photographs illustrated his escape from the pain he had captured in the photos taken in Vietnam. He shared the cow faces only with kindred souls. Obviously, Nancy thought, he had not felt that Belle's soul was kindred.

Still, she repeated the mantra, "Don't take it personally" to Belle and patted her on the shoulder. "Take this opportunity to enjoy some time alone before supper," she said. "Don't you have some schoolwork to do?"

Belle nodded her head, but her focus remained frozen on the barn as she walked back across the yard to George's house.

* * *

Carrie stopped by Rachel's office to pick up a copy of the first draft of the new employee handbook Rachel started before she left on her honeymoon. As she walked in the front door, Georgia ended a phone conversation and returned the receiver to its cradle.

"What's the scowl about?" Carrie asked.

Georgia shook her head and hesitated before she answered. She chewed on whether to share her concern or keep it to herself. Years of work in a law firm taught her the importance of tight lips.

"For God's sake, what is it?" Carrie pushed. "Has something happened in Taos? Is it Ricky? Tell me. You can trust me, you know. I'm practically part of the firm. A member of the family almost."

Georgia nodded and reached for a Kleenex from the crochet-covered box she kept on the corner of her desk for clients. Most people, who came to see Rachel, saved their tears for her secretary after they completed their business in the inner office. "I'm worried about Stan," Georgia confessed after she blew her nose several times. She pulled out another tissue and wiped her eyes. "Did you notice anything different about him at the wedding?"

"No, but I was pretty distracted by Horace. He was like a kid who'd forgotten to take his Ritalin that day."

"Speaking of Ritalin, maybe that's all Stan needs. Some simple pill."

"What in the world are you talking about, Georgia? What's wrong with Stan?"

Georgia rose from her desk and walked over to join Carrie on the sofa. She sat, hands folded in her lap, and listened to the traffic pass on the street outside. Not one to create unnecessary alarm, she chose her words carefully. "Stan's memory seems to be failing. It's been going on for some time now. Nothing major. A few missed deadlines, and I've had to call to remind him about several cases he was working on. But his condition seems to be getting worse."

Georgia paused. She wished Rachel sat on the sofa beside her to share her fear for Stan, but she knew that Carrie, too, cared deeply for the private detective who always managed to work his way into everybody's heart.

"Yesterday he got Lily's name wrong. He called her 'Ruth'."

"Ruth?"

"His wife's name. The woman's been dead ten years. He called his granddaughter 'Ruth'."

"Well, we all make mistakes like that, Georgia. I do it all the time. Especially names. And that's a logical mistake. You know how much he loves Lily, and to call her by his wife's name seems like a natural thing to do. Maybe he was just tired."

"I know all that, but it was his reaction when I corrected him that worries me. He kept insisting he was taking Ruth—not Lily—to the toy store. He actually became angry and hung up on me."

"Oh, dear. That does sound bad."

The two women looked at each other. The same thoughts raced through their minds.

"Have you talked to Rachel about it?"

"A little, but the woman's on her honeymoon. She's already obsessing about Ricky. I don't want to add to her list of things she has no control over but which she's determined to fix despite the fact she's all the way on the other side of the country. The Stan problem can wait. No restraining order will make any difference with him, I'm afraid."

"Afraid? What are you afraid of, Georgia?" Susan demanded as she bounced through the front door of the office.

Georgia and Carrie looked at each other, and, at the same time, as if on cue, said, "Nothing."

"Good. Cause I've got something for you to help me with. Something fun, and something that needs to be done in a timely fashion. Can't involve people who are afraid. Don't want to bring any bad juju to this project. You do understand, don't you? It's not that I don't care about whatever it is you're afraid of. Don't get me wrong. But this project needs lots of positive energy around it, or it will fail, sure as my name is 'Susan'."

Carrie and Georgia sat wide-eyed and open-mouthed as Susan spun around the office in circles like a pink jogging-suited tornado. Her pink tennis shoes patted out a frantic rhythm back and forth across the hooked rug.

"Stop, Susan," Georgia finally commanded. "Tell us what you want."

Susan stuck out her bottom lip like a child who had been reprimanded but then settled into the rocking chair beside Georgia's desk. "I'm putting together a care package for Ricky," she beamed. "I just know you both want to contribute some little something. You, Georgia, should contribute some chocolate chip cookies, for instance, and, you, Carrie, should think of something to send." Here, Susan stopped and looked puzzled. "Well, surely you have something you could send the poor boy, couldn't you? Money, maybe?"

Carrie laughed. "When are you sending this care package, Susan? Do we have a little time to give this some thought? Aren't there restrictions about what he can get?"

"Restrictions? What do you mean 'restrictions'?"

Georgia stood up from the sofa and walked over to her desk where she sat down in front of her computer and Googled the name of the hospital where Ricky had been admitted. "We should probably call and ask them," she said. "When are you sending it?"

"I'm not sending it. I'm going over there tomorrow. I figured he probably needs some company. Some cheering up. Maybe a poem. Maybe his new friends there need poems, too."

Georgia held up her hand to signal for quiet as she punched in the number of the hospital. After a few minutes of recorded instructions, she hung up. "Well, I'm off the hook. No homemade cookies allowed. Susan, you can bring poems. And Carrie, here's a list of things you can send. The good juju also passed muster, but it can't be individually wrapped."

Carrie looked at the list and then over at Susan. "Need someone to go with you? I guess Jim will stay with Ben, right?"

"Sure, that sounds like fun. What time can you be ready? Eight?"

"Make it nine, and you've got a deal."

Susan gave a sharp military salute, rushed out the door and left it open in her hurry to return home. When Georgia stood up to shut it and looked down the street, the pink jogging suit was nowhere in sight. She laughed. "That woman is what my father used to call a 'force of nature.' You're a brave woman to offer to ride with her. Prepare yourself for an adventure, and you won't be disappointed."

"I can use some distraction. Horace is driving me nuts with all the plans for the move. A change of scenery will do me good, even if it's a trip to a mental hospital. Should make me feel more sane. Some days, the thoughts of all the changes at work, of getting married and of moving from where I've lived for so long, all combine and give me the crazies."

"When are you two getting married? Still doing the justice of the peace thing? No wedding?"

"Yes. And then a trip to Hilton Head Island for the weekend. We plan to start the final packing when we get back. The closing date is on Valentine's Day."

"What a wonderful gift. Your first home together. I know Rachel is looking forward to having you as a neighbor."

"I'm sure I'll never take Susan's place, but I do hope Rachel will give me a chance."

"Nobody will take Susan's place, but Rachel is open to change. My goodness, her life has been nothing but change recently. Finding Ralph. Falling in love. Becoming a mother at sixty-two. The woman is the poster child for 'Anything is possible.' You'll be fine."

"I hope Susan will leave behind some of her good "juju," as she calls it."

"Oh, she will. And you'll find it when and where you least expect it."

Chapter Nine

After their day on the river, followed by a shared hot shower and a short nap, Rachel and John headed for Doc Martin's. The dim lights in the small dining room provided the perfect ending to a perfect day, Rachel thought. Then she remembered Maria's expression when they had mentioned their plan to eat at the restaurant.

Rachel looked around. Nothing seemed to have changed since her last visit. When her favorite waitress approached the table to take their drink orders, she bubbled in her usual vivacious way.

"See, nothing's wrong," John whispered as he read Rachel's mind.

"Pam is an actress, John. The world could have just ended, and she'd still be cracking jokes if that were the role she had assigned herself for the evening."

"Okay, but please try to relax and enjoy your meal. No probing questions tonight. Let Pam entertain us."

Rachel gazed around the room in silence and then looked at her husband. She leaned toward him. She smiled. "You were an excellent paddler today, John Turner. I must say, I was impressed."

John reached across the table and stroked her cheek. "And you did a great job of restraining yourself when I wasn't. Even when I almost turned the canoe over."

"Hitting that rock was tough."

"But you were the picture of cool and calm. I love you, Rachel Turner."

Pam approached the table with their wine glasses and set them down with a flourish. "What did I just hear? What's with the 'Rachel Turner' line? Something happen I haven't heard about since your last visit?'"

"Pam, this is my husband, John Turner."

Pam dramatically fell limply into the extra chair at their table and pretended to faint. "Tell me you're kidding. You were my model of the single woman, happy in her solo lot in life. Now, you've gone and betrayed me. Changed the story?" Rachel laughed. "I think your line is supposed to be 'Congratulations,' honey."

"Sorry. You know it's all about me. But, hey, I'll get over it. Congratulations, Mr. and Mrs. Turner. Drinks are on the house. What you gonna have for dinner?"

After Pam headed to the kitchen with their order, John reached in his pocket and pulled out a long slim box and pushed it across the table toward Rachel.

"What's this?" "Open it and find out."

"John, you spoil me too much."

"Never too much. Open it. I found it at the little gift shop near Cafe Tazo."

Rachel lifted the lid and gasped at the turquoise necklace that lay tucked inside the orange tissue paper. She clasped it around her neck and felt it fall heavily between her breasts.

"A stone for every year we have ahead of us," John said.

"Lots of stones, here, John. I don't know if I want to live that long."

John smiled. "Eternity is a long time, my love."

"Now, that's a line I'm going to steal," Pam said. "'Eternity is a long time, my love.' Simple. Easy to remember. But very, very deep."

"Yes, that's me. Simple," John laughed.

"But deep," Rachel giggled. She looked at Pam, averted her eyes from John and asked the waitress about the restaurant's business.

Pam made a production of scraping bread crumbs off the table top. She hummed tunelessly while she worked. Rachel waited patiently. She hoped John wouldn't interrupt the story she knew was about to unfold. The truth behind Maria's concern. Finally, Pam seemed to resolve whatever inner conflict she suffered about whether to confide in a customer the news about the restaurant's business.

She sat down again in the extra chair and leaned toward Rachel so that their conversation wouldn't be overheard. "Sylvia has breast cancer," she whispered.

Wow, no working up to the shocking news slowly, Rachel thought. But I shouldn't be surprised. Pam loves the dramatic value of shock.

"She and Peter aren't sure how it's going to affect the restaurant. All that treatment after the surgery and everything. They're at the age where they were thinking of retiring anyway, so they may just shut it down. Of course, the rest of us are hoping they'll find someone to take over so we can keep our jobs. And we're all worried about Sylvia, too, of course."

"Of course," Rachel said. "I'm so sorry. Are either of them here tonight? I'd like to speak to them, if they are."

"No, they've been staying pretty close to home since they got the news. They're so private, you know. In fact, I'd probably lose my job if they knew I'd told you, so don't say anything, please."

Rachel promised she'd keep the secret. When Pam walked back to the kitchen to check on their order, John gently punched her shoulder. "Just couldn't control yourself, could you?"

Rachel sipped her wine and didn't answer. Her mind raced in all kinds of directions, none of which she chose to share with John.

* * *

As the newlyweds lay in each other's arms later that night and enjoyed the view of the desert that stretched around them outside the four glass walls of their room on the top floor of the inn, Rachel purred like a kitten.

"What was that noise?" John laughed.

"I'm so happy. I didn't know it was possible to feel so good."

The moon over the Taos Pueblo land shone its light across the bed, and Rachel snuggled closer. The house spread silently below them.

"Think you can hold on to this feeling after we get back to the city? Maybe we should buy the restaurant, send for Ben and Ralph, and stay out here," John said. When Rachel didn't respond, he realized with a sick feeling that his wife had actually considered the idea as a serious possibility. "Rachel, I'm joking," he said. He sat up in bed and looked down at his wife. "You've spent too much time with Susan. Forget I even mentioned such a wild idea. We have too many ties to DC. We can't move to Taos. Don't worry. Someone will buy the restaurant, if that's what's needed."

Silence filled the room.

"It won't be us, Rachel."

Rachel propped herself up on one arm so she could look John in the eye. "There you go getting bossy again," she teased. She pecked him on the cheek and then wrestled him down into the pillows with her. She wrapped her fingers in his hair and drew his face close to hers. She kissed his eyelids and lingered there, her breath warm on his face. She hovered over him and savored his scent and the flicker of the candles in the kiva. The night was unseasonably warm, so they had decided not to light a fire. The candles provided just enough light to add to the glow of the stars and the moon.

"We are so lucky this room was available when we made our reservation," John said. "The view is truly amazing."

"Magic," Rachel said. Suddenly, the memory of George's magic lesson washed over her in a rush. She pictured George as she splashed with him in the river at the base of the rock tower he too her to see. She remembered the childlike joy she tasted for the first time in her life. As she lay in her husband's arms, she recognized an alarming sense of loss.

"Hold me, John. Hold me close," she said as she refocused on the steady sound of her husband's heartbeat.

* * *

Ralph pulled on his leash and dragged Susan along behind him. "Hold on, Ralph. What's the rush? You know something going on at the Circle that I don't?" Instead of slowing down, the dog quickened his pace. He didn't even stop to sniff his usual spots along the way.

"Wait! What about the lamppost?" Susan huffed as she almost jogged to keep up with the dog as he rushed down the street on a mission. When the two reached the Circle, Ralph ran straight to the hotdog stand where Ricky stood beside Deejee. The hotdog vendor added one last squirt of mustard and handed the man his breakfast. Susan stopped in mid-stride. Her mouth hung open, and, for once in her life, she remained speechless.

"Surprised to see me?" Ricky asked, his mouth full of hotdog. Deejee stood silently and flashed Susan a warning look. Her lips pursed and her eyes darted as if to say, "Careful. Don't push him." Susan heeded the wordless stop sign.

"Well, yes, I guess I am surprised to see you, Ricky. When did you get home?"

"Home? What exactly do you mean by 'home?' If you mean the homeless shelter, the bus driver just let me off there about an hour ago. If you mean 'home' like where you live, 'home' like where my family, Belle and Mary, live, guess I haven't quite arrived yet."

Ricky bit fiercely into his hotdog again and stared at Susan with red-rimmed eyes that shifted from her to Deejee and back again like nervous jitterbugs. Ralph sniffed at Ricky's pants legs and finally sat back on his haunches to wait for Deejee to give him his daily handout.

"Even Ralph has a home," Ricky mumbled. He rolled up the empty aluminum foil, stuck it in his pocket and squatted down to rub Ralph behind the ears. "Lucky dog. You're one lucky dog. You know that, don't you?"

Susan looked at Deejee for some clue as to what she should do or say to find out why Ricky had been released from the hospital so soon after his suicide attempt. As if he read her mind, Ricky stood up. "Vacation cut short. Funding cut short. No health insurance means mini-vacations. But you wouldn't know anything about that, would you, Susan? No money? No health insurance? Vacations cut short?"

Ralph licked Ricky's hand as if he sensed the anger and wanted to wash it away with his rough tongue. But Ricky refused to be comforted. He yanked his hand away from the dog and stepped back to put some distance between himself and the loving energy he had been offered. But Ralph—being a dog—wasn't ready to give up. He followed Ricky toward the bench where he was headed and leaned against his leg. Susan, still with a tight hold on the leash, was forced to follow.

Ricky tried to ignore the dog, but, even through the fog of the last pill he'd swallowed before he left the hospital, he felt Ralph's heart.

"Maybe he wants you to pet him," Susan whispered.

"Me? Why would he want me to pet him when he's got you?"

"I don't know why. Maybe 'why' isn't important. Maybe the only thing that's important is that he does, and that you do."

Deejee walked away from her hotdog cart to stand closer to where the other three had moved. "Maybe Ralph knows you and he are alike. Brothers. He feels connected to you in a way he doesn't connect to the rest of us. Maybe he loves you in a way he doesn't love the rest of us. Cause he knows you've been where he's been. Seen what he's seen."

"Okay, okay," Ricky said as he smeared mustard across his cheek in an attempt to brush a tear away. "Now, you're sounding like an AA meeting. I get it. You can stop." He knelt down beside the dog and wrapped his arms around Ralph's neck. He buried his face in the clean-smelling fur and inhaled. When he finally stood up, the anger had disappeared from his eyes. "You gonna tell Rachel I'm back, I guess. Warn Belle to keep Mary away from me."

Again, Susan looked at Deejee for guidance. The black woman shook her head.

"I don't know, Ricky. I guess I'll have to think about it. What do you want me to do?"

Ricky stood still and stared down at Ralph. "Tell her I'm back and doing fine," he said. "Tell her she knows where to find me, if she wants to talk. I won't bother her. I've got things to do."

Not able to stop herself, Susan asked if he still had a job at the law firm.

Ricky nodded his head. "Yeah, I guess lawyer Rob is kinda like Ralph. He's been where I've been."

* * *

Miles away, Nancy listened to George stomp his boots several times on the back porch. She looked up as he opened the door and walked in. She watched him slip off his black leather hat and hang it on the back of one of the kitchen chairs. "Coffee?" she asked.

"No, thanks. I've drunk about all the coffee I can handle. Couldn't sleep last night. Been up since four, drinking coffee."

Nancy nodded. "Full moon last night. Does it to me every time."

"I think it's more than the full moon, in my case."

Nancy didn't respond. She knew George would talk when he was ready. "Are Belle and Mary still asleep?" she asked.

"Yeah. Don't think those two would ever make it as country girls. They sleep right through the rooster crowing like it was a signal to burrow further under the covers."

"Give them time. You never know about people. For some, it takes time."

"Not Rachel."

Okay, here it comes, Nancy thought as she rinsed out the oatmeal pot and stuck it in the dishwasher. I knew whatever went sour between George and Belle had Rachel in the middle as a main ingredient. Still, she waited for George to go on.

He picked up the paper and flipped through the classified ads. Just when Nancy gave up any hope that she would hear George acknowledge the reason for his sleepless night, he slapped the paper down on the red-and-white checkered oilcloth table cover and glared up at her.

"She just doesn't get it," he said.

Nancy knew George meant Belle's reaction to his photography. Belle had spoken almost those very same words. Still, she waited to hear George's version.

"Guess I was expecting too much. Hoping to fill my needs with a woman half my age. Even less experience in living life than in the number of years, themselves. She just doesn't get it."

"You can't compare Belle to Rachel, George. That's not fair."

George's face darkened, and his shoulders slumped.

"You need to move on. What you and Rachel felt was special, but you need to move on."

"Magic," George interrupted.

"Yes, maybe, but magic comes in different packaging. Look at Simon and me. Our life may not look like magic to you, but it's a good life. You know that. You've seen us."

George walked across the kitchen to where Nancy stood at the sink. He wrapped his arms around her and hugged. She stroked his back. "Thanks, but it's hard to forget the Rachel kind of magic, if you've ever felt it." And then George shoved his hat back on his head and limped out the door and down the steps.

Nancy watched him walk toward his truck, rev the engine and back down the driveway. She watched him aim the old Ford pickup toward town and shoot forward like a bullet.

I'd hate to be his target, she thought and said a silent prayer for George and all the wounded hearts in the world. Including the two still asleep in his house up the hill.

Chapter Ten

H ere, boy. Come on, boy. Come to Ben. Come on, Ralph."
Upstairs in her bedroom, Susan heard Ben's voice grow
louder and higher with each shriek. She dashed the finishing
touches of her lipstick and rushed down the steps and to the back of
the house. She stopped in her tracks when she saw the tears stream
down the child's red face. "What is it, Ben?"

"I can't find Ralph. He's run away again. He's lost again. It was
my job to take care of him, and I've lost him. Ralph! Ralph!" Ben
left his post at the back door and dashed out into the yard. He
frantically raced from one corner to the next and periodically stopped
to yell the dog's name or stoop to look under a bush.

Susan followed him. She tried to balance his hysteria with a
calmness she didn't feel. She approached the child slowly and
reached out to touch his shoulder. Ben jerked away. The look he shot
Susan turned her blood to ice.

"Where is he? Why don't you do something? It's all your fault.
Big people aren't supposed to let dogs get out." Ben threw himself
down to the ground and curled into a ball.

Where the hell is Rachel when I need her? I have no idea how to
handle this, Susan thought desperately.

And then she remembered the days, the weeks, when she felt
trapped in her own nightmare, convinced of her husband's affair. She
remembered how Rachel simply held her. How wise her friend had
been to know that what she needed most was to be allowed to feel
what she needed to feel, even though Rachel doubted that her pain
was based in truth.

Susan lay down on the cold ground beside Ben and held him until the little body no longer shook with sobs. She pulled out a Kleenex and wiped his tears. As she tucked the balled-up soggy tissue into her jacket pocket, Ben sat up. A wide grin spread across his freckled face. "I know where he is," the child shouted as he jumped up and ran back into the house.

Susan struggled to rise from the ground. The cold had seeped into her bones, and she heard them crack as she stood up and hobbled back to the house. When she opened the kitchen door, a wild reunion scene greeted her as boy and dog chased each other around the granite-topped island in the middle of the room.

"Careful there, buddy. You don't want to fall and crack that hard head of yours against the counter top."

Ben laughed, grabbed Susan's hand and pulled her into his dance of joy. Breathless, Susan finally stopped and asked the adult question, "Where was he?"

"You're not going to believe it," Ben shouted. "You're really not going to believe it!"

"Try me. And lower your voice a little. No need to shout. I can hear you perfectly well."

Ben's face turned serious. "He was sitting in the window seat in your living room, staring at Rachel's house. Waiting for Rachel. He misses her so much, he wouldn't even come when I called." Ben leaned down and patted Ralph's head. Then he dropped to his knees and buried his face in the dog's fur. When he looked up at Susan, his eyes filled with tears again.

Oh, no, here it comes, Susan thought. She braced herself.

"Susan, we have to call Rachel and tell her she needs to come home. That Ralph is sad. That he needs her here."

When Susan didn't answer, Ben jumped up and raised his voice in anger. "We need to call her now!"

Susan silently cursed Rachel for the fact that she left her to care for a child who still grieved his parents' death. A little boy ill-equipped to deal with his grandfather's absence and the fear it provoked. A boy who didn't understand the importance of a honeymoon. This is just too hard, she thought. Ben watched her struggle, lost patience and stomped to the phone. "What's the phone number? I'll call," he shouted.

"Tell you what," Susan said. "We'll call and let Ralph hear Rachel's voice. I bet that will help. And you can talk to your grandfather, too. Would you like that?" Susan braced herself for Ben's continued insistence that the only answer to the current problem was for Rachel and John to cut their honeymoon short and come home. She was surprised when he looked down at Ralph. He studied the dog for a few minutes to gauge his feelings. When he finally returned his attention to Susan, he smiled.

"He thinks that might work," the little boy said. "At least, he's willing to try."

"Sometimes that's all it takes," Susan said. "A good try sometimes works well."

Susan called the Mabel Dodge Luhan House and asked to be connected to the Turners' room." Remember they're in a different time zone. They may not be in their room right now," she said to Ben while she waited to be connected.

"But we can leave a message, right? Ralph could maybe do a bark. Rachel likes it when he does that. She probably misses him, too, and if she heard him bark, she'd probably want to come home. Don't you think so?"

Susan held her fingers to her lips and signaled Ben to be quiet.

"Rachel, hey there. It's Susan. Surprised to catch you in your room. What? Oh, nothing's wrong."

"Yes! Something is wrong," Ben shouted as he grabbed the phone. "Rachel, you need to come home. Ralph misses you bunches. I thought I'd lost him. I looked and looked and looked and called and called, and he wouldn't come and guess where he was." Ben stopped long enough for Rachel to ask "Where?" and then forged on with the sad story of Ralph as he pined away on Susan's living room window seat. Finally, he stopped and listened to Rachel at the other end, on the other side of the country. "Yes, we've been medidating, and it doesn't help. Susan thinks maybe you should talk to him. Maybe we could try. I'll put the phone to his ear, and you tell him you love him, okay?"

Ben held the phone to Ralph's ear. The dog's tail wagged, and he opened his mouth and panted. Finally, he let out a happy yelp.

"See, it worked," Susan said. She started to reach for the phone, but Ben wouldn't let it go.

"Susan thinks it worked, but I'm not so sure. Maybe you'd better call again in about an hour. He might forget." Ben stood in silence and looked doubtful. "Yes, I can talk to Granddad." More silence while Rachel handed the phone to John. Ben smiled when he heard his grandfather's voice. He repeated the story of the lost dog and how he had found him in such a pitiful position of pain. "How many more days does he have to wait?" he asked. His mouth turned down at what sounded like a very long time. "Okay, but I don't' think I'll tell Ralph. I don't think he can count, anyway. Rachel always says, 'One day at a time' makes things easier." Ben listened and smiled weakly. "I love you, too. And Rachel." He handed the phone to Susan.

"Hey, John. Glad you were there. Yes, we're fine now. What? Okay, we'll expect your call in an hour. Yes, I'm sure Ralph will appreciate it. Bye now."

Susan hung up the kitchen phone and looked at Ben.

"Sure hope this works," he said. "We don't want Ralph to be sad, do we, Susan?"

"No, but we don't want Rachel and your grandfather to be sad because they had to end their honeymoon either, do we?"

Ben thought about that for a while and then shook his head. "No, but adults do sad better than dogs," he said.

And little boys, Susan thought with a sinking feeling.

* * *

Georgia rose from the chair behind her desk and greeted Stan with a hug. As soon as she wrapped her arms around his neck, she felt the tension. Even through his heavy pea jacket and wool plaid scarf, Georgia felt the tight muscles in the man's shoulders. She took a step back from him and looked into his face. Stan averted his eyes.

"When's Rachel coming back?" he asked.

Stan asked the same question every day. Maybe he's just got a lot on his mind and that's why he can't remember things, Georgia thought. Maybe it's a normal confusion. Maybe it's nothing to worry about. "Next week. Next Friday night. Late."

"Good," Stan said and turned to leave.

"Wait a minute there, buddy. You can't just waltz in here, ask 'When's Rachel coming back?' and then leave. What's going on? Have a seat. Talk to me."

Georgia was surprised and relieved when Stan didn't argue. Like a man with the weight of the world on his shoulders, he trudged over to the rocking chair in front of Georgia's desk and plopped down in it. Georgia waited for the man to speak. Just as she was about to give up and accept the fact that perhaps he wouldn't say anything, he did. "My family wants me to retire," Stan said and looked up from the hands he clutched in a fist in his lap.

Georgia waited for more, and, when more didn't follow, she leaned across her desk and patted his arm. "Well, what do you want, Stan? Are you ready to retire? Spend more time with Lily maybe? Relax? Have some fun? Travel?"

Stan sat in silence, head bent, until he finally looked up again at Georgia, his eyes dark, deep pools of misery. "They won't let me take Lily out alone anymore."

"What? Why? What do you mean?"

"Something's wrong. Something bad. I'm losing it, Georgia."

Georgia didn't have to ask what "it" meant. She'd seen the signs with Stan for weeks. And the same signs with members of her own family and friends. Dementia took many forms. She hoped Stan's was one of the kinder, gentler ones. "What do you need from Rachel, Stan? How can she help?"

"I need to get some things in order. Papers signed. Hell, I don't even have a will, Margaret."

Georgia ignored the fact that her old friend had called her by the wrong name and opened Rachel's calendar. A terrifying thought crossed her mind. "Stan, you're not about to give up, are you?"

"No, I'm not going to do myself in, if that's what you're thinking. But I want to get things in order before I totally lose my marbles." Stan laughed the old deep raspy laugh that Georgia counted on all the years she worked with him. The laugh that lightened so many heavy loads she and Rachel shouldered in the law firm. During the times when they both felt like they couldn't stand another heartbreaking moment, Stan cracked a joke in a child custody case and made it possible for them to continue to forge ahead. Now, in his own dark hour, he still had that gift. Still had the ability to bring humor to a story that Georgia feared might not have a happy ending.

Georgia erased the name in Rachel's first appointment slot on the Monday she was scheduled to return to the office. "Can you be here at nine that Monday?" she asked as she pointed to the date on Rachel's calendar.

Stan nodded.

"Good. I'll call Mrs. Richards and reschedule her for later in the week. Her latest tiff with her home owners association will just have to wait."

Georgia filled out an appointment card and handed it across the desk to Stan. "I'll call you Sunday to remind you."

"Better call me Monday morning, too," Stan said. "For Rachel's sake. I'd hate to ruin our 20-year relationship by keeping my girl waiting. Hate to ruin my track record, you know."

"See you Monday, Stan."

"Thanks, Margaret. You're a good woman. Don't know what you see in an old fart like me, but I'm sure glad you do."

Georgia smiled as she walked Stan to the door. Before he left, he turned around, and the fog seemed to lift. "Did I just call you 'Margaret'?"

"It's okay, Stan. Really."

"No, it's not okay, Georgia, but thanks for saying so. See you Monday."

* * *

"I wonder if we could get a reservation for a night here before we leave," Rachel said as she and John stood in the bedroom of the model Earthship.

"Are you serious?"

"Yes. Don't you just love it>" Rachel asked as she ran her hand over the bottom of the green bottle that stuck out from the stucco wall. "Isn't it one of the most fabulous places you've ever seen?" She rushed to the bathroom and called for him to follow. He found her where she sat in the deep well-like bathtub and smiled at him with a come-hither look. Candles lined one side of the rim, and lush white towels lay in an inviting stack in an alcove behind her. "Pretty sexy, isn't it?"

John looked down at the rough concrete tub and then at his wife as she beamed like a child. "Don't you think it's a little cold in here? What about our nice warm room back at Mable Dodge? Remember the view at night? The stars? The moon?"

Rachel crawled out of the tub and into her husband's arms.

"John Turner, how many times do you get to stay in an Earthship? We don't even have Earthships in our part of the country."

"We don't know that. Maybe we do. I don't know why we'd want to, but maybe we do."

At that moment, the young woman who welcomed them when they arrived—and showed them a short pre-tour video—walked into the room. "Any questions?" she asked.

"Yes. Do you have any Earthships available for a night sometime during the rest of this week? We'd like to stay in one before we leave," Rachel said.

John started to protest but instead said a silent prayer that all the Earthships were booked until long after they left New Mexico.

"As a matter of fact, we just had a cancellation on the one next door for tomorrow night," the tour guide said.

Rachel whipped out her credit card, handed it to her and said, "We'll take it. How soon can we check in?"

"Three o'clock. But if you call, I can let you know if it's ready earlier."

As John and Rachel walked up the steps and back to ground level, Rachel turned and came nose-to-nose with a very large Doberman that sunned himself on the roof. She gave a shriek that startled herself and the dog, which stood, yawned and lay back down.

"Sure you want to give up the luxury of city life in Taos for the wild desert?" John teased. "Can't promise I will be able to protect you from the likes of that mongrel. Or worse. Who knows what lurks out here after dark, my little city girl."

"You don't scare me, John Turner," Rachel said as she eased her way slowly past the dog toward the car. "That's why I married you. To take care of me."

John laughed and listened as the sound echoed across the desert. "That's the funniest thing I've heard in a long time. We both know you don't need anybody to take care of you."

"But it sure is nice to know you would, if I did," Rachel said as she climbed into the driver's seat and headed the car back toward town.

"Want to stop at the Millicent Rogers Art Museum while we're out?" John asked.

Rachel reached over and squeezed his hand. "Not only is it nice to have you to protect me, but you read my mind, too. I was just thinking the same thing. But I didn't realize you knew the place. It's one of my favorite stops while I'm out here. I try to make it a point of coming at least once each trip."

John nodded his head. "And the views are as beautiful as the art inside. We can eat our picnic lunch Maria packed for us there, if you like."

"I'd like that very much. Of course, picnics with you are always fun anywhere we eat them."

John smiled, but Rachel thought she noticed a tenseness. "What is it?" she asked. "Is something wrong?"

"Talking about picnics reminded me of the picnic we enjoyed at the zoo with Ben. Guess I miss the little guy. And I'm a little worried, too."

Rachel pulled into the museum parking lot and switched off the engine. She turned to face John. "We can leave early, you know. We can go home any time you want. I miss him, too."

"And deprive you of a honeymoon you've waited sixty-two years for? No way."

"It's not like I've been pining away for a fairytale wedding all my life, John. I've done just fine without one, I'll have you know."

When John's mouth turned down, he looked just like his grandson, and Rachel laughed. "You know what I mean, darling. I've never been happier in my life, but it's not because we're on our honeymoon. It's because I'm with you, and we have a life together. That life includes Ben, and if you think we should go home to be with him, we will. Right after our night in the Earthship would be fine with me."

John laughed and reached across the seat to grab her in a huge bear hug. "This is why I married you, Rachel. You're my kind of woman."

Chapter Eleven

As soon as she and John returned to their room, Rachel called to tell Susan they would return to DC in a couple of days.

• "I'm not at all surprised, but what caused you to change your plans? What happened?" Susan asked.

"I think it was the picnic, but who knows with men."

"The picnic?"

Rachel reminded Susan of the Washington zoo adventure and told her that their New Mexico picnic without Ben had made them miss him more than they thought they would. "He's a big part of our lives. In fact, I wish we'd brought him with us. He's one of the reasons I married John. Why I fell in love with him. To leave Ben behind was a big mistake."

"Well, just to let you know, he's doing fine. But change your plans, if you want to." Susan smiled as she watched Ben brush Ralph's shiny coat. "Right now, in fact, Ben is grooming Ralph. He's decided the dog needs to be brushed every time we make the trip to the Circle. Ralph isn't doing anything to discourage the attention."

Rachel laughed. Susan considered whether to tell her friend that she ran into Ricky but decided to end the conversation on a lighter note. She knew her friend would have plenty of time to think about how to handle that situation—and Stan's retirement—when she got home.

After Susan hung up the phone, she returned to her recent morning routine. She intended to pack one box a day, and, so far, she managed to stay on schedule. She opened a cabinet and started to take out glasses and wrap them in newspaper.

"If you pack all the kitchen stuff, what are we going to drink out of?" Ben asked.

"Good question. But for every good question, there's a good answer," Susan said. With a flourish, she pointed to the picnic basket that sat on the counter near the back door. "That's what we're going to do," she said as she whipped off the top to reveal a full set of dinnerware. "The rest of our days here in DC are going to be one big picnic. Won't that be fun?"

Ben looked doubtful. "Susan, sometimes you act like you're more of a kid than me," he said and then slapped his hand over his mouth. "Sorry," he said as he dropped Ralph's brush and rushed over to hug Susan. "I'm sorry. That wasn't very nice of me. I didn't mean to make you feel bad."

"It's okay, honey. Lots of people have told me the same thing, and I take it as the highest compliment. If more folks would make life a picnic, life would be lots of fun, don't you think?"

Ben nodded his head, relieved he hadn't insulted his friend. Ralph leaped to his feet and danced around them as if he sensed a celebration.

"I think Ralph knows the good news," Susan said. "Want to hear it?"

Ben's eyes grew wide, and he clapped his hands. "Granddad's coming home today?"

"Not today, but real soon. Early. They're coming home early. Day after tomorrow. And we've got lots to do to get ready, so hop to it, kid." Susan handed Ben a glass and a wad of newspaper and showed him how to wrap and pack. "We want to have all this work done before they get home, so we'll have time to do nothing but play after they get here."

"Susan, I'm glad you're just like a kid. You're more fun that way."

"Thanks, buddy. That's quite a compliment—especially coming from a kid like you."

* * *

Mary watched the hour hand inch its way to the four, and, as soon as it hit its mark, she leaped to her feet. "Bye," she shouted to her mother. Belle smiled as she watched her daughter run to meet George at the barn. Her first love, she thought. As long as she lives, she'll never forget the way she feels about that man.

Then a sadness swept through her. For weeks, she fantasized about a life for Mary on the farm with George. But, as suddenly as he appeared and made such a big difference in their lives, the feelings between them changed. Belle struggled with whether she should talk to George. Find out if he felt the shift, too, and see if she could salvage the fantasy of a life on the farm.

As she watched Mary disappear into the barn where the cows waited to be milked, she thought about Rachel's affection for Ben and how it led to her love for his grandfather. Maybe I'm just trying to copy that love story, Belle thought. Just because it worked for Rachel doesn't mean it will work for me. George is wonderful with Mary, and she adores him, but something has changed between the two of us.

And then Ricky's face floated into her mind.

The more time that separated Belle from Ricky, the more often her thoughts wandered back to DC. She wondered whether he was back at work. Wondered if he attended AA meetings. Whether he was alive. Whether he thought about her—and Mary. They shared a history. And not all of it was ugly.

Belle remembered the disappointed look in George's eyes when he showed her his photographs. I've never seen that look on Ricky's face, she thought. I'm not sure what it means, but I'm sure I don't want to see it again.

She turned from the window to see Nancy at the door. "Mary's run up to the barn to help George milk," she said. "That little girl sure loves farm life."

"Yes, she does, but at that age, she loves almost everything about life. I wish I could protect her so she could hold on to that enthusiasm forever."

"I wouldn't worry. You're doing a great job, seems to me." Nancy walked closer to Belle and laid her hand on her shoulder. "You look blue. Anything wrong?"

Belle paced to the sink. She stalled for time. She rinsed out the cup that sat there and placed it on the drain board.

"What is it, Belle?"

Belle shook her head and fished for the words to explain what she, herself, didn't understand. "I think I want to go home. I miss the city. I miss Ralph. I miss my own little apartment. You and Simon have been so kind to make us feel welcome here, but I just don't feel like me."

"And you miss Ricky."

"I know that sounds crazy, after all he's done, but, yes, I miss Ricky. I need to be there for him."

"You don't 'need' to, but if you want to, then that's where you should be. I'm sure George will drive you back whenever you decide to go." Nancy walked to the door but stopped in the hall and turned back. "George is a good man, Belle, but if your heart still belongs to another man, don't hurt him. He's been through too much already."

"I don't think my leaving will hurt him," Belle said. "Something's changed between us. I can feel it."

Nancy didn't argue with what she knew to be true. You can't argue with magic, she thought. You'll never win.

* * *

Deejee did a double-take at the sight of the two men walking toward her hotdog stand. She recognized the taller man as Rob White, the senior partner of White & Townsend. The younger man looked like a white-washed version of Ricky. And the remake wasn't confined to the new suit and fresh haircut. His color had faded from the bloodshot red she last saw to a healthy glow. And even from a distance, she could see the clear eyes. He walked with a spring in his step.

"Where you off to, all dressed up?" Deejee asked. "Morning, Mr. White."

Ricky hugged Deejee, careful not to wrinkle his new suit. "Rob is taking me to court with him this morning. The paralegal is out sick, and I'm going to assist with document presentation." Ricky beamed like a child on Christmas morning.

"Wow. Movin' on up in the world, aren't you."

"We're lucky to have Ricky," Rob said. "He's a natural."

"Yeah, as long as I can stay clean and sober, things seem to go okay," Ricky laughed. He looked down at his watch. "We better get to the courthouse, Rob. Don't want to be late."

"You're the boss," the older man joked as the two left Deejee and headed for the metro station.

Deejee shook her head and said a silent prayer. Susan called her the night before to tell her Belle and Mary would arrive the next day. Please, God, keep this boy on the path. She watched him disappear down the metro escalator. Please, God, for Mary's sake.

* * *

When Carrie stopped by Susan's house to measure windows for shades to replace the existing curtains, she felt surprised to find her friend curled up on the window seat in the living room. Susan didn't sit very often, and Carrie couldn't remember a time when she actually caught her in the act. "Tired?" Carrie asked.

"A little. But mostly, I'm feeling lost. I've lived in this house on this street across from my best friend for so long that I feel absolutely lost on a sea of where-the-hell-am-I-going. But, I'm floating. I haven't sunk yet."

"Susan, you can still change your mind, you know. We don't have to go through with the sale. You can stay here, and Horace and I can find another house."

Susan hung her head, and her shoulders dropped. "No, Jim is determined to move to the beach. He's talked about this move ever since we met. It's his dream. I can't take that away from him. And I'll be fine. I'll adjust."

"Sure, you will. You'll make friends quickly. And you'll have lots of weekend guests, I'm sure." Carrie walked over and sat on the window seat beside Susan, close enough so their knees touched. "Have you found a place yet?"

Susan pulled a brochure out of her apron pocket. On the cover, a youthful retired couple swung golf clubs. In the background, cluster homes lined the fairway. "'Paradise' is what Jim calls it," Susan said, but her expression, as she scanned the brochure cover, belonged more to someone who faced the fires of hell than the pearly gates of paradise. "We were lucky to land an end unit. Jim says we were lucky. Jim says it's prime property."

"Have you actually seen it?"

"Oh, yes. We've seen everything. And everyone seems very nice. We may even get a dog."

Carrie, caught off-guard by that announcement, sat in silence. She waited for the rest of the dog story.

"I know. I know. I've always said I'd never have a dog, but Ralph...Well, you know."

"Yes, Ralph does have that effect on people. Of course, you realize there's only one like him."

Susan nodded and stood up. She stuffed the brochure back into her apron pocket.

"Maybe you should just borrow Ralph every now and then. Visitation rights. See how it feels before you commit to adopting your own."

Susan stopped to give the concept some thought and then shook her head. "No, I couldn't do that to Ben. He's had too much separation in his short life. We'll find our own dog without putting that child through losing his best friend—even for a weekend. We'll find our own Ralph. There's a Ralph for everybody, if you believe there is. Just got to be in the right place at the right time.

* * *

Ralph peered out one of the two long windows that flanked the front door and watched as Rachel and John walked up the sidewalk. Susan brought him inside earlier so he'd be there to greet them. Rachel heard him bark even before she opened the car's passenger door. As she inserted the house key, she heard him jump up and down on the other side.

"Brace yourself for a tornado," she warned John.

Before the door was open even an inch, the dog pushed it wide, leaped into Rachel's arms and licked the face of his long lost friend. After he kissed every inch of his mistress, he turned his attention to John.

"Sure, I get the leftovers. I'm the villain. The one who took her away from you. I know, I know. Sorry, old buddy, but at least I brought her back to you."

A squeal echoed from across the street as Ben burst from Susan's house.

"Look both ways!" Susan screamed. "Watch for cars!"

Ben skidded to a halt at the curb, looked from right to left and then dashed over to where Rachel and John unloaded luggage from the car. John picked his grandson up in his arms in a long embrace. Finally, he set him down to share the homecoming with Rachel.

"Wow, you're back! You came back!"

"Of course, we did. We told you we would, and we always do what we say we'll do, right?"

92

Rachel saw the dark cloud pass over Ben's face and knew what he thought. She wondered when the memory of his parents' death would fade further into the background. They, too, had said they would come home. But they didn't. Before Ben could sink deeper into the blackness of that trauma, Rachel pulled a bag out of the trunk of the car. "We brought you a surprise, big boy. Come on in the house, and you can see what it is."

Ben raced to the front door as Ralph nipped at his heals like a puppy. Just for a minute, the ache in the dog's hips seemed to disappear with the pure joy of the family reunion.

"What is it? What is it?" Ben shouted as he spun in circles in the hallway.

"Come on in the den, and you can find out," John said. Ben sat on the sofa, hands folded in his lap. He patted the cushion beside him. "Come on, Ralph. You can share the surprise with me."

Rachel handed Ben the large brown paper bag, its handle tied with a ribbon. Ben took his time as he untied the colorful twine, and, when he finally managed to pull it off, he fastened it to Ralph's collar. "There, now Ralph has a present, too."

Ralph did, indeed, look very pleased with the twine. He sat up tall and straight, his eyes fixed on Rachel with the look of adoration that only a dog can manage. Rachel smiled. She looked at John. "I'm so glad we're home," she whispered.

"Me, too," John answered.

Unable to stand the suspense a minute longer, Ben ripped open the bag and dug into the paper wrapped around its contents. Finally, he pulled out a kaleidoscope. "What is it?" he asked. He turned the long cylinder first one way and then another. He shook it and spun it, still not able to understand what he had been given.

"Look through the hole at the end," John explained and showed him how to hold it. "Now, turn it and aim it at the light, like this."

Ben held his breath. He spun the tube, and, as he spun, he let out the air in his lungs in a long slow whistle. Then he held his new treasure up to Ralph. "Look, Ralph. It's magic. It's a magic world. Rachel and Granddad have brought back a magic world."

I hope so, Rachel thought. I sure hope so.

Chapter Twelve

S usan smiled at the scene she found in Rachel's den. *I'm glad they didn't listen to me when I told them to stay in New Mexico as scheduled,* she thought in a rare admission of misguided advice.

From the crowded sofa, Rachel looked up at her friend and beamed. "Thanks for holding the fort down while we were gone. How are things here?"

"Not sure where to begin," Susan said in another rare moment— one of restraint.

"How about starting with you. How's the packing coming along? Are you still on schedule for the closing and the move, itself? When should I expect to see the Mayflower guys across the street?" Rachel decided to practice a joking attitude about the move. "Act as if" she told herself as she tried to believe that her best friend's move to the beach would be a gift to everyone involved.

"The closing is Thursday afternoon. The movers arrive Friday. I've been packing all week."

"And I've helped, haven't I?" Ben yelled. "We're going to the beach!"

Susan and Rachel's eyes met over the little boy's head. They knew that "we" was a far cry from the truth. "Ignorance is bliss," Rachel had heard her grandmother say so many times. Ben had no idea how much his life was about to change after Susan left.

"When are Carrie and Horace planning to move in?"

"The end of the month. They want to get painters in to change colors in some of the rooms. But I wouldn't be surprised to see Horace in the yard Thursday afternoon doing some landscaping work. He's so excited."

"And when are they getting married?"

"Haven't you heard? They went to the justice of the peace a couple of days ago. It's a done deal."

"I knew they were going to keep it simple, but I didn't know it was going to be that simple," Rachel laughed.

"They wanted to wait for you to come back so you could be the witnesses, but then they decided just to get it over with."

Once the door had been opened, the rest of the news Susan had tried to restrain rushed out.

"And Belle and Mary are coming home tomorrow. Did you know that? And Ricky is back at work at the law firm. Did you know?"

"Whoa, there. Slow down. One thing at a time. I thought Belle was in heaven, living on the farm. She told me she was even thinking about moving out there and turning into a farm girl."

"Something happened between George and her. I don't know what exactly, but, last night when I talked to her, she was very definite about her decision to come home. George is driving them back." Susan looked at Rachel as though she might know the answer to the mystery.

"Why are you looking at me like that?" Rachel asked. "I've been on the other side of the country. You're the one she talked to. And if you can't pry the reason behind the change in plans out of her, Susan, nobody can." Rachel laughed and rose from the sofa to cross the room to where her friend stood. "Don't look so worried. Everything is working out. Belle is a big girl, and she knows what she's doing."

Susan shut her eyes and sighed deeply as she leaned on her best friend's shoulder.

"And so are you. When will you have your guestroom ready? I'll just leave my bags packed."

Susan's eyes popped open. "Are you serious? You'd come that quickly?"

"Sweetie, I may load myself on the Mayflower van. You just never know about me."

* * *

Georgia sat at Rachel's desk and organized phone messages and mail into priority piles. She looked up with a smile when her boss walked in.

"Been gone only one week, and you're taking over my job," Rachel joked. "Tell you what. You can have it. I think I'll move to the beach with Susan."

Georgia ran around the desk, and the two women held each other. They rocked back and forth without a word. Rachel tried not to look at the piles on her desk. Georgia read her mind. "Don't worry. It's not as bad as it looks. Half of the phone messages are from Stan, forgetting he'd already called. And most of the mail is junk."

"How is Stan? Has he seen a doctor?"

Georgia picked at the sleeve of her sweater until Rachel grabbed her fingers and pried them loose from their nervous task. "Tell me, Georgia," she said.

"They're not sure. They're never sure, I guess, but the doctor is recommending retirement, and his children want him to move in with them. Early stages of some form of dementia, they say. He forgot to turn off one of the burners on his stove a couple of days ago and burned up a teakettle. Could have set the house on fire if his neighbor hadn't seen the smoke pouring out the open kitchen window."

Rachel dropped down to her desk chair and started throwing unopened envelopes into the trash. Finally, she looked up at her secretary. "How's he taking it?"

Georgia pointed at all the pink slips of paper with Stan's name on them.

"I see," Rachel said. "Not well. Old coot. But surely, living with Lily is the carrot at the end of the string for him."

"He's losing his memory, but he's still no fool, Rachel. He knows he's giving up his freedom. Even Lily can't soften that blow."

Rachel looked at her calendar. "Is he still driving? Can I call and ask him to come in, or should I go over there to see him?"

Georgia shook her head. "He shouldn't be, but he's still driving."

"Call him for me, will you. Ask him to come in at three. I've got a little something I picked up for him in Taos." Rachel rooted around in a bag and pulled out a roll of tissue paper tied with yarn. "And for you."

Georgia wrapped herself in the soft lilac shawl Rachel bought for her. "Think I'll head for the rocking chair," she said. "Goes perfectly with the picture of me relaxing after you retire to the beach."

"Not yet we don't," Rachel said. "What's this I hear about Ricky being back in town? Do we need to file another restraining order?"

Georgia shared Deejee's daily report that Ricky regularly showed up for work and attended nightly AA meetings. "He's living with his AA sponsor, who seems to be keeping a close eye on him."

Rachel and Georgia looked at each other, a similar thought in each of their minds. But what will happen when Belle and Mary get home?

"Let's just take it one day at a time," Rachel finally said. "Right now, Belle's not back home, but looks like you and I both have lots to do. You call Stan. I'll tackle what's left of this pile of mail."

"Yes, boss," Georgia said with an exaggerated salute. She turned back as she neared the door. "And Rachel."

"Yes?"

"Welcome home. I missed you."

"I missed you, too, Georgia. More than you know. I think this trip out west finally convinced me that I could never move to New Mexico permanently. I have too much I love right here."

Georgia smiled.

"Now, get to work. Obviously, Stan needs a phone call," Rachel said as she waved six phone messages at her secretary's back.

* * *

When Stan entered the office an hour later, Rachel bit her lower lip. The pain distracted her from the sight in front of her. She tasted blood on her tongue.

"What's wrong, Rachel? You look like hell. I thought you'd look like a blushing bride, but instead you look like someone who's just witnessed a train wreck."

Stan walked over to Rachel's desk and pulled her out of her seat. In his arms, she inhaled the scent of Prince Albert. "Why, Stan, I believe you've started smoking your pipe again," she said.

Stan looked puzzled. Like a lost child. "Pipe?"

"Maybe it's just my imagination. I thought I smelled tobacco smoke on your jacket. Thought maybe you'd taken up the pipe again. But I guess it's just leftover smoke."

"Yeah. That's it. Leftover smoke," Stan said.

God, I hope so, Rachel thought as she battled images of a fire started by an unattended lit pipe. She tried to put the fear behind her with a pat on her friend's shoulder. "I brought you something from Taos, Stan. Here, open it."

Stan beamed like a child as he tore into the bag and pulled out its contents. "It's just like yours," he shouted as he unfolded the woven blanket and wrapped himself in it.

"Not exactly, but close enough. I know you've always admired mine. Now, you have your own." Rachel stalled for time. She folded the tissue paper and bag and crushed them into the trash basket beside her desk. "How have you been, Stan? What's gone on while I've been out of town?"

"What do you mean?" Stan asked as he walked to the window

and stood with his back to Rachel. She saw the hunched shoulders and felt her friend's fear even from across the room. She walked over and laid a hand gently on Stan's back. When he turned to face her, his eyes brimmed with tears.

"Hell, Rachel. I'm losing it. Losing my edge. My daughter wants me to retire."

Rachel waited. The two stood together in silence. Finally, she took his hand. The knuckles were swollen with arthritis, the palms callused with age and years of work in his garden. She squeezed. "What do you think? What do you want?"

Stan shook his head and then looked her in the eye. "I'm afraid she's right, but I don't know what I'd do if I didn't work."

"Play with Lily? Garden?"

"Rachel, they won't let me babysit for Lily anymore. Hell, they won't even let me pick her up from school. She can't ride in the car with me." Stan stopped, a scowl on his face. The tip of his tongue poked out between his teeth.

"What? What, Stan?"

"I don't know. I just lost what I was about to say."

Rachel nodded. "It's okay, Stan. Maybe it's time. You've taken care of a lot of people—me included—for a very long time. Maybe it's time to just stop. I'll be lost without you, you know that, but we can spend more time doing things friends do and less time working. We can rest. I may retire, too."

Stand didn't look at all convinced. Just as he was about to speak, Georgia walked in with a plate of chocolate chip cookies. "Who wants tea?" she asked.

"What?" Stan seemed startled by the question and the simple fact that a third person had entered the room. For a minute, Rachel suspected that he didn't recognize Georgia at all. Then, just as abruptly as the fog had rolled in over Stan's mind, it lifted. "Chocolate chip cookies and tea. A tea party. Perfect welcome home for the lovely Mrs. Turner. And yes, a celebration of my impending retirement. You two ladies can be the first to know. Stan Berninger is taking down his shingle."

As if to emphasize his point, Stan took a huge bite of cookie and laughed his huge Stan Berninger laugh. Cookie crumbs flew across the room. "Yes, ladies, I think it's time. Maybe I'll crawl in the moving van and head for the beach with Susan." Stan picked up his blanket and folded it into a tight square. "Got my beach blanket. All I need is a Speedo."

Rachel and Georgia laughed with relief. "I've got one more job for you, Stan, before you take your shingle down," Rachel said.

"What's that? You know I'll do anything for you."

"Keep an eye on Ricky. I hear he's back in town, and Belle and Mary are headed home tomorrow."

"You got it, boss lady. Do you want pictures? Reports? Anything detailed? Anything particular you want me to focus on?"

"Just keep an eye on him, Stan. You know the routine."

"Yes, I sure do. I'm your man."

"You'll always be my man, Stan Berninger. Always. Now get out of here. I've got work to do."

Stan grabbed two more chocolate chip cookies on his way out the door. He turned back before he shut it. "When did you say Melinda was coming home?"

Rachel and Georgia looked at each other. Georgia took a sip of tea.

"Belle," Rachel said. "Belle's coming home tomorrow, Stan."

Stan shook his head and shut the door behind him.

* * *

Ralph leaped at the door when he heard Rachel insert the key in the the lock. Dog nails scratched on the inside, and, as soon as she opened the door a crack, he ran out to greet her. She tried unsuccessfully for months to break him of the habit, but the peeling paint remained as evidence of the dog's one vice.

When she complained, Ben reasoned that everybody should be allowed one bad habit. The family decided as a group that the leap at the front door would be Ralph's. It was, after all, a habit based in joy, and bad habits based in joy weren't really bad at all. At least, that was Ben's reasoning, and Rachel and John found it hard to argue with him

In fact, a time finally came when Rachel looked at the claw marks on the panel beside the door and saw them as a symbol of the purest love. The love a dog feels for his person.

"Hey, big boy. Let me put my briefcase down and get your leash. We'll walk to the Circle and check on your friends."

Ralph ran back inside the house and straight down the hall to the kitchen where his leash hung on the pantry door handle. Rachel spotted a note on the kitchen table and picked it up. "Gone to the gym. Back by 6. Will bring home pizza." The note was signed by John and Ben. Rachel smiled at the two hearts under each name.

"Come on, Ralph," she said. "We're on our own."

A cold wind at their backs pushed them down the street at a fast clip, and when they arrived at the Circle, Rachel wasn't surprised that the benches weren't as crowded as usual. She was surprised, however, that she didn't see Deejee's hotdog stand.

"Herman, where's Deejee?" she asked one of the two old men huddled over a checkerboard.

"Don't know. Haven't seen her all day."

"Has anybody checked to see if she's okay?" Rachel asked. Both men shook their heads and pretended to focus on their game. "Ralph, you stay with Herman while I go in the drugstore to see if they know anything. Something must be wrong. She's always here."

Rachel tied Ralph's leash to one of the bench legs and ran across the street to the Revco. The clerk at the check-out counter looked up and smiled at her.

"Afternoon, Mrs. Turner. How was the honeymoon? When did you get back? Thought you weren't due home til next week."

"Came home early, Thomas. But what's going on? Where's Deejee?"

Thomas looked out the window. "To tell you the truth," he said, "I've been so busy all day I hadn't noticed she wasn't there. Want me to call her?"

"That's okay. I've got my phone with me," Rachel said. "I'll call." She punched in the numbers but finally ended the call when Deejee didn't answer. "No answer," she told Thomas. "That's strange. Do you know where she lives?"

Thomas said he did and wrote the address on a piece of paper and handed it to Rachel. "But you don't want to go over there by yourself. Take your husband with you."

Rachel promised she would follow his advice and that she'd call Thomas after she found out why Deejee hadn't been at her spot all day. When she walked back to retrieve Ralph, he lay asleep under the table where the checker game wound to an end. She untied and tugged on his leash. "Come on, boy. We've got a mission."

Herman and his friend both snorted, accustomed to Rachel's "missions." A missing hotdog vendor didn't even register on their life-on-the-streets radar screen, a place where missing people were a daily occurrence.

Ralph trotted in the direction of the spot where the hotdog cart usually stood, but Rachel pulled hard on his leash. "Not today, Ralph. Tomorrow." Rachel said a silent prayer that she was right, and that tomorrow Deejee would be back and ready with Ralph's daily treat.

Please, God, let her be okay, she whispered. Ralph tugged on the leash.

Chapter Thirteen

By the time John and Ben returned home from the gym, Rachel had practically worn away the tile on the kitchen floor as she paced back and forth. Before they even had time to take off their coats, she herded them back out the door to the car.

"What about the pizza? I'm hungry," Ben whined.

Rachel grabbed the pizza box and pushed Ben toward Susan's house. John trotted along behind them. Susan answered the door on the first ring of the bell. "Don't have time for lots of explanation, but can Ben stay with you while John and I go check on Deejee?" Rachel asked as she pushed boy and pizza box through Susan's front door. "She hasn't been at the Circle all day, and she's not answering her phone."

"I want to go, too," Ben whined.

"No, you stay here with Susan. We'll be right back," John said as he pulled Rachel toward the car. "We'll call you as soon as we find out what's going on."

Susan looked as disappointed as Ben that she wasn't included in the adventure. The two waved forlornly from the porch as John and Rachel drove away. Rachel shared with John what little she knew and handed him the slip of paper with Deejee's address scrawled on it. "I'm glad you didn't go dashing over there by yourself," John said as he squeezed her hand.

"Yeah, I guess I've turned into an old married woman."

"My old married woman, and I want you to stay safe."

The two settled into comfortable silence as John maneuvered through traffic to the other side of town. When they finally found

Deejee's street, they could barely read the numbers on the row houses. The paint had long ago faded from most of them. Some of the windows were boarded up and shingles hung like broken wings.

Rachel smiled with relief when she was able to read the address that matched the one written on the piece of paper she clutched. Freshly painted a glossy red, the numbers stood proudly over the door. Plastic red geraniums perched in the green metal window boxes.

"Isn't that Ricky's bike?" John asked as he inched the car into a parking space across the street from Deejee's house.

"Oh, dear," Rachel said. "It is. This doesn't look good."

"You stay here in the car while I go see what's going on."

"No way, buddy," Rachel said as she leaped out of the car and ran across the street before John even had a chance to unclasp his seat belt. She stepped around the day's newspaper and a pile of plastic trucks to reach the front door. She knocked several times and then heard someone hurry down the hall toward her. Ricky opened the door and stepped aside as she pushed her way into the cluttered entrance hall. The hotdog vending cart blocked the passageway that led to the back of the house.

John nodded at Ricky but allowed Rachel to lead the charge. "What's going on? Where's Deejee?" she asked, hands on hips and voice heavy with an iciness John had never heard.

"Back here, Rachel," Deejee called from a room deep inside the house. Rachel followed the sound of her friend's voice until she found her, stretched out on a plastic reclining lawn chair, one leg elevated on pillows. Deejee looked at her friend sheepishly.

"What happened?"

Deejee shook her head. "Fell. Finally fell. After all these years of dragging that cart up and down those steps, it finally happened. Fell down the steps, and the damn thing landed on my leg." Deejee's left leg lay, purple and swollen, under a pile of ice bags. "Nothin broken, thank the Lord, but, honey, let me tell you, it hurts like hell." She stopped and pointed at Ricky. "If it hadn't been for Ricky, don't know what I would have done."

Ricky blushed and hung his head. He moved to his patient and adjusted the pillows behind her back.

"I think the angels sent him down my street right as I hit the bottom step. Lord, what a mess. Hotdogs, canned drinks and tons of ice all over the pavement and me not able to move. It was a miracle the way he appeared."

"Have you been to the doctor? How do you know your leg isn't broken?" Rachel interrupted.

"I called the firm, and they sent a runner over to take us to the emergency room," Ricky answered. "They did x-rays. Nothing broken."

Rachel looked at Ricky. "I owe you an apology," she said. "I saw your bike and assumed the worst."

"Yeah. I know what you thought, and it's okay. I'm sure it'll take a long time for you to trust me, after all I've put you through. But I'm trying. All I ask is that you give me a chance. Like Deejee."

Eyebrows raised, Rachel looked at her friend.

"Ricky's going to take some time off from the law firm and operate my hotdog stand until I get myself back on my feet. In fact, you'd better get on to the store now and stock up on supplies for tomorrow," Deejee said as she handed over a fistful of one dollar bills and a list.

Ricky nodded and stuffed the money in his pocket. "When they get back to the city, tell Belle to bring Mary by, and I'll treat them to lunch."

Rachel hesitated only a moment. "They're coming home tomorrow. You don't have long to wait," she said.

Ricky looked like someone just handed him a million bucks as he rushed down the hall. As the door slammed behind him, Deejee beamed at Rachel and said, "I think he's got it this time, Rachel. I really do."

"For Belle's sake, I sure hope so."

"For all our sakes. We all need evidence of miracles in our lives, girl."

"Speaking of miracles, Ralph sure will miss you. How long do you think you'll be out of commission?"

"Doc said at least a week, but if Ricky does okay and likes the job, I'm thinking about retiring. Turning the business over to him."

Rachel dropped down on the floor beside Deejee's chair and looked up at her friend. "I know, I know," Deejee said. "You think I'm crazy, I'm sure. But I've been doing that meditation business you talk about all the time, and the other day it came to me, clear as a bell. It's time. And you don't know this part of my story, Rachel, but that old cart and $50 to get me started was given to me by the old man who used to sell hotdogs in the Circle before me. Now, it's my turn. To pass it on. If Ricky wants it, that is."

Rachel pondered the dangers to Ricky if he worked all day every day at the site where he spent so much of his past. Where he drank and drugged. But she held her tongue. She didn't want to introduce any negativity into what Deejee saw as a gift of gold. And maybe it is, Rachel thought. Maybe it is.

* * *

George lifted a sleeping Mary out of her car seat and carried her toward the basement apartment. Belle dragged the suitcase behind him. As she descended the stairs, the loud bumping noise of the wheels woke the child. "Home?" she mumbled and rubbed her eyes with tiny fists.

"Yes, honey, we're home." Belle looked at George and saw him flinch. Or maybe my imagination sees something that's not there, she thought. Maybe he's glad to get rid of us.

"Ralph? Ben?" Mary squeaked.

"Let's go potty and get you something to eat, and then we'll run upstairs and see if they're home," Belle said.

In response to the voices in the basement, a bark echoed along the upstairs hallway. George laughed. "Guess we've got the answer to at least one question. Ralph is definitely home, but I didn't see John's car in the drive when we got here. May have to wait awhile for the rest of the family." George paced the apartment like a caged tiger. Belle noticed his restlessness.

"You're probably itching to get back on the road, George. Don't feel like you have to wait around with us. We're fine," Belle said. George walked over to where she stood.

"I'm sorry things didn't work out between us, Belle. I really thought they might."

"Stop. You don't need to say anything. I understand. I feel the same way. Well, maybe not the same way since you never told me how you feel, but I felt the shift, too. And, like Rachel always says, 'All is well.' I'm fine. Mary's fine. And, I'm sure you're fine. We appreciate your friendship, and all you've done for us."

"Can we continue to be friends? Will you come visit us at the farm?"

"Milk cows," Mary chimed in.

Belle laughed. "Guess you've got your answer there."

"Good. I'll keep the guestroom ready for you."

* * *

Susan saw John's car pull into the driveway across the street and ran outside. Before she could launch her barrage of questions, Rachel told the story of Deejee's fall and Ricky's rescue. "He's going to take over the hotdog business. Maybe permanently." Susan reacted to the news in the same way Rachel had earlier, and Rachel surprised herself by how quickly she took on Deejee's reassuring role. "We need to give the boy a chance," she said.

Before Susan sputtered out all the reasons he shouldn't be given another opportunity to disappoint them all, Rachel stopped her. "I'm headed upstairs to meditate. It's been a long day, and my mind is wild." Rachel gave her friend a quick peck on the cheek. "See you tomorrow. I want to hear all about the new condo."

"Let me show you the pictures."

"Not now, Susan. Please. I can't take in one more piece of information. My head's about to explode. Tomorrow. I promise. You'll have my undivided attention. I'll call you in the morning, and we'll make plans for lunch."

Rachel felt a twinge of guilt as she turned her back on her friend and walked across the street, but she had learned a long time ago to take care of her own needs first. She noticed the lights on in the downstairs apartment and felt tempted to check on Belle and Mary but resisted the pull. Even Ralph's enthusiastic leaps and face licks didn't stop her for long.

"I'll take him for a walk," John said. "You go upstairs."

Rachel smiled at her husband. "Join me when you get back, if you like. Ralph knows the routine."

"Thanks. How about me? Do I know the routine?"

"Yes. You know the routine. Well."

Rachel turned and mounted the stairs to her third floor room, relieved to be home. Relieved to be surrounded by the familiar, even if it felt slightly askew at the moment. As she lit a candle, settled on her meditation cushion and pulled her shawl around her shoulders, she felt her breath slow. And her wild mind unwind.

"All is well," Rachel whispered. She believed the words more deeply each time she repeated them. She didn't set a timer and allowed herself the luxury of a meditation that lasted as long as she wanted it to last.

She didn't know how much time had passed when she heard

Ralph jump onto the window seat and felt John settle onto the cushion across from her. She opened her eyes and smiled. John returned the smile, took a deep breath, exhaled and closed his eyes.

All good things come to those who wait, Rachel thought as she looked at the man who sat cross-legged in front of her. In a million years, I wouldn't have dreamed this scene. I would never have pictured me, the loner, with a desire to share this, my most special place, with anybody else. Except maybe Ralph. Ralph grunted from the window seat as if he had read her mind.

Rather than the distraction she had feared, John's soft steady breath added an element of comfort to the setting, she realized. Much of what she knew now about love proved to be so different from what she imagined earlier in life. A shared house was not an intrusion. And the early return home felt like a light warm blanket instead of the dark heavy pall she dreaded.

Rachel opened her eyes and peaked again at John, who sat Buddha-like on the cushion she bought him in Taos. Slowly, she eased off her own seat and crawled on her knees over to her husband. She wrapped her arms around his shoulders and tucked her head under his chin.

"Is this a new routine?" he whispered.

"Maybe. Do you like it?"

"A little distracting, but, yes, I think I like it a lot," John whispered back as he pulled the two down to the floor. Ralph grunted from across the room and fell back to sleep.

Chapter Fourteen

R achel saw Carrie's car parked across the street the next morning and hesitated. Maybe they need to work out some of the moving details and don't want to be bothered by a visit from me, she thought.

"Why are you just standing there like that?" John asked from the bottom of the stairs. "Forgot something?"

"Carrie's over at Susan's. Maybe I should wait until she leaves before I go over."

John shook his head and laughed. "For someone who meditates as much as you do and aspires to the simple life, you sure can complicate things sometimes. Go on over, silly. If they don't want you there, they'll tell you."

Aha, Rachel thought. Fear of rejection. That's the real problem. She threw her shoulders back, opened the door and marched forward.

"I'll be here if you need me," John shouted behind her.

How well that man knows me, Rachel thought. And in such a short time. Maybe that's the way falling in love at a mature age is supposed to be. Never know how much time you have, so you dive in to a crash course in loving all the nooks and crannies.

"What are you smiling about?" Susan asked when she greeted her friend at the front door. "You look like the cat that swallowed the canary."

"Nothing. Everything. I saw Carrie's car. Hope I'm not interrupting anything."

"She's measuring the windows. Come on back to the kitchen. I'm packing boxes, but I need a break. We can look at the condo brochure together."

111

As the two passed by the den, Rachel waved at Carrie. "Need any help?"

"No, I'm almost finished. How was the honeymoon? Surprised to see you home early."

"That's the operative word—home," Rachel answered.

Carrie laughed and followed Rachel and Susan to the kitchen. "Horace is like a kid with a new toy," she said. "It's all I can do to keep him from coming over here and starting to plant stuff."

Rachel looked at Susan to gauge her reaction to the impending changes to her yard and was relieved to see a smile play at the corners of her friend's mouth.

"No need to wait," Susan said. "If your loan falls through, I'll have yard improvements in the bank. And the closing is in only a couple more days. No need to torture the boy any longer. As long as he doesn't get in the way of the movers."

Susan picked up a slick brochure from the kitchen table and opened it to a colorful centerfold. She stabbed at a corner townhouse and moved her finger to a little flag a few yards from it. "That's our place, and that's the ninth hole. Jim is hysterical, he's so happy."

Rachel raved about the location, the landscaping, the architectural style, the brochure design and was about to launch into a whole new litany of other attributes when Susan interrupted her.

"Stop. You really don't need to do all that now. I'm fine. Actually, I'm really looking forward to being a beach bum." She pointed to the far side of the drawing to a space behind the row of townhouses. "That's the ocean." And then she pointed to a townhouse with a large red X slashed across it. "And that's your new home, Rachel Turner. It's empty. Or will be in a month. The current owners are moving to Virginia to be closer to their children, and you better grab it quick because they're selling it for a ridiculously low price so they can move it fast." Susan looked at Rachel. "Don't just stand there," she said, shoving the brochure at Rachel. "Take this across the street and show it to your husband."

Rachel stood with her mouth open. She held the brochure gingerly, as if it were a hot poker.

"Maybe I should go with you," Susan sputtered. "You don't look too sure of yourself." She tugged on Rachel's sleeve. "Come on. What are you waiting for?"

Rachel shook her head and allowed herself to be pulled back across the street to her unsuspecting husband. When the two walked in, John stood at the kitchen sink where he washed his coffee cup. "Oh, dear, this looks like trouble," he said as he tossed the dishtowel onto the kitchen counter. Rachel held the brochure in front of her at arm's length. Neither woman said a word. "What's this? Dare I look? You're both acting like you're handing me a court summons—or worse."

Susan realized that Rachel hadn't perfected her assigned role of promoter, so she took her cue to spring into action. "It's the brochure for the resort community Jim and I are moving to at the beach," she said. "Just so happens that there's a condo being sold at a real cheap price right near ours."

"And you thought Rachel and I would make good neighbors?"

"Well, I know you both have careers, and Ben's in school."

"Not a problem. None of that's a problem. Where do I sign?" John asked.

Rachel stood, speechless. "Close your mouth, Rachel. You'll swallow a fly," John laughed. "I'm not the sticking point, Miss Susan. Your friend here is the one who's going to take some convincing."

"But Stan is sick and Georgia—what about Georgia?"

"See," John said as he folded the brochure and stuck it in his back pocket. He turned Susan around and headed her toward the door. "You go on home and let me work on my wife. I have a few tricks that might just work."

Susan hugged her friend. "Just open your heart, Rachel. Isn't that what you're always saying. And Ralph would make a great beach dog."

Ralph heard his name and ran into the kitchen and barked his agreement.

"See. I told you so," Susan laughed. Rachel picked up the kitchen towel and threw it at the retreating figure.

"Are you out of your mind?" she shouted at John. "I"m not ready to retire and neither are you. I've got clients who depend on me."

"You've got me. And Ben. And Ralph. Wherever you go. Let's sleep on it, shall we?" John pulled his wife toward their bedroom where he shut the door with Ralph on the outside. "Later, Ralph. I have a few tricks to work in here first."

* * *

Belle held Mary's little hand in hers as they crossed the street. Dupont Circle bustled on an unseasonably warm winter afternoon. Rachel shared the news that Deejee had fallen and that Ricky was in charge of the hotdog stand, so Belle wasn't surprised when she saw him wrap a hotdog in aluminum foil and hand it to the first customer in a long line. Several minutes passed before he had a chance to look up and notice Belle whisper to Mary that they should wait for the line to get shorter before they took their turn.

Ricky waved to them, and Mary looked up at her mother for approval. When Belle nodded, the little girl raced across the concrete and leaped into her father's arms. Belle heard her squeals and the man's laughter echo across the Circle. She smiled and walked toward them.

"Morning," Ricky greeted her. "Hotdog?"

Belle's first thought was to refuse. She didn't want to start something—something even as simple as accepting a hotdog—but a voice in the back of her head nudged her, and she surprised herself when she said, "Thanks."

"Me, too! Me, too!" Mary shouted. Ricky grinned as he prepared the hotdogs—one plain for Mary and one loaded for her mother. A third for himself made a family meal. He flipped over a "Back in five minutes" sign and closed up shop.

"Let's go sit on that bench in the sunshine, shall we?" he suggested as he gestured to the other side of the Circle. Mary ran ahead of her parents and hopped up on the bench to wait patiently. A smile spread across her face.

"I wish adults could forget the past and forgive as quickly as children," Ricky said. "Think there's a possibility you can follow her example and give me another chance, Belle?"

Belle looked at her daughter and shook her head. "I don't want her hurt again, Ricky. It's not just you and me, you know."

Ricky nodded his head. "We'll take it slow. We'll take it one day at a time. But, as Rachel says, 'All good things come to those who wait.' I'm waiting, Belle. And you're my good thing."

Belle sat beside Mary and patted the bench beside her. "Thanks, Ricky. I'm proud of what you're doing," she said as she nodded toward the cart. "I guess if Deejee can trust you with her business, I can try to let go a little, too."

"That's all I'm asking. Try. I sure am."

"What you tryin', boy?" a voice boomed behind them. Belle looked up to see Stan stumble toward them, a big grin on his face. "Heard about Deejee's fall. Came down to see if it was true you were selling dogs for her. Looks to me like you're slacking off already." Stan stooped down in front of Mary. "How about giving an old man a bite," he teased.

Mary picked off a small bit of bun and handed it to Stan, then looked to her mother for approval. Belle smiled. "Maybe he'd like a little hotdog with that bread," she laughed.

"Oh, no. This is perfect, little missy. You know everything Lily does is perfect in Grandpa's book."

Belle and Ricky looked at each other, but neither corrected Stan's mistake. Neither wanted to embarrass Stan by pointing out that he had just called Mary by his granddaughter's name. Stan struggled to stand and looked confused for a few minutes before he spoke. "Rachel and John at home? Since I'm in the neighborhood, thought I'd stop by and report on a few cases I'm working on."

Belle told him she thought they were at the house but suggested he call first.

"That's right," Stan laughed. "Don't want to surprise honeymooners during afternoon siesta time." The old man dug around in both pockets but came up empty-handed.

"Need to borrow my phone?" Ricky offered.

"Nope. I must have left mine in the car. Good to see you, boy. Keep up the good work. No slacking off. I'm watching you, you know."

Ricky laughed and promised to have a special hotdog waiting for Stan the next day. He shook his head as the old man stumbled off toward the area where he always parked his car.

"What are you thinking?" Belle asked.

"I don't know. Seems like sometimes you wait, and all good things don't always come, Belle. Doesn't seem fair."

"It's not. Who said it was?"

Ricky reached for her hand. "Gotta get back to work. Stop by and get a drink before you leave."

"Me, too?"

"You, too, little one. Especially, you."

"Thanks, Ricky," Belle said. "Thanks."

Ricky answered with a smile. As Belle watched him walk away, she thought she saw a new posture. His spine seemed straighter and his shoulders broader and stronger. She looked down at Mary as she stared at her father's back, a serious expression on her face, her mouth sprinkled with crumbs. Mary turned to Belle. "Daddy a good boy?"

"Yes, honey, Daddy's a good boy."

"George a good boy?"

The question startled Belle until Mary spit out a long list of names of other good boys. "Yes, they're all good boys, but the most important question is, are you a good girl? And the answer is, you most certainly are. Mary Mason, you are a very good girl, and don't you ever forget it. And don't you let anybody ever convince you otherwise, okay?"

Mary hopped up and down on one foot and smiled up at her mother. "Mommy a good girl, too. And don't you forget it."

Out of the mouths of babes, Belle thought. Out of the mouths of babes.

"Mommy tired?"

"Yes, Mommy is very tired. But Mommy knows what to do about being tired. She may not know what to do about everything, but tired is simple. Naps are in order for these two girls."

* * *

Rachel looked out her bedroom window and felt her heart sink like a heavy rock to the bottom of a very deep well. The Mayflower moving van stretched as long as a beached whale beside the curb in front of Susan's house. The back opened in a huge mouth and an army of movers fed furniture into it, piece by piece.

"My God, what time do you think they got started?" she asked John as he walked out of the bathroom and over to where she stood, pressed up against the window. The two stood side by side, wrapped in a shadow cast by the giant maple tree that spread its branches across the front yard.

Suddenly, Susan burst out her front door. She frantically waved a clipboard at one of the men.

"What is she saying?" Rachel sniffed.

"I don't know. Can't hear, but you can bet it's not good from the look on her face."

"I can't watch anymore. You ready for coffee?"

"Sure. Want me to make it?"

"No. I need something to keep me busy. Keep my mind off what's going on across the street."

John lifted the hair off his wife's shoulders and sifted it through his fingers. He let it drop back into place, softly fanning it like a silver frame around her face.

"On second thought, I think I'll take you up on that offer," Rachel said. "I'm going upstairs to meditate. I'll join you in a little bit."

"Take your time, sweetheart. I'll wait for you."

Before Rachel could even blow a complete whistle out of her mouth, Ralph had joined her as she trudged up the steps to the third floor. The dog stayed close by her side as she climbed. Goosebumps ran up and down her spine. "There's a shift in the air, Ralph. Do you feel it?"

The dog rubbed her leg in agreement.

"It's as if a huge black hole is opening across the street and sucking up Susan. What are we going to do, buddy?"

Ralph dashed over to his window seat, plopped down in his usual place, laid his head down on his front paws and closed his eyes.

Rachel laughed. "Right. I know. Sit." And she did.

* * *

Forty minutes later, Rachel and Ralph joined John in the kitchen where he read the *Post* and sipped coffee. Ben sat at the table with him, lips pursed as he worked on his new Scooby Doo coloring book. John crossed to the counter where the coffee pot sat. He poured his wife a large mug of hot French Roast.

"Better?" he asked.

Rachel smiled. "How's the progress across the street?"

John waited until she sat down before he spoke. "The truck just left. Susan and Jim are still there, though. Do you want to walk over and say good-bye? I'll go with you."

"Where are we going?" Ben piped up. He'd been so quiet that the adults had forgotten he was in the room. Rachel looked at John and silently questioned whether a good-bye scene was a good idea. He shrugged his shoulders and smiled. He knew that the good-bye scene would be much harder for his wife than his grandson.

"Sure, come on. Let's go see Susan and Jim. Don't you have something you want to give them? Something you made?" he asked Ben.

"Yikes, I almost forgot. The picture I drew for their new house," the boy yelled. He ran upstairs. Ralph raced at his heels.

"Are you going to be okay? Got anything you want to give Susan to take with her?" John joked gently in an attempt to lighten the moment.

"She's got everything of any value I can possibly give her," Rachel said. John knew what his wife meant and took her hand and squeezed it.

"Want me to take a picture of the three of you standing in front of the house for the last time?"

Rachel looked like she'd just bitten into a piece of very bitter fruit. "Surely, you're kidding. Why in God's name would I want anything to remind me of this day." She pulled away from her husband and rushed out the front door.

"Hey, where's Rachel? Why didn't she wait for me? I hurried as fast as I could. Why did she leave you?"

"I think I said something that made her mad, buddy. Sometimes we make mistakes and hurt people."

"Well, why did you do that?"

"Like I said, sometimes we make mistakes."

"Now, what do we do? Can I still go give Susan my picture? Is Susan mad, too?" Ben clutched the crayon drawing of Susan's house to his chest like a security blanket, and his eyes filled with tears.

"Nobody's mad at you, little guy. In fact, I'm sure your present will make Rachel as happy as it will make Susan. Happiness is contagious, you know. When one person feels it, everybody around them feels it, too."

"Well, let's go quick. I don't like it when Rachel is mad—specially at you."

"Me either," John said and followed his grandson out the door and across the street to where Rachel sat on the front steps with Susan and Jim.

Ben ran to Susan and presented the drawing with a flourish. "For your new house. So you won't forget this one. And that's me and Ralph. So you won't forget us."

Susan and Jim admired the drawing and took turns as they hugged Ben.

"See, Rachel. See the drawing and how happy it made Susan. Are you happy, too? You're not still mad at Granddad now are you? Did I fix it?"

Rachel laughed and nipped at Ben's freckled nose. "The picture is beautiful, Ben. I'm sure Susan will find a very special place for it in her new home."

John was aware that she hadn't answered the question about whether she was still mad at him. He might have to work on that later. Little boy magic didn't work on some things, he knew.

"So, when are you coming to see where we've hung his gorgeous picture? Soon, I hope," Susan said. Everyone looked at Rachel to gauge her mood. John realized he'd have to be the one to carry the boat over this rocky place.

"Think you can have the spare bedroom ready by next weekend?" he asked.

Rachel's face brightened, but she still didn't speak.

"Of course," Susan said. "We'll roll out the red carpet. In fact, I can make an appointment for you to see the unit that's available. You'll want to see it while you're at the beach, right?"

"We're moving to the beach, too?" Ben shrieked. "Ralph, we're moving to the beach!"

"Not much gets by that boy," Jim laughed.

"Right, and now you two are going off and leaving, and we're stuck here to answer that question for the next week. Thanks." Rachel gave Susan and Jim a quick hug and turned and ran back to her house.

"What was that all about?" Susan asked John.

"Sorry. You'll have to forgive Rachel. Your leaving is hitting her pretty hard."

"Guess my picture didn't make her happy, after all," Ben said.

"Maybe not Rachel, but it sure made me happy," Susan reassured him. She stooped down for one final hug. "Thanks, Ben. I know exactly where I'm going to hang it."

"And we'll be going to see it soon. Real soon. Now, let's go home and take Ralph to help Rachel. Some hurts need a little black dog magic," John said.

"Tell Rachel I'll call her when we get to the beach."

"Will do. I'm sure she feels terrible about the way she acted. By then, she'll have settled down and will want to apologize."

"No apologies necessary. We've been through a lot worse than this. And I understand. Trust me."

"You're a good friend, Susan. We'll both miss you. Jim, take care. I envy you, man. But you've earned this time, and I'm not far behind you. I'll watch you and depend on you to show me how this retirement thing is done."

"I don't think it will be you who has trouble grasping the retirement concept. Rachel may be another story."

* * *

121

From deep in the bubbles that filled her garden tub, Rachel heard John and Ben open and close the front door. Ralph raced up the stairs and sniffed along the bottom of the bathroom door.

"What's Rachel doing in the bathroom so long?" she heard Ben ask after several minutes. Ralph knew and had stopped scratching after a few last swipes.

"I bet she's taking a bubble bath," John answered.

"Why? It's not time to go to bed. Why's she taking a bath now? Did she get dirty?"

"No, she didn't get dirty. Bubble baths relax her. She needed to relax."

Relaxation was not a concept Ben had grasped yet, and he looked puzzled. John tried another explanation. "She's sad because her best friend is leaving. The bubbles make her feel good."

"I'm sad, too. Can I take a bubble bath? Bubbles make me feel good. In fact, I like blowing bubbles even better. Can I go outside and blow bubbles with Ralph? Blowing bubbles make dogs feel real good."

Rachel smiled as she listened to John open and close drawers as he looked for the bottle of bubbles. Finally, the back door slammed shut, and the house was quiet. She heard John climb the steps and timidly knock on the bathroom door. He waited for her to respond.

"Yes," she answered. John eased the door open only wide enough to extend his hand. In it he held a sign with the word "Sorry" written in big black letters and bordered by red hearts. Rachel giggled.

John poked his head around the door. "Need someone to scrub your lovely back for you?"

"Sounds good to me."

John reached for the loofah that dangled from the towel rod over the tub and gently massaged away the tension in Rachel's shoulders. "Honey, I'm really sorry."

"No, John. Stop. I'm the one who needs to apologize."

"Why don't we just let it go. Seeing a friend leave is hard."

"But bubbles help."

"Ben says blowing them is even better," John said as he dipped his hand into the bubbles, scooped up a pile and blew them in a cloud at his wife. Rachel blew back, and soon the bathroom was filled with bubbles and the bathtub had two people in it instead of one.

Chapter Fifteen

Ricky's favorite AA meeting—his home group, named "Back to Basics"—met every night at six o'clock in a church basement within walking distance of the office where he worked and the Capitol Hill townhouse he shared with his AA sponsor. On most days, the two men left the office together and used the four-block walk as time to decompress from the day. After the meeting, they often stopped at a small cafe on the way home, grabbed a bite to eat and talked about what they heard in the meeting.

On the rare occasions when a late appointment with a client kept Rob from the meeting, Ricky attended by himself. Alone on Tuesday, he approached the group of smokers who sat outside on a picnic bench. The day had been hectic, and Ricky felt no desire to engage in the usual small talk. He craved silence to balance the hours of ringing telephones and the regret he felt about a missed deadline that had been his responsibility.

The day stretched his raw nerves to their outer limits.

He tried to dodge the good ole boys who found their kicks these days in tortuous teasing. As a newcomer, he often fell victim to their good-natured pokes and prods. Tuesday, he knew his tolerance for their form of fun hung low and dark. He smiled, shook a few hands and started down the stairs when a big burly biker named "Wayne" called out his name.

"Hey, Ricky, hold up there. Heard you've gone part-time at the firm. Got so good now that you're sober you can do twice the work in half the time, is what I heard."

"Yeah, and I heard you pushed poor ole Deejee down her steps and are selling hotdogs the other half of the day," another old-timer laughed.

Ricky knew he'd never hear the last of the story if he didn't play along, so he climbed back up the stairs and joined what was fondly called "the meeting before the meeting."

"Yeah, God's been mighty good to me. Deejee's not hurt bad. I'm helping her out, and she says it's a relief to have somebody she can trust with the business. Another miracle of sobriety, I guess."

"Sure you're not playing with fire by hanging out in your old playground with all your old playmates?" Wayne asked between drags off an unfiltered Camel cigarette. "And where's your sponsor? You pushed him down the steps and taken over the firm, too?" Wayne laughed and coughed a deep, racking smoker's cough.

None of the others joined in his fun. They saw the edge Ricky teetered on and knew enough to back off. "Go easy on the boy," said a scrawny old man known only as "Spunky." "Looks like our boy Ricky might have had a hard day. Go on inside, son. Get yourself a cup of that good AA coffee. John's made his famous brownies with chocolate icing. Take two. You deserve them."

Ricky smiled and bit his tongue. He worked hard on his resentment about the AA members who didn't have a job. The ones who drew disability checks and loafed all day, every day. He and his sponsor talked about the anger he felt and the fact that their behavior made him look at the wreckage of his own past.

Tuesday the anger seethed just below the surface as he looked at the little clique he had labeled "bums." The group of men who took such pleasure when they teased him about his work.

He ran through the Serenity Prayer in his mind, hit what AA members referred to as the "pause button" and barely escaped down the stairs and headed for the coffee pot and pan of brownies. Two were left. When he reached for a napkin and the spatula, he sensed someone behind him. Before he had a chance to scoop out even one brownie, he heard a woman clear her throat.

"Don't even think about it," she warned in a husky whiskey voice.

"Think about what?" Ricky asked. He turned and looked into a pair of ice-blue eyes, level with his.

"Don't even think about taking the last brownie. I kill for chocolate."

"Help yourself," Ricky said. "Ladies first."

"Just for that, I'll take both of them."

"Just for what?"

"I ain't no lady. You know it. I know it, and most of the bums out there know it," she said as she jabbed a long red-polished thumbnail toward the picnic table. "But ain't no need in rubbing my nose in it." The girl took a vicious bite out of one of the brownies.

"Hey, I don't even know you. Give me a break," Ricky said. He poured himself a cup of coffee and stalked over to his favorite folding metal chair in the corner under the clock. He took a deep breath and closed his eyes. He missed his sponsor, who always sat next to him. The empty chair felt like the "big black hole" he heard so much about since he started recovery. But when the mouthy redhead plopped her tightly blue jeaned bottom down into the chair—his sponsor's chair—he thought, there are worse things than black holes.

Surprise hit him between the eyes when the girl shoved her second brownie at him. She didn't say a word. Just sipped her coffee and stared straight ahead.

"Thanks," Ricky muttered.

"Sorry," she muttered back. "I'm still new at this."

"Me, too," Ricky whispered as the chairperson started the meeting with the Serenity Prayer.

The girl stumbled over the words, but her "Amen" rang loud and clear.

Amen, indeed, Ricky thought and shoved the rest of the brownie into his mouth and tried to ignore the girl beside him as she slowly licked the icing off each of her fingers.

* * *

When Ricky walked into the apartment, he found Rob in the den. His sponsor turned off the television, looked at his watch and then up at Ricky.

"How was the meeting?" he asked.

"Good."

"Topic?"

"Forgiveness."

"Did you share?"

"No."

"Did you get something to eat after the meeting?"

"No."

Rob stood up and walked over to where Ricky leaned against the wall. Ricky actually heard himself being sniffed.

"Then where did you go? It's almost nine o'clock. Why are you so late?"

Ricky pushed off the wall and brushed past his friend. He plopped down on the sofa and put his feet up on the cushion.

"And get your feet off my sofa."

"What is this?" Ricky shouted. "I feel like I'm being interrogated. I'm your sponsee, not the opposing party in a capital murder trial. Give me a break, man."

Rob walked closer and sniffed again.

"And I haven't been drinking if that's what you're thinking."

The older man sat back down in the recliner and stared at him.

"No, I don't smell any alcohol. And I know where the cigarette smoke came from. But there's another smell, and to a newcomer, it can be more deadly than booze or tobacco. I'm pretty sure that smell I smell is the smell of a woman. Some kind of perfume, and it's on you in a way that doesn't come from a sisterly hug. Where one arm's around you and the other has a coffee cup at the end of it. No, brother, this smell seems to be coming from your hair, like some young perfumed thing's been running her fingers through your hair."

Rob stopped to give Ricky the chance to respond. Instead, Ricky looked down at his hands. He picked at a cuticle and then rubbed the back of his neck. He moved his feet off the couch and sat up straight.

"So? What have you been up to? This program is based on honesty, remember. I asked you a straight question, and I deserve an honest answer. Why are you late, and where have you been?"

Ricky looked up at his friend and jutted his chin out. "Walking. I've been walking."

"With whom?"

Ricky jumped up, his hands clenched in fists at his sides. He towered over Rob in silence. Words raced around in his mind like whirling dervishes.

"Just give it to me straight," Rob said softly. "I've been where you are, remember."

Ricky's shoulders slumped. He knew his anger was no match for his sponsor's loving concern.

"Okay. Her name is Felicia. She's new. I know. I know. No 13th stepping. But, damn. I'm lonely. Belle's giving me no hope of us getting back together. She's moving on. I just know it. And this girl. I mean, you should see her, man. She's just so sweet-smelling and soft and tiny."

"Hold on there, buddy. Slow down. Take a deep breath." Rob rose from the recliner and disappeared into the kitchen. He returned with two mugs of steaming coffee and handed one to Ricky. The two sat in silence and sipped. Ricky waited for his sponsor to speak first.

"Okay, like I said, I know where you are. What you feel. Because I've been there. Lonely, rejected, young and horny." He took another gulp of coffee, a faraway look in his eyes as though he stared at memories of his own Felicia. Finally, he focused again on Ricky.

"Did you have sex with her?"

When Ricky hung his head and didn't answer, Rob gently set his mug down on the coffee table and moved over to the sofa to sit beside the younger man.

"How do you feel?" Rob finally asked.

"Great. I feel great, man. I haven't had sex with a woman in I don't remember how long. I mean, she was so sweet."

Rob motioned for him to stop. "Okay. So the sex was great. I'm sure it was. But let's just sit with this a minute or two. Just be quiet and let what you've done roll around in your heart and see what happens."

Ricky picked at his cuticles.

"Are you willing to look at it with me, Ricky?"

Ricky cleared his throat a couple of times as if something foul-tasting were stuck there. After one last gagging sound, he nodded his head and closed his eyes. Rob leaned back against the sofa cushions beside him, and the two sat.

* * *

Later that night, as Ricky lay in bed, propped up against a mountain of pillows, smelling the clean, freshly changed pillowcases at his back, he looked down at the notebook on his lap. Every night since he picked up his last white "surrender" chip at an AA meeting, he followed his sponsor's suggestion to review the day on paper.

As he looked at his most recent entry, he realized that his handwriting reflected the crazy roller coaster he rode that day. The words sprawled across the pages, left the lines and raced across the margins as he let out his feelings of frustration at work, anger and resentment at the bums at the meeting, the ecstasy when he took Felicia on the sofa in his sponsor's office. Followed by his shame when he admitted that abuse of the trust Rob showed him when he gave him the keys. And the shame when he realized he gave free rein to his selfish sexual desires when he used a newcomer.

Fortunately, he thought, the roller coaster ride ended when he made amends to Rob and Rob forgave him. Finally, he felt relief when he let go and forgave himself.

The last step, he knew, was to make amends to Felicia.

He looked down at the napkin on which she carefully printed her phone number. He promised to call her the next day. As he looked at the heart with which she had dotted the "i" in her name, he felt a new wave of shame at what he did. He realized he acted just like all the other bums who used the woman. He remembered the hope in her eyes. Hope that he would be different.

He knew she was too new in the recovery program to realize what he should have—that any kind of mature relationship— anything other than physical satisfaction—was almost impossible until she cleared all the wreckage of the past that drove her to that church basement. And Ricky knew he still faced a long process of work on his own self-centered isms.

That Tuesday night proved it.

* * *

Early the next morning, he dialed the number. When he heard Felicia's groggy voice answer the phone after five rings, he realized she had been asleep. He apologized, but when she sounded so excited to hear his voice, he felt more guilty about the purpose of his call than the fact that he woke her.

She agreed to meet him at the hotdog stand at five o'clock.

"Great. I'll buy you a dog and we can walk to the meeting together," Ricky said as he tried to keep his voice light. When he hung up, he prayed for the courage to do what he knew was necessary for his sobriety—and for hers—but he dreaded the long day ahead. And the even longer night after he made his amends and faced the fury of a woman scorned.

Rob assured him that even if Felicia reacted with anger—which she had every right to feel—that Ricky needed to take this step to ensure his own sobriety. That not drinking was just the first step in his recovery. He needed to stop using people to make himself feel better.

And, in the middle of the night, he realized that included Belle and Mary.

Off and on throughout the morning at the office and throughout the afternoon as he smeared ketchup and mustard on hotdog after hotdog, he felt like an automaton. A machine going through the motions. Every time he thought about his meeting with Felicia, he broke into a cold sweat, and his heart raced like a runaway train. A couple of times during the morning when he passed Rob in the hall, the two exchanged a look. A look that combined a warning of the impending storm and a "You're doing the right thing" smile.

When he left the office to pick up the vending cart Deejee still stored at her apartment, he felt like he carried the weight of the world on his back. He wondered how he'd manage to pull the cart and his emotional burden.

"What in the world is the matter with you, boy? You look like death warmed over," Deejee said when she opened the door and saw his face.

"Nothing much," Ricky muttered as he pushed his way past Deejee to the cart.

"Sure you're up to doing this today? You don't have to, you know. The world won't come to an end if you don't sell hotdogs every day."

Ricky assured her he was fine and that he took his job seriously. "I don't want to let you down, too," he said.

Deejee saw the hurt look in the boy's eyes but didn't pry.

"Okay. Do what you need to. And when you bring the cart back,

I'll be out. A friend's taking me to dinner. The spare key's under the flower pot around back. Let yourself in and put the key with the cart."

Ricky hesitated at the thought of being trusted with another key.

"Are you sure you want to leave the key out like that? I'm sure Rob wouldn't mind my bringing the cart home for one night."

"Sure I'm sure. Why not?"

Ricky hung his head, and Deejee knew he harbored a secret heavier than the cart. Still, she didn't ask.

"You do what you're comfortable doing, Ricky. If I get home and the cart's not here, I'll know you're sleeping with the damn thing. Suit yourself. I'm fine either way."

Ricky looked up and smiled. "Thanks" he said and allowed himself to be hugged. Deejee's arms—and the love he felt in them—gave him the courage he needed to make the trip to the Circle and the step he would take there to set himself free.

Chapter Sixteen

Ricky felt Felicia's presence before he saw her. He looked up. She stood on the opposite side of the Circle and stared at him. The sun shone like a spotlight on her flaming red hair. The rest of the cast of characters in the scene that afternoon faded into black and white around her. Even the sounds receded into a drab background of car horns, sirens and the shouts of two angry chess players. All became a dull roar of background noise against Ricky's loud heartbeat.

Felicia's eyes reminded him of a scared animal as they peered out from under their heavy purple eye shadow and dark black mascara.

The girl took a deep drag off a cigarette, held the smoke for a minute too long and disappeared behind the cloud she exhaled.

Ricky saw her turn to leave. She knows, he thought. She knows the AA program well enough to realize why I asked her to meet me here. Oh shit, what have I done?

He also heard Rob's voice as he encouraged him forward and he ran toward Felicia.

"Stop," he called out. "Please, stop."

Felicia turned, her black leather jacket zipped tightly under her chin and her hands jammed into her pockets. Tight black denim jeans clung to legs spread wide in a fighter's stance.

"What?" she hissed.

Ricky hesitated only a minute, long enough to silently whisper the Serenity Prayer.

"Thanks for coming," he began.

"You asked me. I came."

"Yes. Well, you could have refused, but you didn't."

"Why would I refuse? Why say 'no' to what you got," she purred. She shifted a hip so it came to rest against his crotch. Ricky stumbled back, caught off-balance by the girl's sudden shift from fighter to flirt.

"Cunning and baffling," he heard Rob say so many times about alcoholism and all its manifestations. Ricky looked at the manifestation who stood in front of him and took a deep breath.

"Here, sit down with me for a minute," he said.

"Cigarette?" Felicia offered as she lit a second Camel off the short stub of her first.

"No, thanks. Quit in rehab. Trying hard not to pick up again."

"Well, aren't you something. Pretty hot shit, aren't you? Guess you think you're too good for me, don't you?" Felicia blew smoke in his face and tilted her chin up at him as though she dared him to hit it.

Ricky sucked in another deep breath and launched into the amends Rob helped him prepare the night before.

"No, Felicia, I don't think I'm too good for you, and I don't think I'm hot shit. In fact, if I was hot shit, I wouldn't have done what I did. I wouldn't have to tell you I'm sorry."

"Sorry for what?" the girl interrupted. "I thought you got off last night. I sure did."

"Felicia, I had no business taking you to my boss's office like that. I abused his trust in me. And I used you. It wasn't right. You deserve better than a one night stand, and I don't have more than that to offer." Ricky paused. "I need to focus on staying sober and not on being with a woman. And so do you. Hell, you're even newer at this than I am."

"Can't we help each other? I mean, do we have to stop having a good time just because we're not using? What's the point of staying clean if we can't have a good time doing it?"

Ricky looked off into the distance. The traffic light cycled from green to yellow to red before he found words. Felicia smoked and waited for him to answer her question. Her body twitched beside his.

"Yes, we can have fun," he finally said. "Jut not like we did. We need to find new ways to make ourselves feel good. Ways that don't hurt other people—and ourselves."

Felicia jumped up from the bench and jerked her black leather bag over her shoulder. "You're no different than the rest," she shouted at him as she ran toward a bus stopped at the corner. Before he could catch her, she boarded the bus, paid the driver and moved to the rear. She didn't look back. And as the bus pulled away from the curb and disappeared into traffic, Ricky knew Felicia was gone.

* * *

Rachel turned out the light on her side of the bed and pulled the covers up under her chin. When the phone rang, she hoped it was the call she'd waited for all day and grabbed the receiver.

"That was fast," Susan said on the other end. "I didn't even hear the phone ring. Are you up? Did I wake you? You and John aren't in bed, are you?"

Rachel laughed. "Susan, you're fine. No, we're not asleep and no we're not doing anything else either."

"Well, good."

"What took you so long to call? It's ten o'clock. I've been on pins and needles all day, dying to hear how the move went."

John sputtered next to her. "That's an understatement," he muttered.

Rachel swatted at her husband.

"The move went great," Susan said. "Not a hitch. All the furniture survived in one piece, and everything fit in the condo perfectly. Even got the king-sized mattress up those narrow stairs I was worried about. You know, thing's always have a way of working out so much better than we think." Susan went on with a long and detailed list of all the other "things" that worked out well in her new home on the ninth hole. Rachel felt herself doze off to sleep to the drone of her best friend's voice. John started to snore on his side of the bed.

"And then, right as the movers shut the back door on the van, a group of our new neighbors popped over with a potluck supper and several bottles of welcome home wine. In fact, they just left."

Rachel's eyes flew open, and she sat straight up in bed.

"Rachel? Rachel? Are you there? Did you hear me?"

"Yes. Yes, I heard you," Rachel said as she swung her legs out from under the covers and over the side of the bed. "How nice for you. A welcoming committee. That was fast."

"Yes, and word is that somebody's very interested in that end unit. I don't know if it's a good idea for you to wait until next weekend to come see it, Rachel. Maybe you and John should drive down tomorrow. And, if you can't do that, maybe I'd better make an offer to the sellers for you, contingent, of course, on you and John liking it."

"Slow down, Susan. It's way too late for me to even think about something like that. And you must be dead tired. Neither one of us is thinking straight at this time of night. Let's talk tomorrow."

"But, Rachel, waiting might not be a very good idea."

"Susan, thanks for calling. I'm so glad to hear your voice and to know everything worked out. I'll call you early tomorrow morning. Tell Jim congratulations on a dream come true. Love you both."

Rachel hung up the phone and heard a timid knock on the bedroom door. She turned the light back on and walked across the room to unlock the door. Ben stood in the hall and rubbed the sleep from his eyes. Ralph stood at attention beside him.

"What's wrong?" the little boy whispered.

Rachel knelt down on the floor beside him and stroked Ralph behind his ears. She realized the phone must have waked the child. He became a very light sleeper after his parents' accident. His therapist couldn't say how long his sleep problems would last.

"What's wrong?" he asked again, louder the second time. "It's night time. Who's calling us so late? What's happened?" he shrieked.

John climbed out of bed and joined Rachel in the hall. He, too, crouched down to Ben's level and pulled his grandson to him.

"Nothing's wrong, son. Everything's right, in fact. Susan called to tell her best friend that the move into the new house is done. Wasn't that nice of her?"

"Susan is Rachel's best friend?"

"Yes, you know that."

Ben looked at Ralph. The dog looked back and wagged his tail. Ben leaned over and whispered in his ear and then patted his head. Ralph leaned into the boy's pajama leg.

"Ralph was a little sad," Ben explained. "He thought he was Rachel's best friend. But he's okay now. I splained to him that we can have more than one best friend."

"Smart boy," Rachel said. "Thanks for helping Ralph. I'm sure he'll have a much better night's rest now that you've made him feel better."

After a warm milk and graham cracker snack, the three climbed back into their beds. Rachel relaxed in John's arms, her head tucked under his chin.

"Out of the mouths of babes," she thought as she remembered the twinge she felt when Susan told her about the welcoming committee. Remembered her fear that she had already been replaced in Susan's life. Remembered Ben's words to Ralph as he reassured the dog that "people can have more than one best friend."

"John," she whispered. "Are you awake?"

She felt him nod his head and mumble into her hair.

"Hold me close," she said.

And he did.

* * *

Carrie sat on the side of the bathtub. She stared at the narrow plastic strip in her hand and then at her watch. She shook her head in disbelief as the innocent white turned bright pink minutes before the prescribed time was up and her fate was sealed.

"Pink for pregnant," the instructions read.

Maybe I should try again, she thought. Just to make sure. She had bought two pregnancy tests, just in case. She ripped open the outer packaging and sat down on the toilet again. Nothing. Guess I'm nervous, she thought. She pulled her panties and jeans back up and washed her hands. She ran downstairs to drink a glass of water. Several glasses of water later, she sat down again, strip in position and tried to force at least one drop. A different drop. After what seemed like an eternity, she felt her bladder release what would be a verdict in a matter of minutes.

Why am I so nervous, she wondered. Horace will be delighted. We're married. We both want children. We talked about having a family on our first date. Well, not having a family together, but that we both wanted children.

Just not when. They hadn't talked about when they would start trying. Certainly, not this soon.

Am I just being a control freak? Carrie worried as she stared down at the second bright pink strip of color. She remembered that her mother and several of her older friends warned her that if you wait for the perfect time to have children, you'll never have them.

Okay, so this is the deal, she thought. I'm pregnant. I can go see a doctor, and he'll verify what I already know. In fact, I think I even know when I got pregnant. That night after Rachel's wedding party.

Too much champagne. Did we use a condom? I don't think so. I'm almost positive we didn't. In fact, I think we were out of condoms, and I said not to worry because I'm sure it's safe.

And, now I'm pregnant.

Should I call Horace now or wait until he comes home? I'll call him. I can't wait. No, this is not news to be shared over the phone. I'll make a romantic dinner. His favorite meal. Candlelight. Champagne. Wait. I can't drink. I'm pregnant. Well, surely, it won't hurt this early in the game. Heck, I wouldn't even know I'm pregnant if I'd had to wait to see a doctor and getting an appointment could have taken days. We'll sip champagne in front of the fire. I'll sit in his lap. I'll say, "Horace, do you think maybe I've gained a little weight? Do I feel heavier to you?" and he'll say something sweet.

"Honey, I'm home," Horace yelled from downstairs. Carrie sat on the side of the tub. She held the two test strips in her hand. When she didn't answer him, he ran up the stairs and rapped on the bathroom door.

"Carrie? You in there? Why do you always close the door when you're home alone? Carrie? Carrie, are you okay?" Horace opened the door and peered around the edge. His wife huddled, white-faced, her hands behind her back.

"What is it? What are you hiding behind your back?"

Carrie stood and slowly raised the two pregnancy test strips in front of her husband's face.

"What?" he asked. "What are those?"

Carrie waited for the truth to sink in. Waited for the same shock to hit Horace that hit her just minutes before. Finally, she realized the man had no idea of the meaning of the two strips she held in front of his nose like flags.

"Horace, don't tell me you don't know what these are. Don't know what this means."

"No. I don't, but you obviously do, and, from the look on your face, it's not good. Are you sick? What's wrong? Tell me."

"These are pregnancy tests. I tested positive. I'm pregnant. We're going to have a baby."

Horace sank down onto the side of the tub in the same spot his wife had just left. His mouth dropped open, and his cheeks flushed bright red. Then, he let out an Indian war cry and grabbed Carrie in a mad dance down the hall and threw her on the bed, landing on top of her in a tangle of arms and legs.

"Oh, dear," he yelled as he rolled off her and fell to the floor. "I'm sorry. Are you okay. Did I hurt the baby? Should we get you to the hospital? I'm sorry. I didn't mean to squash you. I'm just so excited."

Carrie smiled at her husband and breathed a sigh of relief. She allowed herself to absorb some of his enthusiasm and felt some of her own fear seep out of her pores.

"Don't worry. I'm okay. The baby's okay. You didn't hurt anybody."

"Have you told anybody yet? Who should we call first?" Horace sat up on the edge of the bed and reached for the phone.

"Hold on there, big boy. Let's not rush things."

"What do you mean?" Horace stared at his wife as a look of fear washed over his face. "Wait a minute. Aren't you happy?" When Carrie didn't answer right away, Horace replaced the receiver on its cradle and moved closer to where she propped herself up on the pillows.

"Aren't you?"

"Aren't I what?"

"Happy that we're pregnant?"

Carrie pulled Horace closer and laid her head on his shoulder so he couldn't see her eyes. He stroked her back and waited, then tilted her chin up so he could see her expression.

She returned his stare.

"Let's not tell anyone quite yet. Let's wait until I've been to see the doctor and he confirms the results of this with a real test."

"Well, how long will that take? A day? Two days? I don't want to wait too long. I want to shout the good news from the rooftops. I want to call Mom. Don't you want to call your parents? How about Rachel? At least, let's tell Rachel, for God's sake."

"Horace, I'll try to get in to see the doctor tomorrow. As soon as we get a confirmation—a real test—you can tell anybody and everybody you want to tell."

"And you're happy, right?"

"I'm happy." Carrie paused. "I just wish your father were alive."

"Horace Gilbert the third. He'd love it."

"What if it's a girl, silly?"

Horace frowned.

"What? You don't want a girl?"

"Only if she has your eyes. And your lips. And your everything."

"Okay, okay. I get the point," Carrie laughed as her husband planted kisses on all the parts he identified as perfect for his baby daughter.

Chapter Seventeen

W hen Rachel walked into Carrie's office, she felt the change. The air seemed to vibrate around her. She assumed her imagination had shifted into overly active mode, but she could swear she saw a halo-like glow around Carrie's head. The young woman smiled at her visitor and pulled out a chair so the two could sit at the small round table that nestled in the corner and overlooked the sun-filled patio below. Several employees sat outside to enjoy the unusually warm winter afternoon during their afternoon break.

Rachel looked down as a group of three women laughed as a fourth practiced balancing a hula hoop. Carrie said the latest fad had caught on at the office and that the staff benefited from the combination of exercise and competition.

"Sometimes the simple solutions work the best," the young woman said as she handed Rachel a stack of documents signed by the employees who accepted the incentive packages. Business seemed to be back to normal at The Gilbert Companies.

"And how about you?" Rachel asked. "You seem to have an extra twinkle in your eye. You look like a woman in love with just a little extra spice in the mix. What's up? I know you're excited about closing on your new home, but this glow just doesn't smack of real estate to me."

Carrie hesitated only a fraction of a second before she broke down and blurted out the news that she was pregnant.

"But you can't tell a soul," she made Rachel promise. "We

haven't even told our parents yet. Not until after I've been to the doctor and had a real test. You never know. Maybe I'm not."

"You are. I can tell, But, no, I won't say a word. Not even to John. Not until you give me the okay, and then I'll join you and Horace on the rooftop to shout it to the world. Horace must be about to burst."

"He is. And he'll be so glad I told you. He wanted me to call you last night, but I was still so shocked that I just couldn't."

Rachel reached across the table and stroked Carrie's clenched fist.

"Of course, I've never been where you are, but I would think you'd be a little scared. Good things can be that way. Scary, that is."

Carried nodded.

So much change in such a short time, Rachel thought. The engagement. Horace Gilbert's death. Inheriting his company from her future father-in-law. The break-up and then make-up, followed by the trip to the courthouse for a quickie wedding. And now this. The poor girl must feel like she's been hurtled up and down in the middle of a cyclone.

"How are you feeling? Any morning sickness?"

"No. I seem to have been spared that, so far. Which is one of the reasons I'm afraid the test I used at home may have shown false results. But I have an appointment with the doctor this afternoon, and they'll be able to tell me right away."

"Well, call me as soon as you get out of the office and let me know. I'll be dying to hear."

Carrie promised she would and glanced down at her watch. "In fact, it's time for me to leave now."

Rachel watched her graceful stride and smiled as she thought of the changes that would transform the slender young body in the months to come.

"Think you'll take some time off to be with the baby after he's born?"

"He? Why does everyone assume it's a he?"

"Oh, Horace Gilbert wouldn't allow his first grandchild to be anything other than male," Rachel laughed. "Of course, I'm joking. But what are your plans for the business? Do like the old field hands and squat down, pop it out and keep on working?"

"I don't know," Carried answered. "In fact, there are so many things to consider. It's pretty overwhelming, actually."

"Don't let it be," Rachel said. "Keep it simple. I know that's easier said than done, but try. You made it through taking over the business with flying colors. You can do this. Zillions of women have babies every day. So can you."

"Thanks, Rachel."

"Not like I know what I'm talking about," Rachel admitted," but let me know how I can help."

"Just be my friend."

"You can count on that, and I think Ben will give me a very good babysitting reference. As long as I don't have to change diapers."

"Not sure how we'll manage that, but, okay, no diapers," Carrie laughed.

As Rachel snapped her briefcase shut, she noticed the brochure for the beach condominium tucked in one corner. One more reason not to move, she thought.

* * *

Ricky clicked from channel to channel and back again to where he started to surf. After three complete cycles, he punched off the power button and tossed the television remote control onto the coffee table. He jumped up from the sofa and walked over to the mantle where a snapshot of Belle and Mary sat propped next to a larger studio portrait of Rob's parents. Ricky snorted at the comparison between the two family pictures.

Belle and Mary, captured in black and white, squinted into the sun. Mary, bundled in blankets, huddled in a stroller. Belle clutched its handle like she dared anyone to get too close.

Next to them, in a glossy black enamel frame, Rob's parents stared wide-eyed at the photographer. Smiles frozen, they wore their Sunday-go-to-meeting clothes and appeared as uncomfortable as Ricky felt when he looked at them.

He turned from the fireplace as he heard the front door open and close. Rob entered the den, set his briefcase on the floor beside the coat tree and flopped down on the closest end of the deep leather sofa.

"So, how did it go?"

"What?"

"Felicia."

Ricky groaned.

"Did you make your amends or did you not make your amends?"

"I made my amends."

"Then, the answer to my question is that it went well—as long as you haven't taken a drink. I didn't ask how Felicia took it, did I?"

Ricky shook his head and slumped down at the opposite end of the sofa, as far away as he could sit from Rob without a move to another seat.

"So, now you can cross her off your eighth step amends list and move on. Make sure you don't put her—or some other woman like her—back on the list. Got it?"

Ricky nodded again.

"And how's Deejee doing?"

The change of topic lightened Ricky's spirits, and he chattered on with details of Deejee's latest visit to the doctor and his advice that she continue to stay off her feet for another couple of weeks.

"She's talking about retiring, you know. Wants me to take over the business. What do you think?"

Rob kicked off his loafers and wiggled his toes inside his socks.

He sighed the sigh of a man who is tired inside and out.

"I don't know, Ricky. What do you think?"

Ricky snorted.

"You sound like that shrink at the hospital," he said. "What do you mean 'What do I think?' That's what I asked you, man. I'm looking for advice here. I'm asking for help. That's what I'm supposed to do, right? Ask my sponsor before I make major decisions?"

Rob rolled his eyes and sighed again, deeper this time. He sat in silence so long Ricky wondered if he had fallen asleep. Just as the younger man was about to poke his sponsor, Rob opened his eyes.

"Ricky, you know I can't give you advice. I'm only supposed to share my own experience, and I can't honestly think of a time when I've ever been faced with this kind of decision. Guess I've always played it safe. Worked for "the man." I'm not the entrepreneur type. Not sure I could deal well with all that freedom. I like structure. An office. Punching the clock. Timesheets. Budgets. Meetings. Files."

"Okay, okay. I get it. You can stop now. I understand."

Rob sat up straight and turned his body so he faced Ricky.

"How about you? How does all that freedom feel when you look at it? Think you're ready? Only you know the answer to that."

Ricky shook his head. The two sat together in silence.

"How does this sound?" Rob started. "Do it like we do everything. One day at a time. Don't make a big deal out of it. Try it, and if it doesn't work—if you start feeling the itch—tell Deejee she needs to find someone else. How does that work for you? It's a hotdog stand, after all, not some multimillion dollar global business."

"Yeah, but."

"Don't 'yeah but' me, kid. You can do it. In fact, you don't even have to do it today. We're talking the future here. We're talking tomorrow. Right now, we're here. On the sofa. What's for supper?"

"How 'bout a hotdog?"

"Make mine all the way, and you've got a deal."

* * *

Rachel rolled over and kissed John good-morning. He stretched his body like a cat that begs for more. Some sound close to a purr escaped from under the covers he had pulled over his head during the night.

"Are you awake?" Rachel whispered as she snuggled even closer to her husband. When he didn't answer, she eased away from his body toward the edge of the bed.

"Just where do you think you're going?"

Rachel jumped.

"Good grief, John. Don't scare me like that. I thought you were still sleeping."

John pulled his wife back under the covers into a tight embrace.

"Well, I'm not," he said.

"Good. I need to talk to you."

John groaned. "I need to talk to you" were not words he liked to hear early in the morning.

"Can we get some coffee in us first?" he asked. "In fact, how about a good-morning kiss. Or even a little more action than a kiss. What's so important that you need to talk when we haven't had our caffeine."

"Okay, I'll go start the coffee."

"Don't be long," John smiled and focused his best bedroom eyes on his wife.

Ralph padded downstairs with his mistress and stood beside his food bowl.

"Ralph, do you think you'd like to trade walks to the Circle for walks on the beach? Get sand between your toes? Chase seagulls instead of squirrels? Learn to body surf?"

Ralph ignored the questions and headed for the backdoor. While he stopped at one bush after another to sniff the activities of the night before, Rachel measured out the coffee grounds, filled the Mr. Coffee machine with water and hit the "on" button. By the time the last drip had dropped, Ralph stood at the door again, ready to come back in.

"Did you give my questions some thought? Do you need more time to make your decision?"

Ralph wagged his tail and gave a short bark.

"Quiet. We don't want to wake Ben. He doesn't need to be part of the decision-making process. But you, Ralph Springer-Turner, are key to this adventure. You are a dog to be trusted."

"Who are you talking to?" John asked as he pushed open the swinging door into the kitchen.

Rachel let out a little shriek. "What are you doing down here? I wanted to serve you your coffee in bed."

John stood back a few paces and looked Rachel up and down.

"Who are you, and what have you done with my wife?"

Rachel laughed and jabbed John on his shoulder.

"Don't be silly," she said. "I've served you coffee in bed before. This isn't the first time."

John shook his head.

"No, but coffee-making is usually my job. We both know I make a better brew than you do."

Rachel pretended to be hurt. She stuck her thumb in her mouth and sucked for a few minutes before she dropped the pretense and answered John's question. "I was talking to Ralph. About something serious. Now, it's our turn."

"Can we do it in bed? I really like my weekend coffee in bed, and if you've already consulted Ralph, this must be serious."

Rachel placed the two mugs of coffee on a wooden tray. She centered between them a single yellow rose and baby's breath arranged in a cobalt blue bottle. John surprised her with the arrangement the day before. She picked up the tray and led the way back to the master bedroom. As an afterthought, she stopped to grab the bag of chocolate croissants she brought home from Dean & DeLuca's earlier in the week.

"This must be serious," John muttered as he trailed along behind her. "Caffeine and chocolate."

"Quiet. I don't want to wake Ben. He doesn't need to hear what I want to talk about. Not yet anyway."

The two settled themselves in the bed. Pillows propped behind them and a candle cast a soft glow across the bed. After a couple bites of croissant, chased by half a cup of the dark roasted coffee, she began.

"I dreamed that we moved to the beach," she said and paused. When John didn't speak, she continued. "I saw Ralph and Ben running along the shore, right at the edge of the water. They looked so happy."

Rachel glanced at John again to gauge his reaction. He sipped his coffee silently, afraid to break the spell. He remembered his words to Susan when she introduced the idea of their retirement and relocation. He insisted that Rachel—not he—would be the sticking point.

What he hadn't figured into the equation was the significance Rachel placed on dreams. Now, she'd dreamed of a move to the beach and—even more importantly—Ralph was in the dream. And Ben. And they looked happy.

John smiled.

"I know the whole idea of us uprooting ourselves—especially Ben—I know we shouldn't even think about it. Silly to think of a move to the beach just because Susan and Jim moved. Silly."

John lifted the coffee mug out of Rachel's hand and popped the rest of her croissant in her mouth to stop her speech.

"Too many 'shouldn'ts,'" he laughed. "Let's try to be open-minded. Like when you brought Ralph home and when you moved

Belle and Mary into the downstairs apartment."

"And you."

"And me."

"Yes. All those worked out, and I've been thinking—what with the dream and all—that we should—could—go ahead and drive down to see the condo. Just look."

"Sure. When do you want to go?"

"This afternoon."

John grabbed the bedside table to steady himself and the mug of coffee that teetered on its edge.

"What's wrong?" Rachel asked. "I thought you were the one ready to take the plunge?"

John shook his head and rubbed his eyes as he stalled for time.

"I just didn't expect the move to be so sudden."

Rachel told him about her conversation with Susan the day before. About the news that a potential buyer was rumored to be about to make an offer.

"Susan said we should take a look at it this weekend. I think she may be right. Wouldn't hurt to look. I mean, after the dream and all."

"Yes, certainly. After the dream."

"Great. I'll go wake Ben and we can get started."

"Oh, no, you don't. Not so fast. I had a dream, too, last night, and you were in it. I looked very happy. We both looked so happy. Here, let me show you how it went."

Chapter Eighteen

The soft afternoon sunlight lay across the fairway in a golden glow. Golfers had all headed for the clubhouse by the time Rachel and John arrived. The lush green carpet spread out before them in a picture of peace. The ninth hole flag fluttered in the breeze.

John and Rachel held hands as they stood at the sliding glass doors to the patio a mere steps from the green.

"Do golf balls crash through this window sometimes?" Ben asked as he broke the peaceful spell. "Or hit people on the head when they're outside playing? Where's the swing set? And the pool?" he asked the realtor.

Rachel didn't like the look the realtor gave Ben. A smug, sniffing-a-bad-smell look. Rachel suspected the woman would ignore the questions, and she felt her mother hen protectiveness flair up.

"Ben, that's a smart question. Good thinking," Mrs. Jordan said in what sounded a little too condescending for Rachel's taste, but she held her tongue. "That's what's so nice about this location. By the time the golfers get to this point in the course, their balls are rolling and not crashing." Mrs. Jordan smiled a satisfied smile and began to herd the group into the next room.

"What about the pool?" Ben shouted.

"The pool is right around the corner of that building," Mrs. Jordan said through gritted teeth. "You can run over there in a matter of minutes. But let's look upstairs at the bedrooms before I give you a tour of the clubhouse and other amenities."

John squeezed Rachel's hand. "Good job," he whispered.

Ben ran ahead of the three adults. His tennis shoes sounded like large, heavy hammers on the bamboo floors. Rachel was glad Susan and Jim had offered to keep Ralph with them during the condo showing. She couldn't help but wonder what dog toenails would do to the soft flooring. The floors not covered with bamboo were tiled in soft earth tones and appeared equally susceptible to damage. Every room was decorated to create a natural feeling, but Rachel feared that nature didn't include dogs and children.

The kitchen, in contrast, was designed in black and white. Black and chrome appliances with white walls and tile floors. White cabinets with glass panes. Rachel looked over at John as they passed through on their way to the upstairs and knew he made an effort not to drool. The man loved to cook, and the kitchen was a cook's dream. A large island sat in the middle of the space, with chrome bar stools pulled up to it. Rachel imagined friends—Susan and Jim and all the new friends they would make once they settled in—as they sat deep in conversation while John prepared one of his favorite meals.

Upstairs, three bedrooms opened off a wide hall. The master bedroom overlooked the golf course, and its bath featured the garden tub Rachel insisted she couldn't live without. On the drive down, John assured her that one could easily be installed if the unit didn't already feature it.

But there it was. A sand-colored tile garden tub that matched the sand-colored tile floors and appeared to grow out of them like a living being. Rachel wasn't sure until she could measure, but she was almost positive that it was even larger than the one they had in DC. Plush cream-colored towels stood stacked neatly in an alcove beside the frosted window set in the wall behind the tub.

"Wow," Ben yelled. "This bathtub is big enough for all four of us."

"Four?" Mrs. Jordan asked.

"We have a dog," John couldn't resist saying. He winked at

Rachel. Horrified, Mrs. Jordan turned on her heel and headed for the door.

"But where will Rachel medidate?" Ben shrieked.

Rachel and John looked at each other.

"Out of the mouths of babes," Rachel said.

"Excuse me?" Mrs. Jordan asked.

"We have a third floor in our home in Washington, and I enjoy a room there where I meditate. Ben was asking where I could meditate here. Thanks, Ben, for reminding me."

"Well, there's the sunroom near the living room on the first floor. Perhaps that would suffice," the realtor suggested.

"Does it have a window seat?" Ben asked.

Mrs. Jordan pretended she hadn't heard the question.

"Excuse me, Mrs. Jordan," John said. "I believe my grandson asked you a question about a window seat in the sunroom."

"To tell the truth, Mr. Turner, I don't remember. Follow me, if you will, and we'll go see. One, of course, could be added if Mrs. Turner prefers to mediate on a window seat."

"Actually, it's for the dog," John said.

"I beg your pardon?"

"Ralph, the dog, needs the window seat for his meditation practice."

* * *

"So, what did you think?" Susan asked. She opened the door to her condo before Rachel, John and Ben even had a chance to knock. Ralph bounded out and ran circles around his family.

"Does he need a walk?" Rachel asked.

Susan assured her friend that the dog walked to the clubhouse and back earlier and already made lots of new friends, including several other dogs that lived along the row of condos between Susan and Jim and the empty unit. "Dog Row" was the name the residents affectionately called that section of the community.

"Come on in. Tell me all about it. What did you think? Did it have a garden tub? Where are you going to put your meditation room?"

"Hang on there, Susan," John stopped her as everyone rushed through Susan's front hallway toward the kitchen. "We're feeling a little overwhelmed by the realtor you dumped on us. We need some down time. Maybe a drink?"

Susan looked like she'd been slapped in the face. Rachel walked over to her friend and pulled her close. She flicked the brim of the hot pink tennis visor Susan still wore hours after her tennis lesson.

"This your new look?" Rachel teased.

"Why? Don't you like it?"

"Of course, I like it. You look adorable. You're always the cutest friend I have. Just don't give up the tap shoes. Promise?"

"Promise. Okay, what do you want to drink?" Susan aimed the question at Rachel, but John was the first to pipe up with an answer.

"This is the beach. Aren't we supposed to drink margaritas or daiquiris or something with lots of crushed ice and little umbrellas?"

Susan stared at John with a look that would kill. Rachel jumped to the rescue.

"Whatever you're having will be fine. We do want something that will relax us. Mrs. Jordan was definitely a little intense. Maybe herbal tea would be in order. Jasmine, maybe?"

"With a shot of whiskey for me," John insisted as he passed by the two women and headed for the bathroom upstairs. Ben tagged along behind his grandfather. Ralph brought up the rear.

"What's up with him?" Susan asked as she set the tea kettle on the back burner of her new stove. "Don't you just love the flat surface on these stoves here?" she asked. "Oh, that's right. You have a flat surface on your stove in DC, don't you. Well, it's new for me, and I love it. I love everything about this place, Rachel. A hop, skip and a jump, and I'm at the beach right across the street. In fact, why don't we leave your grumpy old husband here with his whiskey, and you and I can take our tea party out to the waterfront."

"Sounds like an excellent plan," Rachel agreed. She ran upstairs to tell John where the two were headed. Ben wanted to join them, but Rachel was able to divert his attention to his favorite television show that was about to start.

As she rejoined Susan in the kitchen, she remembered Ralph and grabbed his leash. "Come on, boy. Let's see if you'll make a water dog. What do you think?" she asked Susan.

"Absolutely."

"What are you grinning about?"

"Nothing. Nothing at all."

"Well, you sure don't look like 'nothing at all.' You look like the friend I've loved for years and who has always got something up her sleeve."

"Who knows. It all starts with a dog," Susan laughed.

Rachel tugged on Ralph's leash while Susan poured tea in a thermos and loaded two mugs in her beach bag. The walk to the beach from Susan's condo offered Rachel the opportunity she needed. Quiet walking meditation. Susan knew her friend well enough to give her the silence she craved. The sounds of Ralph's plopping paws and the pair of human footfalls worked. Rachel matched her breath to the rhythmic sounds and, by the time the group passed out of the gated community and crossed the highway to begin their walk down the public beach access, her heartbeat had slowed. As they crested the dunes and began their decent to the shoreline, she turned to Susan and said, "Let's sit here for a few minutes and sip our tea before we walk."

"Great idea," Susan agreed. "We can leave the thermos in this clump of beach grass and lighten our load."

Ralph rushed down the water's edge while Rachel and Susan

spread the reed mat they brought with them.

"Isn't it wonderful to be able to let him off his leash like that to run free?" Susan said. "Look how happy he is, Rachel. Like he was born to be a beach dog."

Ralph did, indeed, look happy as he ran up and down the waterline. He chased seagulls. He dug in the sand. He jumped like a puppy at a fish in the water. After each adventure, he looked back at Rachel to make sure she appreciated his latest accomplishment.

Rachel smiled but didn't answer her friend. Some things are obvious between friends and don't need to be spoken, she thought. Susan knows I know what she's up to. We'll just sit with it for a while. Let it percolate.

A warm breeze blew the loose strands of hair around Rachel's face. She pushed them back and realized her fingers were wet.

"Rachel, you're crying. What's wrong?"

Rachel stared down at her wet fingers and inhaled the salt air. She sucked it deeply into her lungs and exhaled slowly. Finally, she glanced up at the woman who sat on the dune with her and then out at the dog that danced with the waves.

"Nothing's wrong, honey. I think my heart is brimming over with so many things that are right."

Susan smiled and jumped up. "Great. Let's walk."

As soon as Ralph saw the two stand, he scrambled back up toward them and led the way back down toward the ocean. Whitecaps dotted the crystal coastline. The sun started to set and created reflections of light in the cottage windows lined up like bright welcome signs ahead of them. Rachel shaded her eyes against the glare and didn't see the sign until they were almost past it.

Someone had nailed a weathered board with the hand-painted red words "For Sale" to the end of a handrail of the boardwalk that stretched from the beach to a three-story gray clapboard cottage. Rachel grabbed Susan's arm. "Stop," she said. "Do you see what I see?"

Susan looked toward the ocean where Ralph stopped to flirt with a seagull. Rachel walked toward the sign and the stairs that led up to the boardwalk. Ralph saw his mistress change course and rushed toward her. As he flew past, Susan redirected her gaze, saw the sign and gasped.

"Come on," Rachel said as she pulled her friend up the steps.

"Careful. They look a little rotten," Susan said as she teetered on a loose board. "I'm not sure we should be doing this, Rachel. Feels like trespassing or something. Maybe we should go get John and Jim."

Rachel laughed. "I can't believe you're the one being cautious instead of me. Come on, silly. The house has a 'For Sale' sign in front of it. The owners want people to trespass."

"I don't know, Rachel. This place looks like it's been empty for a long time. Look at the swing set. That rust probably dates back to the fifties."

"Yes, look at the swing set, Susan. Look at it. It's a swing set."

She pulled out the small notebook and pen she always carried with her and jotted down the phone number painted on the sign. Ralph waited at the top of the porch steps fifty feet ahead of them. He wagged his tail in a welcome home wag. The two women turned to each other and laughed.

"Should we call now?" Susan asked.

"Let's look in the windows first," Rachel answered as she raced from one to another. Finally, she gave up. "They're all shuttered."

"Maybe that's a sign."

"Yes. It's a sign we need to call."

"Better wait until we get back to the house and talk to John first. Remember how he felt when you postponed the wedding without including him in the decision. I think your husband is a sensitive man, and you need to be careful. You're not alone anymore, you know. You have to take him into consideration with everything now."

"Everything? I'm just going to make a phone call."

"Everything."

Rachel groaned as she stuffed her phone back into her jeans. As the two women turned to head back to the house, Rachel looked up at the third floor window. She swore, to herself, she saw a window seat. And on it, she swore she saw a dog.

Chapter Nineteen

W hen Rachel and Susan opened the front door, they heard a cue stick hit a pool ball and then John's voice. "Damn. So close and yet so far," he groaned.

"Not bad for an old coot who hasn't held a cue stick in his hands for decades," Jim laughed. "Unless you're playing a trick on me and waiting to show me your real stuff at the last minute and beat me."

The women followed the voices to the den where their husbands played their final shots. Solid-colored balls still covered the pool table, and, from the look on John's face, they belonged to him. Rachel hesitated to bring up the proposal of a phone call to another realtor. She looked at Susan for guidance, and her friend tilted her head toward the kitchen.

"Let's refresh these guys' drinks and pour ourselves something," Susan said as she scooped up the two empty cocktail glasses balanced on the edge of the pool table.

"Better let John have another drink before you mention the house," she said as Rachel closed the door to the kitchen. "Men don't take losing very well."

Rachel acknowledged her friend's much longer marital experience and sat on one of the bar stools at the kitchen island while Susan poured scotch. She thought about the possibility of being able to enjoy similar afternoons with her friend, and her heart lifted. She realized she didn't feel the heaviness until she felt the shift. She smiled.

"What are you grinning about?" Susan asked as she slid a glass across the counter-top.

"Oh, nothing. Everything. Just happy, I guess." Rachel knew all the steps required to make a major change like the one she entertained. They'd have to check on the school system for Ben. To close down the firm would take months of preparation. She couldn't just walk away from her clients in mid-case. And the house on O Street might be difficult to sell since the housing market was down.

Just as a dark cloud started to pass across her face, Jim and John walked into the room.

"Is it warm enough to sit outside?" Jim asked. John followed him into the room. Rachel knew the smile was the forced smile of a loser who tried to be a good sport. She stood and hugged her husband. Susan handed everyone a drink.

"It's a little chilly," she said. "Let's sit in the sunroom where we can see the course and pretend we're outside. Won't be many weeks now before we'll have plenty of time to enjoy the patio."

Rachel and John sat together on the soft white leather couch. Susan and Jim took their seats in the maroon striped wing-back chairs on either side of them. The golf course stretched empty in front of them, except for one lone boy, who searched for lost golf balls.

"Look!" Ben squealed. "It's a kid. Can I go out and play with him, Rachel?"

Rachel looked over at John. He nodded.

""Sure," she said," but don't wander so far that we can't see you."

Ben jumped up from the floor where he built a tower of Legos and pulled the sliding glass doors open.

"Can Ralph go with me?"

"No dogs allowed on the golf course, buddy," Jim said.

"Sorry, Ralph," Ben said. "It's hard being a dog sometimes, but I'll be right back."

The adults watched as Ben raced toward the other child. The two boys immediately continued the intense search for balls together.

"Wouldn't it be nice if adults could make friends so quickly. If they kept life that simple," Rachel said as she snuggled closer to John.

The group sipped their scotch. Only the clink of ice cubes broke the silence in the room. Rachel looked across at Susan. She waited for some signal that would let her know when to broach the subject of a call to the realtor about the beach house they found on their walk.

Just when she thought she couldn't stand another minute's wait, the doorbell rang.

"Who could that possibly be?" Susan said on her way out of the room to answer the door. When she returned, a young man trailed behind her.

"Mr. Hatcher, this is my husband, Jim, and our friends, John and Rachel."

The three shook hands, and Susan asked the newcomer if he would like a drink.

"No, but thank you," he said. "I was out on the beach earlier and noticed these ladies looked at a house I have listed. I'll admit I watched which condo you returned to. The sellers are very eager to find a buyer, and I'm just trying to help them as much as I can." The man hesitated. "Any chance you'd like to see inside?"

Rachel looked at John's open mouth and then at Susan for guidance.

John was the first to speak.

"Sorry, Mr. Hatcher, if we appear rude. This is the first I've heard of a beach house for sale. Rachel, would you care to fill me in?"

Rachel rose and moved across the room to stand next to her friend.

Susan spoke first. "Yes, John. On our walk, Rachel and I did see a house with a "For Sale" sign in front of it. We were just getting ready to tell you about it when this nice young man knocked on the door."

John looked at Rachel. She nodded but took her time as she looked for the right words to break the awkwardness.

"Yes, I didn't want to call the phone number until after I had talked to you," she said.

John raised his eyebrows and stood up to shake the young man's hand. "Looks like you do a good job representing the owners," he said. "Hope we can find somebody as hardworking as you to sell our place in DC."

Susan and Rachel looked at each other and smiled.

"Let me call Ben inside," John said. "We certainly want him to be part of the tour."

"Great," Mr. Hatcher said. "I just happen to have the key with me. Don't always carry it, but, for some reason, I grabbed it today. Looks like I was in the right place at the right time."

"Does seem that way," Susan said with a grin.

* * *

As soon as Mr. Hatcher unlocked the front door and it sat open an inch, Ralph pushed his way through and disappeared down the long hall and up the stairs.

"Where does he think he's going?" John laughed.

"Looks like a dog who's come home," Mr. Hatcher answered on cue. "I don't want to sound pushy, but Ralph sure looks like he knows where he's going."

"And I think I know where," Rachel said. She looked at Susan and the two smiled at each other. "Follow me, honey," she said as she grabbed John's hand and led him toward the stairs.

"Me, too. Me, too," Ben squealed and raced after them. By the time Susan and Jim found their friends on the third floor, the dog and his family all crowded onto the window seat to admire the view of the ocean. High tide rolled in and waves crashed within a few feet of the end of the boardwalk that stretched from the porch out to the beach.

John opened the large window. A breeze blew in salt air and the squawk of sea gulls filled the room. He took Rachel's face between his two hands and kissed her softly on her forehead.

"Welcome home, Mrs. Turner."

Susan and Jim applauded from the doorway where they stood with Mr. Hatcher.

"Don't you even want to see the rest of the house?" the shocked realtor asked.

"I want to try out the swing set," Ben shouted. He ran past Susan and Jim and then skidded to a stop. "Can I, Granddad? Can I swing?"

"Sure, buddy, but stay away from the water."

"I'll go with him," Jim said. "I saw a shed back there I'm curious about."

Ralph rushed after the two, also eager to make his rounds since he had accomplished his most important duty when he led Rachel to their new meditation spot.

"When can they move in? Do the window treatments stay? How about that runner in the hall? Is it included?"

John laughed. "Wait a minute, Susan. We don't even know what the asking price is. And any purchase would have to be contingent on our sale of the house in DC, you know."

Mr. Hatcher stepped forward and handed John and Rachel a glossy, full-color brochure. A professional photographer shot pictures while the house was still filled with furniture. Rachel's hands shook as she took the four-page spread from her husband. Each room, bathed in sunlight, looked like the centerpiece of a *Southern Living* spread called "Gracious Beach Life." She looked at John.

"Almost as tempting as an Earthship, isn't he?" he teased.

"Almost." Rachel turned to the back page and then flipped back to the front again. "But where's the price?"

Mr. Hatcher smiled. "There isn't one on there. The owners want to take offers. As I said, they're eager to sell. The wife inherited the place from her grandmother. It's been in the family since it was built in 1935, so it holds a very special place in the granddaughter's heart. Unfortunately, she lives in California, and there's no other family anywhere near to look after it. I get the feeling that if the right people come along and make a reasonable offer, they would accept it."

Susan interrupted again. "Well, property on the beachfront like this is a lot of work and we'd have to do some checking."

Rachel stepped forward and grabbed one of her friend's fluttering hands. "Susan, we aren't doing anything. John and I are. Now, stop your managing and let's look at the rest of the house. The brochure is gorgeous but I'd like to take the tour, if you have time, Mr. Hatcher."

"I sure do. Let me just close this window and we'll go back downstairs. If you like this little room, you're going to love the rest."

* * *

And they did.

Later that night, Rachel and John lay together in Susan's guestroom, spent from all the excitement of the afternoon. Neither could find the words to express the thoughts that raced through their heads or the emotions that filled their hearts.

The gray clapboard house had been totally remodeled on the inside with all new "everything" as Mr. Hatcher had said. The glamorous brochure had not misrepresented the place they saw on their tour.

"What do you love most about it?" Rachel asked from the dark.

"About what?" John teased.

Rachel poked him in the ribs and then moved into tickle mode.

"Okay. I give up. Stop that," John yelled. Rachel stopped and waited for the answer to her question. "I know what you love most," he said.

"What do you know I love most, Mr. Smarty Pants?"

"The garden tub that overlooks the ocean. I'll never see you again. You'll turn into a prune."

"Well, that's a close runner-up to the fact that I can walk a few blocks to see my beat friend every day."

"Beaches don't have blocks, silly."

"Picky, picky, picky." Rachel started to tickle again.

"Okay, okay. My favorite part of the house is the porch. The wraparound porch. I plan to spend every afternoon in a rocking chair on that porch. I may even take up smoking a pipe."

Rachel interrupted her husband when she turned on the bedside lamp.

"What did you do that for? You're blinding me, woman."

"You talk as though it's a done deal, and we haven't even talked money yet."

As if on cue, a manila envelope slid under the door. Rachel and John looked at each other. Rachel jumped out of bed and yanked the door open. Susan smiled on the other side of it. She looked like a child who has been caught with her hand in the cookie jar.

"What's this?" Rachel demanded as she shook the envelope at her friend.

"Comps. I ran the comparable statistics for you on recent sales of beachfront property."

"Isn't that the realtor's job?" John asked from the bed.

"No point waiting," Susan chirped and then turned on her heel and marched back down the hall to her own room.

"'A force of nature' is what my grandmother used to call people like her," Rachel laughed as she opened the envelope and pulled out ten sheets of information. Susan printed out full descriptions, tax values and prices of property sold during the last six months. "Want to look at these now or wait until morning?"

"Are you kidding?" John gasped as he grabbed for his wife and the listings she dangled in front of her.

The two sat in the bed with papers scattered around them long into the night. Just as a clock downstairs struck midnight, they agreed on an offer and turned out the light to celebrate.

Chapter Twenty

George stood in the middle of the upstairs room and faced the window that overlooked the field between his cottage and the larger farmhouse down the hill. He stared at the giant maple tree that shaded its corner. As he stood, he inhaled the smell of bacon, fried to a crisp, lifted on air currents and carried up the hill toward him.

He squinted his already squinted eyes and imagined a little girl in the tire swing that hung from one of the low-hanging branches of that tree. He closed his eyes tightly and turned away from the vision of Mary.

And her mother.

George turned to face the wall opposite the window and folded his arms across his chest. He balanced himself and braced his back against the window frame so he could examine the photographs. Hundreds of pairs of eyes stared back at him. Beckoned him to move closer.

Slowly, he took a step forward. One step and then another, away from the tire swing and closer toward the faces. One face in particular—the boy with the rifle—pulled him like a fish on the end of a very long line. The piercing black eyes drew him to the shore that was his past.

"I will come back for you," he heard himself say to An, the boy he met so many years ago while he was stationed in Da Nang. "After this war is over, I will come back for you and I will take you away from all of this."

And to the boy's mother, Phuong Phan, he said the same, only with more than words. And he meant what he said. And what his body said.

The landmine changed his life forever. Shattered his body and the boy's dreams. The Army airlifted him out of the foreign territory before he had a chance to say "good-bye" to the two people who became his reason to fight. Who gave heart to the nightmare his life became.

George reached out and touched the photograph of the boy. He covered the rifle with his calloused finger and imagined the young mother in his finger's place. She never allowed George to photograph her. She didn't see the beauty George saw and said she wanted him to remember her through the filter of love and not a camera lens.

She believed I loved her, George thought, and yet I don't even know whether she's even alive. All these years, and I've never even tried to find the two people who trusted me to rescue them. To bring them from their small coastal village of Tam Ky to the land of milk and honey. To bring them to America.

George fell to the floor and leaned his head against the wall and wept.

* * *

Nancy and Simon stared at George in disbelief. Their plates of dinner sat in front of them, untouched. The mashed potatoes sat cold and stiff. The gravy congealed in the silence of the kitchen.

"I know I'm not giving you much notice," George said, " but if I don't go now, I'm afraid I'll change my mind and not go at all. I know there's work to be done around here, but at least planting season hasn't started, and I think I know a young fellow who would do a good job for you and he needs work."

Nancy stood up and walked around the kitchen table to where George stood, fists clasped in front of him. She rested her hand on his shoulder. "Stop, George," she said. "This isn't about the farm. We survived before you came, and we'll manage again after you leave.

But I'm worried. I'm worried about you." She looked to her husband for support, but Simon still sat in shock, unable to speak.

So, Nancy forged ahead. "Are you sure you're not making the decision to return to Vietnam to find this boy and his mother at this point in time because of all that has happened recently? Are you sure this plan of yours isn't purely a reaction to Rachel's wedding and then all the drama with Belle and Mary? The past few months have been a lot for you to process emotionally."

George had confided in Nancy some of the details of his time in Vietnam and his diagnosis of post-traumatic stress syndrome. She knew the ways it manifested itself. She knew about the medication he took to treat the night terrors and the challenges of day-to-day life. She wanted to ask him if he still took his pills but stopped herself.

George read the question in her eyes. "Yes, I'm taking my meds, Nancy, and no, I don't think I'm running away from what's happened here. I don't think my disappointments in the past few months have created a problem. I think they've cracked the shell that's kept me from doing what I should have done a long time ago. Kept me from keeping my promise."

George wrapped his arms around Nancy. They stood quietly. George rested his head on top of his friend's gray curls and smiled at her husband.

"I hope you will give me your blessing," he said. "I appreciate all you've done for me. You've given me a home, given me good honest work and paid me for it, and, most important, you've given me your friendship. I just need one more thing from you now." George pushed away from Nancy so he could look into her eyes. "I need your faith in me. Faith that I'm doing the right thing."

Nancy backed away from the weathered farmhand who had become such a big part of her family. She wiped a tear from her cheek and walked across the room to stand with her husband. She waited for him to speak. She knew George admired Simon's practical approach to life, and that a blessing from him would mean even more than the one he knew she would give him.

Simon seemed to reach down deep into a well of emotion to find the right words to say to his friend. The two shared so much in such a short time. Not just the long hours while they waited for the birth of a calf or searched the fields for lost cows. The two quiet men knew each other from a place deeper than words could reach and in the silence of morning milk time, they connected in that place.

"I'll miss you," Simon said. "We'll miss you," he corrected himself and cleared his throat. "But go. You're a good man. Go and find these people. Find them and bring them back here to Virginia. Here in Virginia would be a good place to bring them. We'll find somebody to take your place temporarily while you look for them, but the job of farm manager will be yours when you get back. That job will always be yours."

George stepped forward, and the two men shook hands.

"But don't take too long," Nancy said. "We need you back here by harvest time at the latest. And harvest time is probably going to come early this year."

"Yes, I have a feeling it will," George laughed as he limped out of the room. "Yes, this year's harvest will most surely come early and will bear a beautiful crop. I feel it in my bones."

He turned at the door. "I've already packed, and I'm ready to leave in the morning."

Simon nodded. "Traveling mercies, George."

As George walked across the field to his house, Nancy called out to him.

"What about Rachel? Does she know?"

George stopped and turned back. "I emailed her last night."

"And Belle?"

George bowed his head, nodded and disappeared into the night.

* * *

Rachel read George's email three times before she shared it with John. The message was short and typically George—to-the-point.

"Rachel," he wrote, "I hope you and John are settling in to married life. I'm sure Ralph is relieved to have you home. And Ben. I hope Ben is doing well. I miss you all. Everything is running smoothly here at the farm. Nancy and Simon send their regards."

George usually wrote emails in one short paragraph. Not this one. At this point, he shifted to a second paragraph. On her first read, Rachel took a deep breath as she sensed the fresh start the new format seemed to signify.

George raced through the news of his departure in the second paragraph.

"I know this may come as a shock to you and to John—and to those you choose to share it with—I leave tomorrow for Dulles Airport to fly from there to Saigon. I don't know how long I will be gone. I am looking for someone. Actually two people. A mother and her son. If I find them, I hope they will come back to the farm with me. Wish me luck. George."

Rachel read the last word of the email and looked up from the computer screen to gauge John's reaction. As she suspected, his reaction mirrored hers. His mouth hung open, and he rubbed his eyes in disbelief.

"Wow," he finally said. "Life is sure full of surprises, isn't it?"

"That's putting it mildly. I guess he kept his passport current."

John laughed.

Rachel looked hurt. "What's so funny about that? You can't just decide to leave the country on the spur of the moment. Your passport has to be current, and, if it's not, it can take some time to get a new one."

"Yes, of course," John said. "I know all that, but I would think you'd be asking yourself more important questions than whether he had a current passport. Like who are these people he's looking for and how is he going to find them?"

Rachel stared into the dark outside the guestroom window. She sat silently for such a long time that John finally asked for her thoughts.

"Belle. I'm thinking about Belle and whether she knows."

"And feels. How she feels. If this seems sudden to us, imagine how it must feel to her."

"I know we're leaving the beach to go back to DC tomorrow after we make the offer on the house, but maybe I should call her tonight. What do you think?" John's answer was interrupted by the ring of Rachel's cellphone. She looked at the caller identification and then up at John

"It's Belle," she said. "Hello, Belle. I was just thinking about you. How are you? Good. John's here with me. May I put you on speaker phone. I know he'll want to be part of the conversation." Rachel waited as Belle hesitated. Finally, she agreed, and Rachel switched to speakerphone. She looked at John and took a deep breath.

"When are you coming home?" Belle asked.

Rachel mouthed the words, "Should I tell her about the house?" John shook his head that she should not. "We're driving back to the city tomorrow. Should get home before dark. Everything okay?"

Belle didn't answer.

"Belle, are you there?"

"Yes. Yes, I'm here. And, yes, everything's fine. It's just, well, it's just that, I don't know how to say it. Did you hear from George?"

"Yes, I got an email from him just now. How about you? Did you get an email, too?"

"No. Well, yes, I heard from him, but not an email. He called me."

"He called you?"

"Yes, he called me. About an hour ago. To tell me he's leaving the country. Tomorrow. Going to Vietnam."

Rachel took a deep breath. "Yes, we got an email about his plan. Did he tell you the reason he's going?"

Again, Rachel's question was met by silence. Rachel heard Mary's song in the background. Belle finally asked her to stop so she could continue the conversation. The song changed to a wail that increased in volume until finally Belle cut the conversation short. "Yes, Rachel, he did. I need to talk to you, but Mary's hungry, and I should put her to bed. Give me a call when you get home. We need to talk." A shriek from Mary prompted a "Bye, Rachel," and conversation ended.

Rachel and John looked at each other.

"Doesn't sound too good," John said.

"Doesn't sound to me like this is a good time for us to be considering a move."

"Rachel, remember Doc Martin's in Taos?""Of course, I remember Doc Martin's. What does this have to do with a restaurant in New Mexico?"

John shifted to the sofa where his wife sat, folded her into his arms and leaned her back against his solid chest.

"Just like we didn't move to Taos and buy the restaurant when we heard the owner was sick, we don't have to change our plans to move to the beach because Belle is upset."

John stopped.

"Belle is what?"

"Well, we don't even know what Belle is, at this point, but whatever's going on with Belle, you don't have to fix it, my darling bride. The only person you have to fix is me." John turned her face up so he could kiss her lips.

"And me," Ben shouted. He burst into the room. Ralph bounded after him and leaped into the middle of the pile of his people on the sofa.

"And Ralph," Rachel laughed. "We definitely want to take care of Ralph."

"Cause Ralph takes such good care of us, right?" Ben asked.

"Yes, Ben, he does take care of us. All of us."

"That's a big job, Ralph. Taking care of all of us. And Belle and Mary. They really need a dog to take care of them. They need me, but they really need Ralph."

John and Rachel eyed each other over the top of the child's head and shared the same thought. Ben didn't realize a move to the beach meant his best friends would be left behind.

Chapter Twenty-One

Rachel stopped and turned around. She tugged on Ralph's leash and the dog dutifully followed her a few steps back toward the yard they had just passed on their walk to work.

"I thought I was seeing things, but I guess not. That forsythia bush has one little bloom on it. See it, Ralph? DC must have had a warm spell while we were gone."

Ralph poked his nose into the bush and nudged the lone yellow flower. He wagged his tail and turned as if to say, "Enough. Time to go to work." He tugged, and Rachel obeyed with a laugh.

"You're a real slave-driver, Ralph Turner." The dog wagged his tail at the sound of his mistress's voice and trotted along the street in front of her. Several times, he stopped to mark a favorite spot. When he saw Mr. Moser walk toward them, he wiggled every inch of his body and barked a greeting.

"Back from the beach, I see. Susan and Jim all settled in? You'll have to stop by the house and give Mildred a report. She's dying to hear all about the move."

"I'll be sure to do that. In fact, I'll drop by in a couple of hours, if you're going to be home. I won't be in the office long. Just want to see Georgia and make sure she's okay."

Mr. Moser snorted and gave Rachel a military salute. "Whatever you say, sir, but if I know you—and I think I do—you'll be at the office a lot longer than you're admitting. We won't hold lunch for you." He patted Ralph on the head and smiled crookedly at Rachel before he tottered off toward home. He raised the morning paper in a final farewell and disappeared before Rachel could challenge his regular accusation that she worked too hard.

"Nobody understands me, Ralph. Maybe you do, but nobody of the human variety. It's hard not to work hard when working hard is what you love."

Ralph stopped and licked her hand, then dashed to the front of her office and waited. Georgia unlocked and opened the door in a wide welcome. Ralph looked at Rachel for permission, and, at her signal, ran past Georgia, circled the room to check for danger and then returned to the two women who stood in the entrance. They hugged as if they hadn't seen each other for months instead of two days.

Georgia stepped back to examine Rachel's face.

"Something felt different about that hug," she said. "Is Susan okay? Did the move go the way she wanted it to? Let me rephrase that. Did they get moved? Nothing ever goes exactly the way Susan wants it to. I've had enough experience with Susan to know that about her."

Rachel laughed and pulled her secretary inside. Ralph sat on the hooked rug and licked the remnants of the walk from all four feet.

John and Rachel decided that Georgia should be the first to hear the news that they made an offer on the beach house and that, within an hour, it was accepted. Rachel felt tempted to tell Belle the night before. As soon as she unpacked the car, she ran downstairs to check on the young woman but the focus of their conversation remained on George.

Shortly after she heard Belle's reaction to George's phone call, Rachel knew her friend didn't need another move to trigger more feelings of abandonment. Belle took the news about the trip to Vietnam—and the motivation for it—hard. Her fight-or-flight reaction was more extreme than Rachel expected, and she took her time as she talked Belle out of her idea to quit school and move out of the apartment. Rachel finally coaxed her out of her desire to run away with a gentle reminder that Ben needed her—a trick that consistently worked. Once again, Belle related to the little boy's loss and avoided her own old familiar self-destructive desire to run.

Rachel sighed as she remembered last night's tears.

"Wow," Georgia interrupted her thoughts. "What was that all about? Did the moving company lose something?"

Rachel laughed and walked into the lobby. "No, the move went fine. Seamlessly, in fact. Even Susan was satisfied."

Rachel sat in the rocker and rocked.

"You look like you're on speed, Rachel. Didn't know that chair could move that fast."

Rachel looked around the room. One chocolate chip cookie sat on the plate covered with crumbs.

"Must have had a lot of company while I was gone,"

Georgia nodded but didn't say a word.

Rachel smiled when she spotted the second African violet Georgia told her a new client sent as a wedding gift. The plant sat in a place of honor on the window ledge near the door.

"The plants look good," Rachel said as she continued to stall.

"You weren't gone long enough for them to do much changing. The fern does have a new frond, I think, but everything else is pretty much the same."

Georgia walked over to the rocking chair and stood in front of Rachel. She dug her hands into her skirt pockets and gripped the Kleenex inside.

"Are you going to tell me what's going on or not?"

"Maybe you'd better sit back down."

"Okay," Georgia said and walked to her desk.

"No, not there."

Rachel rose from the rocker and rushed to the sofa, sat carefully near the middle and patted the seat next to her.

"Sit here. Beside me."

"Yes, boss."

"And don't call me that. You and I both know that title fits you better than it fits me."

Georgia sat on the sofa beside the woman who signed her paycheck since the beginning of her career. She turned to face her. She folded her hands in her lap, the Kleenex still clutched like a security blanket.

"Should I lock the door? Turn off the phones?"

"I'll lock the door. You turn off the phones."

Door locked and phones silenced, the two women returned to their posts on the sofa. They stared straight ahead. Finally, Ralph lost patience with them and barked from his position at their feet.

"Okay, okay," Rachel began, "John and I have bought a beach house."

"Good, Lord, Rachel. You didn't have to fire off that fast. I mean, you could have sneaked up for the kill a little bit slower than that."

Georgia leaned away from Rachel and slumped sideways against the far end of the sofa. She dabbed at her nose with the Kleenex. Ralph leaned his head against her knee.

"Do you have a cold, dear?"

"No, I don't have a cold, Rachel." Georgia threw the soggy tissue into the trashcan beside her.

"Do you need another tissue?"

"No, I don't need another tissue."

"How about a cookie?" Rachel reached for the lone Toll House treat. "Here, we can share it," she said and broke the cookie in half. The only sound in the room was the crunch of cookies.

Finally, Georgia broke the silence.

"When are you moving?"

Startled, Rachel jerked. "What?"

"When are you moving to the beach? I'm not surprised, you know. I've seen this coming. In fact, I'm happy for you, Rachel. I've even started organizing files and purging old cases. I've been getting ready for your retirement ever since you announced that you and John were going to be married."

Georgia walked over to the Boston fern and plucked off a dead frond. "But I guess you're never really ready for such a big change. We've been together a long time, Rachel. Been through so much."

Rachel nodded and then sat up straighter, as though her posture might improve the way the scene looked. "I brought you pictures of the house." She spread the Polaroid shots out on Georgia's desk and the two looked at them together in the quiet room.

"Susan's house is a block that way," Rachel said and pointed to the corner of one picture.

"Nice swing set. Does Ben know yet?"

"No. You're the first to know. Of course, he saw the house, but he doesn't know it's ours. Or will be soon."

"How soon?"

Rachel hesitated. "We close next month. The end of next month. It's a cash deal. No need to wait. John had the money from the sale of his place in New York."

Georgia nodded and fluffed the rest of the fern fronds. "Guess we'd better start letting our clients know right away," she said.

"Yes, that we're closing the firm."

"Actually, that may not be necessary."

"What do you mean, 'may not be necessary?' I'm moving."

"Yes, but Melissa—that new lawyer you've been exercising with—stopped by while you were on your honeymoon and we had a nice visit. She asked a lot of questions about the business, and she said that, when, and if, you ever retired, she'd be interested in taking over the firm. She's not happy in the large practice and wants to try to work solo." Georgia looked down at her desk and rearranged her line of pens. "She even offered me a job. With a raise. If I stay."

When Rachel didn't respond, Georgia looked up. Neither of the two friends spoke.

Suddenly, Rachel jumped up. "We need more cookies to get through this, Georgia Payne. Where are the rest of the cookies?"

"What's the problem? You're retiring and moving to the beach. I'll still have a job. Everything is falling right into place like magic."

"I see two problems, Georgia Payne. Number one problem is that I'm not sure I like the idea of you working for somebody else, and number two problem is that I'm not sure I'm even capable of retiring."

Ralph moaned.

"Rachel Springer—excuse me—Rachel Turner, you can do anything you set your mind to. And I haven't decided what I'll do yet. But that will be my decision."

"Maybe you can retire, too," Rachel said and rushed over to lean across Georgia's desk. "That condo Susan picked out for John and me is still available and you, and Mike would love it."

Georgia laughed. Ralph leaped up, relieved that the mood in the room lightened. He stood with his tongue hanging out of his mouth, panted and looked from one woman to the other. He waited.

"Rachel, you can't move everybody in your world with you to the beach. Are you planning to move Stan? Deejee? Belle and Mary? How about the whole homeless crowd at the Circle?"

"Of course not, silly. But you're special."

Georgia walked around the desk and faced her friend. "Yes, you and I are special," she said, "and a few hundred miles can't change that."

* * *

Georgia promised she would not share the news of her friend's move with anyone other than Mike, but Rachel knew how fast word traveled. She wanted to tell the story to the important people in her life, rather than have them hear it from the unreliable grapevine. On her walk home from the office, she made a mental list of friends she needed to talk to immediately and in order of priority.

Belle topped the list. She would tell Ricky. Next came Carrie and Horace. Deejee. Since they lived out of town, Nancy and Simon appeared further down on the list. They would know how to contact George and would tell him.

Stan. Rachel heaved a heavy sigh as she wondered how many times she would need to tell Stan and how he would react to another major change in his life. She knew their roles had been reversed and that he depended on her now in the same way she depended on him for so many years. With his failing health, the burden of staying in touch would be on her, she realized.

Rachel straightened her shoulders. I'll be the one doing the driving back and forth to see him, she thought. Ralph barked, as if he read her thoughts and agreed that Stan would need special attention.

"Glad we're not moving to Florida, Ralph."

"What's this about moving to Florida? Who's moving to Florida?" Mrs. Moser's voice startled Rachel, and she almost tripped over Ralph. She untangled herself from his leash and debated whether to move the Moser family from the bottom to the top of her contact list. Surely, Mrs. Moser can't spread the gossip before I have time to walk across the street to tell Belle, Rachel thought. She will at least have to tell Mr. Moser, and I'll have plenty of time while they debate the wisdom of my decision and then they'll debate all kinds of scenarios involving who will move in my house and how the neighborhood will be affected.

Rachel made a quick decision and hoped she wouldn't regret it.

"Good morning, Mrs. Moser. Beautiful day, isn't it?"

Mrs. Moser descended the two steps to the sidewalk and stood in front of Rachel as if to bar her way. Ralph sniffed her pants legs, and, when he was satisfied the person who confronted his mistress was, in fact, Mrs. Moser, he lay down in a spot of sun. The dog knew no conversation with his next door neighbor was ever a short one.

"Yes, it's nice now, but the weather girl on Channel 4 says we'll get rain later." Mrs. Moser stopped as a look of confusion flitted across her eyes. She refocused. "Rachel, we don't need to stand here like fools talking about the weather. The weather's going to do what the weather's going to do. I asked you a question. Who's moving to Florida?"

"Mildred?" Mr. Moser yelled from his front porch. "Mildred, what are you doing out there? Oh, good morning, Rachel," he said as he opened the door wider to wave at her. When he saw his wife's worried look, he shuffled down the walkway to stand closer to the conversation.

Good, Rachel thought. I can make sure Mr. Moser gets the news from me and not garbled somehow by his wife's reaction to it.

"How was your visit with Susan?" the old man asked.

"Hush, silly. Somebody's moving to Florida, and I'm waiting for Rachel to tell me who. We're always the last ones to hear things on this street. Rachel Turner, just because we're senior citizens—or whatever you young people like to call us these days—doesn't mean we don't deserve the common courtesy of knowing important news. News that may affect us. News like a move to Florida."

"Now, Mildred, give Rachel a chance to speak, for God's sake. Go ahead, Rachel." Mr. Moser shuffled closer to his wife's side and gripped her elbow. Rachel noticed the gesture more and more recently. She wasn't sure whether he meant to comfort his wife or whether he needed the balance.

"Our visit with Susan and Jim went very well," she said. "Ben loved the beach, and Ralph seemed to shed several years. He ran and jumped at the seagulls like a puppy. Susan and Jim's condo looks like they've lived in it for years, rather than less than a week."

Mr. Moser snorted. "No surprise there. That girl's a powerhouse."

"But what I want to know is who's moving to Florida?"

Rachel laughed, but, before she could answer, Mrs. Moser stepped forward and, nose-to-nose, demanded, "Is it you?"

"No, Mrs. Moser, we're not moving to Florida."

"Thank the good Lord," the old woman yelled. She backed away to stand beside her husband. She reached out to grab his hand. The two smiled at Rachel.

Great, she thought. This isn't going to be easy. She took a deep breath. "No, John and I have no intention of moving to Florida. That's too far away from our friends." She stopped to let that reassurance sink in. "Why don't we go up and sit on your front porch for a little bit. Enjoy this unusually warm weather we're having."

"Well, the weather girl on Channel 4 says it's going to rain. What's that girl's name, Mildred? That cute girl on Channel 4?"

"I don't know her name, honey, and I don't care. Rachel wants to sit on the porch. She must be tired. Come on, now. And get the mail out of the box while we're out here."

Rachel and Ralph followed their neighbors back to the porch. Rachel breathed deeply and prayed for the right words to use. This feels like preparing an opening statement in an important trial, she thought. Feels like make-or-break words. The rest of the case may depend on those kind of words.

Mr. and Mrs. Moser sat in their favorite rockers. Mr. Moser sat in the rocker to the left of the front door, and his wife took her place in the one to the right. Rachel eased down onto the porch swing and patted the seat beside her. Ralph jumped up, turned around his prescribed three times and lay down with his head in her lap.

Rachel inhaled deeply. The old couple stared at her.

"Well?" Mrs. Moser prompted.

"I've got some very happy news to share with you," Rachel began.

"You're not pregnant are you?" Mr. Moser shouted.

"No, silly. That's Carrie. Rachel's not pregnant. What is it,

Rachel?" News does travel fast, Rachel thought, when she heard that her neighbors already knew about Carrie's and Horace's baby. The doctor must have confirmed the pregnancy test or they wouldn't tell people. Now nice. Except a baby will live across the street and I won't be here to enjoy it.

"So, what's your good news?" Mrs. Moser interrupted.

"And if it's good news, why do you suddenly look all pouty?" her husband demanded.

Rachel jerked. "Oh, I guess my mind wandered a little. Sorry."

"Are you okay, dear? Mildred and I worry about you sometimes. Your mind. It seems to wander more than it used to. Do you take vitamins? Mildred and I do and it helps."

"Be quiet, silly, and let her tell us her good news. I'm tired of waiting."

Okay, here goes. You can do this, Rachel told herself. "As I said, Ben and Ralph loved the beach so much, and, actually, John and I did, too. Actually, we loved it. And we saw this house. And it was right across the road from Susan and Jim's condo. On the beachfront. And we made an offer on it. And the sellers accepted it. And so we're thinking about moving. In a month."

Mr. and Mrs. Moser stared across the narrow space that separated their rockers from the swing, and they rocked. Nobody spoke. Finally, Belle's greeting broke the creek of the rockers.

"Hey, guys," she called from across the street. "Beautiful day."

"Booful," Mary mimicked.

"I don't know," Mrs. Moser called back. "Depends," she said. "Rachel's leaving us. Moving all the way to the beach."

So much for my priority list, Rachel groaned.

Chapter Twenty-Two

Crayon drawings covered every inch of Belle's refrigerator door. Ben's stick figures danced across the freezer section in a rainbow of colors. Some frayed with age but still clung to their places of honor. At the bottom, where she could reach and rearrange them, Mary's finger-paint pictures stuck crookedly in a line. Belle joked that her daughter currently exhibited her hand print series. Ten pieces of copy paper showcased a pair of hands, all in the same position but dipped in different colors. Reds, greens, blues, yellows— and all the shades in between—spread out in a joyful parade.

How big will those prints be the first time I come back from the beach to visit, Rachel wondered.

"What's the worried look about?" Belle asked. She set a tray of cookies and tea cups on the coffee table and sat down beside Rachel. When her friend didn't answer, Belle pointed toward the tray. "Why don't you do the honors. After all, it was you who taught me to enjoy afternoon tea. And I've got to tell you, lady, it sure beats afternoon beer. Ah, the joy of jasmine tea. No hangover guaranteed. Just one of the many gifts I have to thank you for." Belle leaned back against the sofa and waited for Rachel to serve. Neither woman moved. "I thought we were going to celebrate," Belle said.

Rachel nodded. "We are. We are celebrating. But you pour. This is your home, and you're the hostess. Pouring is your job. Didn't I teach you that part?"

Belle laughed and then covered her mouth with her hand. "Don't want to wake Mary from her nap. She's been cranky all day. This quiet is a welcome relief."

Belle poured steaming tea into two dainty porcelain cups. Pepperidge Farm Milano cookies balanced on the matching saucers. The two women raised their cups and clinked them together in a gentle toast.

"To your move," Belle said. "May the beach be everything you've ever dreamed it to be—and more."

They sipped in silence, the only sound in the room the crunch of cookies.

"One month," Belle finally said. "That's really quick. I mean, not that I've ever done a move or anything, but how is it even possible to get everything done—whatever everything is—in four weeks?"

Rachel smiled as she remembered Susan's encouragement that they could move even faster if they sold the house in DC furnished and started fresh with a new beach decor. Rachel and John stood firm in a united front in which they assured her that would not happen. They both wanted to continue to live with their old, familiar treasures.

"Actually, the only complicated part of this whole chapter involves the firm," Rachel said," and the way it's working out, that's not even going to be too complicated."

"Wow, I hadn't even thought of that. Are you closing shop? What will Georgia do?"Rachel picked up a second cookie and bit into it. "Remember Melissa? That young lawyer who came with me to visit Mary in the hospital? My work-out partner?"

Belle thought for a moment and then shook her head. "Can't remember much about those days, to tell you the truth. It's all pretty much a blur."

Rachel descried the woman and repeated Georgia's report that Melissa wanted to leave the large firm where she worked and start her own solo practice. The more Rachel considered the concept, the more she liked it. After her initial resistance to retirement from a firm she nurtured for years subsided, a feeling of relief started to take root.

She asked Georgia to draft a letter that would announce the change and she began to work on a contract that would make it official. The only remaining step was to schedule a meeting with Melissa, the woman who would sit in her chair. Maybe she'll change her mind, Rachel thought.

"Will Georgia stay on and work for the new owner?"

That image remained the hardest for Rachel to accept. Her grandmother's saying, "You can't have your cake and eat it, too" popped into her mind, and she smiled. Thoughts of her grandmother always brought a smile, she realized, even in the middle of the most difficult challenges.

"What are you thinking about?" Belle asked. When Rachel mentioned her grandmother and the old adage that came to mind, she nodded. "I was thinking about my own Granny the other day," she said. "Thinking about how proud she'd be of George and what he's doing. Going back to Vietnam to find that woman."

"And her son," Rachel added. "But what does that have to do with your grandmother? The Vietnam war wasn't her era of history. She was already an old woman by the time it even started."

Belle nodded. She opened a drawer in the table beside the sofa and pulled out a photograph. The black and white image was printed on a small square that cracked and faded over the years. Rachel could barely see the faces of the Asian woman and the child she held.

"Filipino?" Rachel asked.

Belle nodded again. She glanced at the picture one more time before she tucked it back inside the drawer. "I can't believe I managed to hang on to that during all my wanderings. I don't even know why I kept it. Granny gave it to me when I was in grade school and we were studying World War II. My grandfather's brother took the photo. The baby was his child. He planned to send for them after the war was over, but he died in a car crash before he could find them. My grandmother was the only member of the family who didn't think of them as family skeletons in the closet. I think she was proud that her brother-in-law was willing to do what she called 'his duty.' Like George."

Rachel raised her cup again. "Like George," she said, and the two touched the edges of their cups together in one last toast.

* * *

Belle had barely locked the door behind Rachel when she heard her phone ring. She rushed to answer it before the sound woke Mary. Ricky's voice greeted her when she made the connection.

"Before you say 'no,' hear me out," he spoke in a rush. "Please. I mean, please hear me out."

Belle clutched the phone to her ear. She swallowed several times. She still tasted bile most of the time when she heard Ricky's voice. Even the thought of him left a sour taste in her mouth most of the time. She tried to follow Rachel's advice to focus on the positive things Ricky had done with his life recently. She tried every day to put the past behind her.

She counted to ten and then she spoke. "What is it? Is something wrong?"

"No. Nothing's wrong." Ricky swallowed his own reaction to that consistent reaction by most people in his life. "I have some time, and I wondered if I could stop by to see you and Mary. I could bring supper. Maybe a pizza? Mary loves pizza. I know she does, and I won't stay too long." Ricky finally paused for breath. He knew his fear of rejection always made him jabber. He learned a lot about fear in his short span of sobriety. About fear and the behaviors it motivated.

He waited while Belle felt her own fear.

Finally, she faced it. "Can you come at five? Mary goes to bed pretty early, and I want her to have time to settle down after you leave."

188

"She gets excited when she sees me? Does she?"

Belle paused again. She didn't want to give Ricky false hope, but she knew she needed to be honest. "Yes, she likes to see you, Ricky. You know that."

"Sometimes, I don't know that, Belle. Sometimes, I need to hear it."

"Let's keep this simple. Just bring the pizza. At five o'clock."

"Pepperoni?"

"Plain cheese."

"Cokes?"

"I've got milk."

Ricky laughed. "You sound like that commercial. 'Got milk.'"

"See you at five, Ricky." As Belle tapped the phone to end the call, she noticed the time. Four-thirty. Half an hour to prepare herself for Ricky's first visit to her apartment since his return from the treatment center. Belle and Mary made daily trips to the Circle to see him while he manned the hotdog stand. Deejee finally made the decision to turn the business over to him, and he was at his post seven days a week. He gave up his job at the law firm and took pride in his life as an entrepreneur.

Belle and Rachel discussed the dangers to Ricky's sobriety by his life in what members of AA called his "old playground." Many of the homeless who spent their days at the Circle were known in similar lingo as his "old playmates."

While Rachel allowed Belle to share her concern about Ricky's return to the Circle full-time, she reminded her that the decision was Ricky's. That she needed to detach and realize she had no control. Rachel even mentioned the fact that, in her experience in the legal arena, alcoholism was as much of a problem anywhere else. Sometimes more.

Belle realized she had begun to obsess once more about Ricky and what was best for him. She shook her head as if to shake away the demons of doubt that continued to plague her. A little voice drifted from the dark bedroom.

"Mommy?"

Belle flipped on the nightlight and smiled as she watched her daughter emerge from under her favorite nap time quilt.

"Nap over?"

"Yes, honey, nap time is over, and Mommy's got a surprise for you. Guess who's coming to see you?"

"Ralph?"

"No, silly. Guess again."

"Ben?" May squealed.

"No, not Ben either." Belle sobered as she thought about how she would be able to help Mary adjust to the loss of her two best friends. Rachel's move to the beach would affect so many of us, she thought. "One more try."

"Daddy?"

"Smart girl. You got it, and he'll be here very soon, so we need to get your face washed and brush your hair so you'll be all pretty when he arrives."

Mary bounced off the bed and raced to the bathroom to wait for her mother. From beneath the washcloth, she muttered something Belle couldn't hear.

"What did you say?"

"Weddy dwess. Mary wear weddy dwess."

Belle laughed. "Sure. I think a pizza party is the perfect occasion for you to wear your flower girl gown."

Mary rushed to the closet and stood on tiptoe, but she still couldn't reach the frilly blue taffeta.

"Daddy will be so pleased to see you got all dressed up for him," Belle said as she fastened the buttons on the back of the dress. Mary looked at Belle's jeans and frowned. She ran back to the closet and pointed to the black cocktail dress Rachel recently gave Belle with the excuse that she couldn't fit into it anymore. Belle resisted with her own excuse that she had no place to wear it. Rachel persisted, and Belle admitted to herself that she enjoyed the effect of the dress in the otherwise drab closet.

She laughed as Mary tugged on the black hem. "Sure, why not. It will look great with these red fluffy slippers."

Mary agreed with a clap of her little hands. She squatted down to rub her fingers through the fur and then beamed up at her mother. "Booful," she whispered.

"Yes, they are beautiful, and you are, too. But, we must be very careful not to spill pizza sauce on our party dresses, okay?"

Mary promised she would be extra careful and began her "extra careful dance" when the doorbell rang. "Daddy," she shouted and ran to the door. She stopped when she remembered the rule about who was allowed to open the door and who was not. She turned to her mother.

"Thank you. That's a good girl. And watch how I look through the peephole to find out who's on the other side." Belle looked. Ricky stood at the bottom of the steps that led down to the door. He held two boxes of pizza in one hand. The other hand hid behind his back.

When Belle unlocked and opened the door, he handed her the boxes. "May I come in?" he asked.

"Daddy! Daddy!"

"Sure, come on in. I'll put these on the table."

"Wait, here's something else."

Belle turned around, and Ricky held out two yellow roses. "For my two best girls," he said and then stopped and stared at them. "Wow, I guess I'd better go home and change clothes," he said as he looked down at his jeans. One leg was spattered with ketchup.

"No," Mary screeched. "Daddy booful."

Belle smiled and closed the door behind him.

* * *

Rachel looked at her watch. She stayed at the office long after Georgia left, reviewed the contents of stacks of files and finally returned them to their cabinets with confidence that all was in order. She wanted to leave Melissa with a full caseload but one that was easily managed. The young woman told Rachel she hoped to add a few of her own cases to the Springer & Associates list, and Rachel knew the natural tendency would be to give the familiar clients preferential treatment.

Another moment of doubt struck, as Rachel thought of the loyalty of the people she worked with during her long career. She hated to think of them shuffled to the side. Georgia assured her that would never happen as long as she sat in the front office. Melissa, as the lawyer, might think she was in charge, but as long as Georgia Payne sat at her desk, she held the reins.

Rachel knew from experience that Georgia spoke the truth.

She glanced down at her watch again. Eight o'clock. She called John earlier to tell him she'd be late and to go ahead and eat supper without her. Ben's bedtime shouldn't be delayed either. The little boy was a creature of habit, and any change in schedule upset him more than it was usually worth.

She looked up at the child's bedroom window and felt relief to see that it was dark. She smiled at Ralph's face pressed against the pane of glass to the left of the front door. Funny how he always chooses the left window as his sentry point, she thought. Claw marks, left before she was able to train him not to jump in excitement at her approach, proved impossible to buff off the pane.

Rachel shivered as she wondered if the new homeowner might replace the glass. She turned away from the front porch to search in her purse for her front door key and saw something shiny at the top of the steps that led down to the basement apartment. She walked across the grass to get a closer look.

Ricky's bicycle lay on its side in the bushes. A chain secured it to the stair railing.

Rachel glanced at her watch for the third time. Past Mary's bedtime, she realized. As she walked back to her own steps, she looked out of the corner of her eye toward the one small basement window. No lights shone in the apartment—except for the flicker of candlelight.

Agitated, Rachel rooted around for her keys. She finally found them in her pocket and ran up the steps and into her foyer.

Ralph yipped with delight and then sat and panted as he waited for her greeting pet. When she forgot and rushed to the den to find John, the dog trotted along behind her, tail between his legs.

"What's the matter with you?" John asked as he rose from the sofa, dropped his book onto the seat and met his wife in the middle of the room. "Ralph looks like he's lost his best friend, and you look even worse."

Rachel knelt down beside Ralph to rub his ears. "Sorry, boy. How could I forget? Please forgive me," she said as she pulled a treat out of her jacket pocket and popped it in the dog's mouth.

"You didn't tell him to sit."

"Sometimes when you screw up like I did, you throw rules by the wayside. I came home and walked right by him without so much as a word. Sorry, Ralph."

Ralph wiggled his forgiveness.

"What's got you so rattled? Long day do you in? Long day missing me?"

Rachel snuggled closer into her husband's embrace. "Of course, I missed you. Sorry I couldn't be here to help get Ben to bed. Did that go okay?"

"Yes. Everything went smooth as silk. You're important, Rachel, but you're not indispensable. Relax."

Rachel broke away from her husband's arms and sat in the warm spot he left on the sofa. John and Ralph joined her, one on each side. The two stared at her.

"Are you going to tell me what's troubling you, or do I have to tickle it out of you?" John finally asked.

When Rachel didn't laugh at the threat, he took her hands in his and raised one, then the other, to his lips and kissed the tips of each finger. He knew she needed time.

"Ricky's downstairs," she whispered.

John sat silently and waited for the punchline.

"The apartment is dark."

Still no reaction from John.

"I think Belle lit candles."

Finally, John spoke. "Have you asked her not to use candles? I don't remember anything in my lease about not using candles."

Rachel looked at Ralph for support. The dog tucked his head under her armpit and sighed.

"John, be serious. May has gone to bed and Belle and Ricky are downstairs—basically alone. They're probably making out."

"Wait a minute. Hold on. Stop the presses. That isn't your story, Rachel." Ralph snorted. "See, Ralph agrees." John hugged Rachel and then stood up and pulled her to her feet. "Ricky and Belle will figure things out. What you need is a nice bubble bath and some leftover meatloaf. Comfort bath. Comfort food. And then, comfort bed."

Rachel allowed herself to be led from the room and up the stairs to the garden tub.

"See you back downstairs. Take your time." Rachel heard John walk away from the door and then walk back. "Okay if I turn out the lights in the den and light a few candles? Or will that make you nervous?"

Rachel opened the bathroom door, threw a towel at her husband and then closed the door softly so as not wake Ben. "Men," she muttered. "He has no idea."

"I heard that," John whispered from the hall. He opened the door a crack. "How about a glass of wine to go with your bubbles?" Rachel smiled. "Some of your ideas are right on target, my dear husband, and that was one of them."

As he closed the door, John smiled down at Ralph. "Magic, Ralph. It comes in many forms. Let's hope some of it is going on downstairs."

Chapter Twenty-Three

Ricky knew he'd been caught. No way around it, he thought. Rachel sees me. He debated whether he should pretend he didn't see her and simply ride off. The sun was barely up. What in hell was the woman doing outside at this hour? Then, he saw her pick up the morning paper and unroll it to glance at the front page headlines.

You're only as sick as your secrets, he remembered his AA sponsor say so many times. Ricky worked hard to let go of so much from his past that burdened him with shame. Shame he numbed with drugs and alcohol. He realized he didn't want to add more secrets at this point.

And he assured himself he had nothing to hide. He spent the night with his family. He loved Belle and Mary and wanted nothing more than to rebuild their lives together.

What business was it of Rachel Turner's what he did?

As if she could hear Ricky's internal debate, Rachel looked up. Their eyes met, and they stood and stared at each other.

"Morning, Rachel." For a fleeting moment, Ricky considered a lie. He could say he'd stopped by to drop something off on his way to work.

"Morning, Ricky." Rachel waited for some explanation as to why the young man stood where he stood at the time he stood there. She knew he slept downstairs. She saw his bike the night before. But, as she watched him squirm, she gave no indication that she knew. She wondered how the man would handle the situation. She wondered what lie he would concoct on the spur of the moment.

"Well, got to get going," he said. "Have a good day."

Rachel's mouth dropped open, and she lost her grip on the newspaper. The sound, as it slapped the ground, caused Ricky to lose his balance and put an end to his escape plan.

"Wait a minute, Ricky. Wait just a minute. We need to talk."

"Not sure why you think we need to talk, but I've got a few minutes."

"What are you doing here at this hour?"

"I spent the night with my family. I deserve a family, just like you do. We hoped you'd give us your blessing but it looks like that won't happen."

"Hold on a second. Not very long ago, you stood on this very spot and almost completely destroyed George's truck. Not very long ago, you were locked up for drunk and disorderly conduct. Not very long ago I had to file a restraining order against you to protect your family."

"Stop. Stop all that," Belle hissed from the stairwell. She rushed over to stand between Ricky and Rachel. "He's right. We love each other, and we want to be a family again. If you've got problems with that, I'll take Mary and we'll move out." Belle looked at Ricky. "Right?"

Rachel watched as a look of panic flooded the young man's face. As far as she knew, he still lived with his AA sponsor, and she doubted Mr. White had room for two more people in his small apartment.

"Okay, what's going on out here?" John asked from the front porch. When he saw Ricky dismount from his bike and lean it against the lamppost, he understood why his wife's face was so red. He walked down the sidewalk and joined the small group at the curb. As he reached them, he saw a porch light across the street flash on. "Let's go inside the house before we have the whole neighborhood out here," he said.

"I can't leave Mary alone downstairs," Belle whimpered.

"Right, so we'll all go downstairs," John said and looked at Rachel. She set her jaw and held the *Washington Post* in her hand like a club. "Rachel, are you coming? Ricky?"

Ricky waited for Rachel to make the first move. Belle watched two of the most important people in her life in their stand-off and knew she stood at a crossroads. "Please, Rachel," she finally said and reached out to touch her. "Do this for me. Come inside. Hear what we have to say."

Rachel glared at Ricky.

"Please," he said.

John saw his wife's jaw relax. He took her hand to offer his support, but Rachel was the one who led the way downstairs.

* * *

Stan rocked in the chair beside Georgia's desk when Rachel arrived at the office later that morning. He looked up from an old copy of *Good Housekeeping* when he heard the door shut.

"Got news for you," he shouted. "You asked me to keep an eye on Ricky, and I've been doing it. Keeping a close eye on him pretty much round the clock, and I hate to tell you this, Rachel, but the boy spent the night in your basement last night. All night. I left the premises at four in the morning, and his bicycle was still chained to your basement stair railing. Sorry to be the bearer of bad news."

Rachel laughed and walked over to where Stan stood.

"What's so damn funny?"

"Yes, what are you laughing about, for God's sake," Georgia demanded. "Stan Berninger spent all night outside in your bushes and now he's come by to give you the worst possible report. I fail to see the humor in all this." Georgia smacked her desk for emphasis.

Rachel placed her briefcase on the coffee table and sat on the sofa. "I'm sorry. How inconsiderate of me."

Stan and Georgia waited while Rachel tried to figure out how to tell them about her morning. She finally decided to keep the story simple. She began with the fact that she saw Ricky's bike the night before and confronted him as he was about to leave at sunrise. She told them about the conversation with Belle and Ricky and about how John was able to convince her—once again—to let the young couple make their own decisions.

"I found out that Ricky is the one who has talked Belle into staying in school. His own hard work has evidently set a good example for her," she said. "And, of course, Mary adores him."

Stand and Georgia stared at each other. Georgia was the first one to find her voice. "What about the restraining order?" she asked.

"I didn't tell Ricky, but it expired last week. Might as well keep him on his toes."

"Guess that means I don't have a case to work on," Stan grumbled. "Back to retirement. Getting too old to be camping out all night, anyway." Stan hobbled over to the door and left without a word.

Rachel walked to the window and looked out. "Where's his car?"

"Family took his keys, remember?"

"You mean he walked all the way over here?"

"Guess so. Not to mention his 'surveillance' as he calls what he did last night in your bushes. Not good, Rachel. Not good at all. We need to do something."

"What we need to do is drink a cup of coffee right now. I can't handle any more lives out of control without at least a half of a pot."

"Think I'll join you."

"Wait a minute. You don't drink coffee, Georgia."

"There's always a first time for everything, and this morning is one of those times."

* * *

Rachel considered whether she should let the phone call roll over to the answering machine. Georgia drove home to enjoy lunch with Mike as a surprise on their wedding anniversary. Rachel suggested she take the afternoon off and spend it with her husband, but Georgia insisted too much work remained to be done before Melissa's appointment next week to sign the contract that would make Springer & Associates her firm.

Her curiosity got the best of her, and Rachel picked up the receiver.

"I miss you," Susan said before Rachel could even open her mouth. "I can't wait another minute. What are you doing? Why can't you just let Georgia handle whatever it is you two are doing and move this weekend. There's a big party at the clubhouse, and I want to introduce you to everybody."

"How did you know I'd answer the phone and not Georgia?"

"I just knew."

Rachel inhaled, exhaled, inhaled and forced herself to remember all the reasons Susan had remained her best friend since their college days.

"Why are you breathing like that, Rachel? You sound funny. You're not sick, are you? You know, the air down here is so much better for you than that city smog. Maybe you're developing allergies. Good think you're moving. Just in time. COPD is a serious disease, you know."

Rachel assured her friend she didn't have COPD and explained why she and John could not possibly push the move forward any sooner than it was planned. John, in fact, learned the day before that his project would require his presence on the site longer than he thought. Rachel and Ben would live at the beach without him for a month, while he made sure his replacement clearly understood the final stages of the hospital construction.

"Okay, so you'll miss the party," Susan rambled on. "We'll have another party after John gets here. How's Carrie?"

Sometimes, Rachel wasn't able to change channels as fast as Susan—especially when her phone call came at a time when Rachel attempted to multitask. She dropped the stack of bills and tried to refocus. "What did you just ask me?"

"How's Carrie? Your new neighbor across the street? Has anyone planned the baby shower yet?"

Rachel laughed.

"What's so funny? Somebody's going to throw her a baby shower, I hope. Or maybe I need to come back to the city and organize it. Do you think I need to do that?"

Rachel assured her she didn't, and that it was too soon for a baby shower. Carrie's due date was still six months away.

"Which room are they going to use as the nursery?"

"You know, Susan, if you want me to move to the beach, I need to get off the phone and get back to work. You've got Carrie's phone number. Give her a call. I'm sure she'd love to hear from you."

Silence, Rachel knew, meant she hurt Susan's feelings. "Susan, I'm sorry. I miss you, too. I'm looking forward to being able to see you every day again."

"Walks on the beach."

"Yes, and I want to meet your friends."

"You're going to love the book club."

"I'm sure I will. Wait. Susan, I hear someone knocking on the door. Sorry. Georgia's not here. Gotta go. Love you."

Rachel hung up the phone before she lost any more time as she listened to the list of plans Susan had for their new life. She shook her head and shoved the bills back in their "to-be-paid" folder before she walked to the front lobby. She glanced out the window before she opened the door. The realtor Susan recommended stood on the other side.

"I'm sorry to pop in without an appointment, "the woman said as she pushed past Rachel, "but we really do need to get this listing agreement signed. I think I have someone interested in buying your house."

Never one to handle surprises well—despite a lifetime of practice—Rachel allowed herself to be pulled back into the lobby by the sheer force of the woman's enthusiasm.

"Actually, Miss Waddell, John and I aren't absolutely sure we're ready to sell. We've even talked about letting the young woman who lives in the basement apartment move upstairs. She and her husband may be getting back together, and, if they do, they'll need more room."

"That's perfect," Miss Waddell gushed, "because the man I know is an investor, and he'd be delighted to have tenants already in place. I'm sure that would seal the deal."

"There's one problem, Miss Waddell. These tenants don't pay rent."

The realtor stepped backwards and stopped. She fiddled with the diamonds on first one hand and then the other. She smoothed a nonexistent stray hair off her forehead. Rachel waited patiently for the woman to recover her composure.

"No rent?"

"Nope. No rent."

"I don't understand. You could be renting that apartment for a couple thousand dollars a month."

Rachel smiled and nodded her head. Miss Waddell looked like she smelled something rotten.

"Well, I guess they could move out," she finally said. "I'm sure the buyer wouldn't have a bit of trouble finding good tenants. People who could pay market rates. People for the main house and another person for the basement apartment."

As a way to encourage the woman to leave, Rachel agreed to accept the listing agreement and promised to talk to John that evening.

"I'll call you tomorrow. Thank you so much for stopping by. Now, if you'll excuse me, I really must get ready for my two o'clock appointment."

As Miss Waddell strutted down the sidewalk to her shiny new black Mercedes, parked illegally in a handicapped spot, Rachel shook her head and picked up the phone on Georgia's desk. She dialed a number and waited for the call to be answered.

"Carrie, it's Rachel," she said. "I need help. What's the name of the realtor you and Horace used to sell your condo?" Rachel paused to listen. "Yes, we did have a realtor. Now, we don't."

Chapter Twenty-Four

The smell of burnt cedar greeted Rachel as she walked to her front door. She looked up at her chimney and the smoke that curled out of it and smiled. She wondered what special occasion prompted John to light a fire with the one cedar log they saved for a time of celebration.

Ben opened the door and wrapped his arms around her waist. He bumped his knee against her briefcase in an effort to hug her and backed off in the dramatic "I'm wounded and about to die" scene he performed when he wanted more attention.

Rachel waited to hear what little boy world crisis stimulated the performance this time. The behavior seemed to come more frequently as the date of the move drew nearer.

Ralph sat beside the moaning boy and looked at Rachel as if to say, "He's you're kid. Do something." The dog didn't wait long, however, before he began to lick Ben's left ear, and Ben's moan turned to a giggle. Rachel joined him on the floor for a laugh she needed after her meeting with Miss Waddell.

"Care to join us?" Rachel asked when John appeared in the doorway to the den.

"I must admit the invitation is mighty tempting, but I've got a better idea. Why don't you three join me in the den. I've got a fire going, and I've just taken the pizza out of the oven."

"I don't know how you do it."

"Do what, my lovely bride?"

"Manage to time supper so well. How did you know when I'd be home?"

"We've got spies," Ben whispered. "We know your every move."

Rachel looked at John. "Is that true? You're having me watched? What will you do after I leave for the beach? Got contacts there too?"

"Believe it or not, the timing of supper was mere luck. I think Mr. Ben is watching too many re-runs of *Get Smart*." John kissed his wife and pulled her off the floor and toward the den. The smell of hot pepperoni, mixed with cedar smoke, spiced the room with a heady aroma.

Rachel settled on the sofa while John and Ben carried pizza and plates from the kitchen and spread the Friday night feast on the large antique trunk that served as a coffee table. Ben passed out napkins, and the three held hands to bless the food.

"And please God, don't let Mary ruin my room. Amen." Ben ended his prayer.

Rachel opened her eyes and stared across the pizza at John. "Something you two know that I don't?"

John rose from his seat to stir the fire and buy himself some time.

"And why are we burning the cedar log we've been saving for so long? What's going on?"

Ben picked up a slice of pizza and bit into it as he waited for his grandfather to speak. He cast his eyes down and moved as far away from Rachel as he could.

"I'm waiting, John."

"It's good," Ben whispered.

"Yes, we all like pepperoni, and you did a fine job making the pizza."

"No, not the pizza. The plan," Ben said, his eyes still focused on his plate.

John finally left the fireplace where the cedar log blazed royally on its bed of kindling. "Rachel, I think we should invite Belle and Mary to move upstairs after we move."

"And Ricky," Ben chimed in.

"We don't need to sell the house right away," John rushed on. "I'm going to continue my consulting work from the beach. We don't need the money from the sale of the house."

"And they need another bedroom for Ricky," Ben piped up. "I just hope Mary doesn't screw up my toy closet."

Rachel laughed as she remembered her conversation with Miss Waddell a few hours earlier. "When did you two come up with this brilliant idea?" she asked.

"Just a couple of hours ago. I was watching Ricky in the backyard with Mary, and he looked so at home there. I'd hate to see them have to move when we find a buyer for the house. He and Belle are both working so hard to create a normal life."

"Whatever 'normal' means," Rachel muttered.

John bit into his pizza. He expected his wife to object. He knew how protective she was of Belle and how doubtful she felt about Ricky's ability to stay sober.

"So, is this why we're burning the celebration cedar?"

John nodded and continued to chew. He watched his wife. Ben watched the adults. When Rachel laughed, they both stopped in mid-chew.

"You're not going to believe me, but at the same time you two were at home hatching this grand scheme to save Belle from a life back on the streets, the identical thought occurred to me at my office across town."

"Two good ideas," Ben shouted. "Two ideas just the same."

"Must mean they're good ideas, don't you think?" John asked and inched closer to his wife.

"Only one missing part of the story," she said.

"What did we miss?"

"Three things, actually."

John and Ben waited. Ralph crept closer to the pizza. Rachel pushed him away before she spoke. "Belle and Mary. And Ricky."

Ben jumped up from the floor and clapped his hands. "We already asked them, and they said 'yes.'"

Rachel stared at John, and he saw the shock in her eyes turn to anger. He retreated to the other side of the room to stir the shrinking log. He felt his wife sizzle behind his back. After he couldn't stall any longer, he mustered enough courage to face her.

"I know we should have discussed this before anything was said to Belle and Ricky, but since you had the same idea, too, maybe what I did wasn't too bad."

"That won't work, John. Not at all. This is still my house, you know. Correct me if I'm wrong, but I believe I bought it long before I met you, and the title is still in my name. In the name 'Rachel Springer,' in fact."

Rachel stood and towered over John, where he moved to the far end of the sofa. Ben felt the heat in the room and was old enough to know that the change in temperature was caused by more than the fire.

"We're sorry, Rachel," the boy whimpered. Even though he didn't know why, the child knew something was terribly wrong, and he wanted to fix it. "We're sorry, aren't we, Granddad?" He ran to John's side and pulled on his grandfather's sleeve. "Tell her you're sorry," he hissed.

Ralph, too, sensed that tempers were about to flare and took sides with a quick shift of position to a place at Rachel's feet.

"We'll talk later, John. After Ben's in bed."

"No!" Ben shouted. "Tell her you're sorry. Now!" He threw himself at his grandfather and began to pelt him with his little fists. John easily restrained the boy and tried to quiet him, but Ben pulled away and ran to Rachel. He wiped his eyes. Pizza sauce smeared across one cheek. Ralph stood on his hind legs and tried to lick him clean. "Okay, Rachel. Okay, Granddad. Ralph and I are going to bed so you can talk."

The boy planted a sticky kiss on Rachel's mouth and ran out of the room with Ralph at his heels. As he rushed past John, he halted. "Tell her you're sorry, and she'll be okay," he whispered.

I wish it were that easy, John thought as he smiled to reassure his grandson. "Thanks, Ben. You're a smart boy."

"Do you need me to leave Ralph down here to help you?" Ben whispered. "I guess he could stay down here, if you need him."

"Go on to bed. I'll be up to tuck you in shortly. And take Ralph. You need him more than I do."

But when John looked across the room and saw Rachel's glare, he wasn't convinced the words he spoke were true.

* * *

Rachel lay awake in John's arms later than night. She listened to his snores and tried to match her breath to his, a trick Susan had taught her during one of their many marriage advice sessions. Rachel shared with her friend the fear that, after a lifetime of sleeping alone, she would have trouble sharing a bedroom—much less a bed—with someone else. She expressed her fear she'd never sleep again.

Susan assured her that the synchronized breath would work and also repeated one of Rachel's grandmother's sayings, "Never let the sun go down on your anger."

The two newlyweds promised each other they would practice that principle—and they had. John's experience in his previous marriage proved that anger allowed to simmer overnight always boiled over in a terrible mess the next morning. Rachel valued the experience of her best friend and her husband and followed their leads.

After John tucked Ben in bed, he suggested he and Rachel meditate together before they retired to their bedroom. By the time they rose from their cushions, blew out the candles and tiptoed downstairs to their bedroom, Rachel felt her body lose some of its tension. She allowed John to coax her to make love and, while she didn't feel the world shake the way she usually did, she felt loved.

They decided to wait until the morning to talk.

When Rachel turned on her side and draped an arm across John's chest, he flipped over so his back faced her. He snorted with pleasure. No, we didn't let the sun set on our anger, Rachel thought, but we still need to do something about the sounds that man makes.

Earplugs, she thought as she finally drifted into a fitful sleep.

* * *

"Granddad let me clean the ashes out of the fireplace."

"And you did an excellent job."

"Wanna see?"

Rachel followed Ben to the den and admired the clean grate. A fresh stack of kindling filled the hopper.

"I did that, too," Ben boasted.

"You've been a busy boy this morning. Thank you for taking such good care of our fireplace needs."

"Granddad helped."

Rachel looked down at the little boy's troubled face and knew he needed reassurance that all was well in the adult world around him. Nobody mentioned the quarrel the night before, but she knew from Ben's scowl that he had not forgotten. Children aren't as resilient as some adults think they are, Rachel thought.

"Your grandfather is good about that. Good about helping."

Ben smiled and bounced from one foot to the other. Finally, he couldn't hold the words back any longer.

"He just wants to help Belle, too, you know. Like you helped Ralph when you brought him home and when you brought Granddad and me here."

Rachel pulled the boy toward her and wrapped him inside her bathrobe. He buried his face in the fur and squeezed her with all his strength. I am so blessed, she thought, and at that minute, she felt the shift. She felt the release. She felt the principle she hung to throughout her sleepless night leave her body as the child squeezed. Squeezed in a way the man's arms weren't strong enough to squeeze the night before. And, in its place—the empty place where resentment had grown and gnawed at her all night long—a feeling of freedom flooded in.

She smiled at John as he handed her a cup of coffee.

"Special blend this morning. Hope you like it," he said.

"I'm sure I will. Smells like heaven. What is it?"

"Not sure it has a name, but I think I'll call it 'Black Dog Magic.' Let's see if it works."

"I think it already has, and I haven't even tasted it yet."

"It's powerful stuff. A little of this and a little of that goes a long way sometimes."

With the perfect timing children sometimes have when they knew adults need to be alone, Ben asked if he could take Ralph for a walk.

"Yes, but just to the end of our sidewalk and around the backyard."

"And put on your hat and gloves."

"And Ralph's coat."

Rachel and John laughed as the boy and dog ran from the room. As soon as the front door slammed, Rachel set her coffee cup down on the trunk and settled herself beside John on the sofa.

"John, I'm sorry."

"No need to talk about it."

"Yes, there is. I need to say a few things. First, thank you for marrying an old woman set in her ways. Second, thank you for marrying a woman who worked all her life in a career in which success is measured in proving you're right and the other side is wrong. Third, thank you for marrying a woman who has a hard time giving up, even outside the courtroom. I hang on, even when the iron gets so hot I can feel it burn my flesh to the bone. I take the opposite side in a debate just so there can be a debate. I've been this way since I was a little girl."

When she stopped to take a breath, John kissed her. "Some of those things are what made me fall in love with you."

"But last night, my stubborn streak hurt us both."

"Didn't bother me all that much. I got a good night's rest. I'm ready for a good day. How about you?"

"No, I didn't sleep at all. I tossed and turned all night."

"What can we do about it?"

"For starters, I think we should go downstairs and ask Belle when she wants to start moving her stuff up here. No need to wait until I'm gone."

"Sounds like the Black Dog Magic brew I made is working."

"The other thing I want is a nice long nap to make up for all the sleep I lost last night."

"Can't promise how the Black Dog Magic will affect that, but you never know. It is, after all, magic."

Chapter Twenty-Five

I f Rachel had entertained any lingering doubts about John's idea, they disappeared as soon as Belle opened the apartment door. The scene that lay on the other side sprang straight out of a Hallmark movie.

Ricky rocked Mary as she napped safe in her father's arms. Ricky's closed eyes—and the mouth curled in a smile—demonstrated pure contentment.

Belle stepped outside to join Rachel and closed the door softly behind her.

"Looks like everybody's asleep except you. Long night?"

Belle nodded.

"Want to go upstairs with me? I've got something to talk to you about."

Belle nodded again. Rachel thought the girl's silence was an effort not to wake her family, but then she saw the red eyes and dark circles beneath them. She stopped at the top of the stairs. "What's the matter, Belle?"

Belle nodded in the direction of the kitchen door and led the way. When the two finally reached the privacy there, she burst into tears. At the sudden outburst, Rachel felt like a pin popped the bubble she floated downstairs inside. Deflated, she stood and held the girl she nurtured so many times before. She remembered the day they met. At the time, Belle was homeless and lived in a shelter with her daughter.

Could whatever caused these tears be worse than what she experienced there, Rachel wondered. Could it be worse than Mary's trip to the hospital and Belle's fear that her child might not come home? Could it be worse than the disappointment when Belle realized her fairytale romance with George was only a fairytale? Could it be worse than the ups and downs of life with Ricky before and after he got sober?

As though she read Rachel's mind, Belle said, "It's Ricky."

Rachel bit her tongue.

"Some tramp named 'Felicia' came banging on our door last night. I'm surprised the noise didn't wake you up. You didn't hear her?"

Rachel shook her head. Guess I slept more than I realized, she thought as she waited for Belle to continue.

"Ricky didn't let her in because we didn't want her to wake Mary. I can't believe she didn't even budge. That child is such a sound sleeper. Thank, God."

Belle paused to blow her nose. Rachel poured water into a tall glass and passed it to her. Belle gulped the cool drink like she hoped it would put out the fire that still blazed inside her. She blew her nose again.

"Ricky took her to Rob's apartment. You know Rob, Ricky's AA sponsor?"

Rachel nodded.

"And he was gone for hours and hours. I thought he'd never come home. Finally, I called Rob, just to make sure Ricky was okay. Do you think that was bad of me? To call, I mean?"

"Of course not. You were scared. You should have called me. I would have been glad to sit with you while you waited." Especially since I wasn't sleeping much anyway, Rachel thought, and then shame swept over her as she compared her complaint last night with the scene downstairs.

"Rob didn't really say much except that Ricky was okay and that he and Felicia had some talking to do," Belle continued. "He said she was drunk. He did say that much, so I figured Ricky must have met her in an AA meeting."

Belle tipped the glass to sip some more water, and Rachel realized she gripped an empty glass. When she stood to refill it, Belle beat her to the sink. She stood with her back to Rachel and drank. Deliberately. Slowly. With the glass drained, she turned to face her friend.

"Ricky fucked Felicia."

Rachel didn't know how to respond to such a naked statement. She planned to offer the happy couple a home. The shock of the sudden entrance of a drunk home-wrecker on the scene left her speechless.

"Only once," Belle rushed on, as she slipped back into her role as Ricky's defender. "When he got back from Rob's apartment, he told me the whole story about how they met a meeting and how he was feeling so unsure about me and George and how he used her." Belle looked at Rachel to measure her reaction. Rachel's frown worked as the final ingredient to dissolve Belle's bitterness. "He made amends to her. He's done his part, Rachel. He admitted he was wrong to use her. He told her, and he told me, and he begged for my forgiveness."

"Did you?"

"Did I what?"

"Forgive him? You don't look like you did. You look like you've been beaten up, in fact."

"Well, yes. I guess. I mean, I feel beaten up." Belle paused. "But not beaten down. If you know what I mean."

Rachel nodded. The two sat together and listened to the wall clock tick. Tick like a time bomb, Rachel thought.

"What about Felicia? What's going to prevent her from coming back next time she gets drunk and beating on your door again? Next time, Mary might wake up. I could file another restraining order, but they don't always work, as you well know."

Belle shook her head and rested it down on her arms. Her shoulders shook with fresh sobs. Rachel reached across the table and took one of her hands and held it. She stroked the fingers, clutched like claws. Slowly, they relaxed and lay limp under Rachel's touch.

"Belle, I walked down here to your apartment this morning to suggest a plan John and I agreed on last night." Rachel almost laughed at the simple way she stated a decision that had been far from simple. She restrained the laugh she knew would be unwelcome in the present circumstance.

Belle raised her head to listen.

"I don't know now if our idea is a good one." Rachel paused. "I want you and Mary to be safe, Belle. Felicia—and any others like her—are a problem."

"She was the only one," Belle shouted. Surprised by her own outburst, she covered her mouth with her napkin. "Ricky promised she was the only one, and it only happened once. Now that we're back together, there won't be any more."

"Where is Felicia now?"

"In jail. She started throwing things at Ricky and tearing up the place. Rob had to call the police. She's locked up, Rachel. She can't come back and bother us."

Rachel looked at her young friend and wondered how she could be so innocent after her life on the streets. Felicia is probably out on bail already, she thought. And I sure don't want her barging into my house and throwing my things around. Rachel took a mental inventory of the valuables she and John agreed to leave behind so Belle and her family would feel at home. They decided to follow Susan's advice to fill the beach house with new furnishings they would select together. "A new start," Susan described the plan.

All that has changed now, Rachel realized.

"What did you want to tell me?" Belle asked.

As Rachel debated whether she should try to make up some story on the spur of the moment or tell the truth, another one of her grandmother's bits of advice came to mind. "Always tell the truth," the old woman warned. "Tell the truth and keep your life simpler because the truth will always come out in the end."

Rachel inhaled a deep breath of air. "We wanted you, Mary and Ricky to live upstairs after we move to the beach."

Belle's face lit up like it had been the focus of a spotlight. Then, just as suddenly as it brightened, it darkened like the spotlight had been turned off by some unseen force above them.

"I guess Felicia fucked more than Ricky," she said through gritted teeth. "No way you'd risk moving three magnets for crazies into your home. You probably wish you hadn't let us live downstairs." Belle rose and shoved her chair back so roughly that it tipped over and fell to the floor with a crash. Belle didn't even stop to pick it up.

"Belle, no. It's not like that."

"Of course, it is. I'm no fool, Rachel. You're a good woman. I appreciate all you've done. But even you have your limits. Sell the house. We'll start looking for a place to move right away."

"Wait a minute. Let's talk."

"Nothing to talk about. Ricky can promise me he won't be unfaithful again, but I can't promise you that his past won't continue to crop up. And I don't want them to crop up in your—in Granny's— little bit of heaven. I don't want it to turn into hell. You'd hate me, Rachel, and I'm not willing to risk that."

* * *

Not a day passed that Rachel didn't miss a visit with her best friend, but she missed her even more during times of crisis. She missed that she couldn't run across the street and share her burden over a cup of tea. A phone call never satisfied the need for Susan's special understanding. An electronic connection didn't come close. They had tried Skype once and both decided they hated it and would leave that technology to Ben.

Rachel picked up her phone and punched in the long distance

number as soon as she heard the downstairs door close.

"Rachel, I'm so glad you called," Susan answered. "I've got the most exciting news. I just talked to the golf pro in the golf shop, and he's going to let me sell poetry on demand there on Saturday mornings. Early, when the golfer's go out, they'll order their poems, and then later when they come in, they can pick them up. Jim's not real sure golfers will appreciate poetry, but I think he's dead wrong. I think everyone will want a personal poem if they're just given a chance. Don't you, Rachel?"

"I think that's a fabulous idea. Good luck. When do you start?"

"Tomorrow. Wish you were here to go with me."

"Me, too. I'd rather be anywhere but here right now."

"Why? What's wrong? How can I help?"

"I could use a friendly ear while I try to process something. Do you have a few minutes?"

"Of course. I do have to prepare for tomorrow morning's pro shop gig. Early tee time is very early, Rachel, but, of course, you will always be more important to me than anything. Even poems. So, go ahead. I'm right here."

Rachel wished "right here" meant across the street and looked at the calendar to count the days that remained before her trip to the beach for the closing on the new house. Six days. Six long days, she thought.

"Rachel, are you there?"

"Sorry. Got lost in my head for a minute."

"What's going on? Is it Ben? I hope nothing's wrong with my darling little Skype buddy."

"No, Ben's fine. And John and Ralph send their love. Georgia is coming with us to the closing. She can't wait to see the house. And you."

"Well, what is wrong? For heaven's sake, Rachel, stop torturing me."

Rachel tried to keep the story of last night's drama short and to the point. She knew Susan would spice it up, herself, so she sped through the bare facts of Felicia's surprise appearance, the scene at Rob's apartment and the police arrest. She ended with the morning's visit from Belle and her tearful defense of Ricky. When she stopped to take a breath, Susan sputtered. "Wait, there's more," Rachel managed to say. "Here's the tricky part. John and I decided to let Belle and Ricky move upstairs with Mary rather than put the house on the market right away. Now, I'm not sure if that's such a good idea."

"What does John think?"

Rachel almost dropped her phone with surprise. She was dumbfounded when she realized she told Susan about Belle's visit before she told her husband. She wondered if she should worry about the condition of her marriage.

"I haven't told John yet," she said, with the hope that her friend would show some concern if concern were necessary.

"Good. Sometimes men don't see the significance of certain things like we do, Rachel. You know what I mean about 'certain things,' don't you, honey?"

Rachel sighed with relief that she confided in the right person first. At least in Susan's opinion. She would tell John when he and Ben returned home from their walk with Ralph. The three left for Dupont Circle to meet Deejee for a pigeon feeding party half an hour earlier.

"So, I guess you're calling me for my expert opinion," Susan continued. "Not that I have much experience with tramps who show up drunk in the middle of the night and accuse my husband of 'certain things,' however."

"No," Rachel agreed, "but you know about friendship and about trust and about faith. And you're always so positive. I want to believe that everything's going to work out for Belle and Ricky. I wanted to move to the beach and be able to picture them living happily ever after, here in Belle's grandmother's house. Instead, she just left my kitchen and headed back downstairs with the intention of telling Ricky they need to find another place to live."

Susan paused. "You're right. I am good at coming up with happy-ever-afters," she finally said.

"Yes, you are. That's why I called you."

"Okay, there are two issues here, Rachel. First, do you want them to move upstairs? Second, how can you convince them to do what you want them to do? Am I right?"

"Well, there's a third issue."

"What's the third thing?"

"Convince John to let them move up here. Remember John?"

"That's right. John was the one who called the police on Ricky right after Belle moved in, wasn't he? Ricky was drunk that night, as I recall."

"Very drunk. And loud."

"Gee, Rachel, this is tough, and talking about it on the phone makes it tougher. We should be sipping tea while we solve this one."

Rachel agreed that a phone conversation was not the best way to deal with important questions but reminded her friend that the closing was only six days away.

"Back to your first point. Yes, I still want them to move up here. Just hearing your voice has lightened things up. It's points two and three that I'm afraid may be out of my control. What would you do?"

Susan giggled. "Remember your wedding dress?"

"My wedding dress?"

"Yes. Remember how many bridal magazines I made you look at and all our shopping trips?"

Rachel moaned. "How could I ever forget?"

"And then, after all I did, remember what happened?"

"I found my grandmother's wedding dress in the attic at the farm."

"That's right. And you wore it."

"And your point is?"

Susan sighed. "As much as I hate to admit it, Rachel, my friend, but the truth is that sometimes we just have to let go and let life happen."

Chapter Twenty-Six

Rachel looked at John and said, "I think the beach has done something to Susan." The two sat on the floor of the den and sorted through Ben's baby clothes. John refused to get rid of them when he moved to DC. Rachel realized that he still struggled in his efforts to let go of anything that connected him to his dead son and daughter-in-law.

When Carrie called earlier in the week and announced that her sonogram showed that her baby was a boy, Rachel mentioned to John that the boxes marked "Ben's baby things" might find a new home.

Even as they sat on the floor, surrounded by a mountain of tiny "baby things," she couldn't believe her husband agreed. As he picked up one of the miniature t-shirts and held it to his nose to sniff the baby powder that still lingered in its folds, he smiled. Then he looked at Rachel. "What did you mean when you said something has changed about Susan?"

"I think the salt air has done something to her brain. She seems to have realized finally that she can't control everybody and everything around her."

"That would take more than salt air. That would take a miracle," John laughed. "But what makes you think the impossible has happened?"

Rachel picked up a pair of blue booties. "How about these?"

"Sure. In fact, I think there are at least six pair just like those. Put them all in the bag. No. Maybe save one pair."

Rachel tossed all but one pair of booties in the bag and then inched closer to John. He looked at his wife, saw her troubled eyes

Leigh Somerville

and dropped a package of unopened cloth diapers in the bag so he could give her his undivided attention.

"Tell me, Rachel. Tell it to me straight. But take your time. I'm not going anywhere."

For the second time that morning, Rachel recounted the Felicia story. She added some of the details she left out during her phone conversation with Susan. She wanted John to hear more about Belle's reaction. She knew his gratitude for the ways in which she cared for Ben would greatly sway his decision about their next step.

Her suspicion proved correct. John jumped to his feet and pulled Rachel with him as soon as she reached the part of the story when Belle left the kitchen to tell Ricky they needed to find another place to live.

"What are you doing?"

"We need to get ourselves downstairs and talk them out of moving before it's too late," John shouted. "Another move would be devastating for little Mary, not to mention what it would do to Ricky's sobriety. Right now the Felicia story is a secret on this street. At least, I hope it is. But if they move and people ask why and they find out the real reason, the shame will push Ricky over the edge."

John spoke from experience. He remembered his wife's struggle with alcoholism and how ill-equipped she was to deal with life's little challenges as the disease progressed. "Sometimes, it's the broken shoelaces that make people take another drink," he remembered someone told him. He knew Felicia—and Ricky's embarrassment over his mistake—would be much more dangerous than a broken shoelace.

"You're a good man, John Turner. This is why I married you."

"Wait a minute. I didn't even ask you what you want to do. That's not a very good husband. How do you feel?"

"I agree with you. I want them here. I can't imagine how I could possibly be able to enjoy our new life at the beach if I had to worry

222

about them back out on the streets."

"And that's what makes you such a good woman, Rachel Turner. And that is why I married you."

Ben ran into the den in mid-kiss. "What's going on? Why are you two kissing again? And what's this baby stuff doing all over the floor?"

"Carrie and Horace's baby is going to be a boy."

"How do they know?" Ben asked.

Rachel and John looked at each other. Each waited for the other to answer the question.

"Why is all my stuff dumped on the floor?" Ben rushed on from one question to another.

Relieved that the hard question seemed to be forgotten, John said, "The baby is going to need some clothes, and you don't need them anymore since you've gotten to be such a big boy, so we thought maybe we'd ask you if we could give them to the new baby."

"And that's what you were kissing about? Gosh, big people sure find some weird reasons to kiss, Ralph."

Rachel laughed with relief. She and John suspected Ben might resist giving away anything from his past. His joke seemed to be a positive sign of progress as he continued to let go of the pain of his parents' death.

"This leg sure slows me down," Deejee said as she limped into the room. "Hope you don't mind me popping in like this, Rachel. I been missing you something fierce and when Ben invited me to join you for lunch, I couldn't resist."

"What a nice surprise," Rachel exclaimed. "You know you're always welcome here. In fact, now that you're retired, you can come more often."

"Aren't you forgetting a small detail?" Deejee laughed.

The move, Rachel remembered. Sometimes, the move didn't seem real. John patted her on the head. "You've got to forgive

Rachel, Deejee. She's getting old, you know. A little forgetful. In fact, I think she's forgotten that we need to step downstairs for a few minutes before we fix your lunch. Do you mind entertaining Ben while we do that? Shouldn't take long."

I hope not, Rachel thought. I sure do hope not.

* * *

When the phone rang later that night, Rachel reached across John to pick up the receiver.

"I can answer it," he said.

"No, it's for me. It's Susan."

"How do you know that?"

Rachel gave her husband "the look" he had learned meant "How could you ask such a silly question?" She picked up the receiver and said "Hello."

"I called your cellphone a million times, but you never answered it. Sorry to call so late. Are you in bed?"

"Yes, we're in bed, but you're fine. We're just reading."

John snorted.

"What was that noise?"

"John. I think he's coming down with a cold."

"I'm sorry to hear that, Rachel, especially with the closing coming up in a matter of days. Better get him to the doctor quick. But that's not why I called. I want to hear what's going on there. With Belle. Why didn't you call me instead of leaving me hanging all day?"

Rachel apologized. She used every excuse she could think of, starting with Ben's baby clothes inventory and ending with Deejee's visit. Finally, after she felt like she had apologized enough, she got to the story Susan called to hear. As always, she tried to keep her conversation with Susan simple. She knew her friend would embellish it enough on her own without help. Sometimes her embellishments were based in fact, and sometimes they weren't. Rachel knew she couldn't control which direction Susan took.

"We finally got them to agree to think about staying," Rachel said. "They're going to talk about it tonight and let me know tomorrow what they decide. I think Ricky wants to stay. Belle's the one who seems to feel like running."

"Where would she run? Where in the world does that girl think she's going?" Susan shrieked.

"I don't think she's figured out that part yet, but she seems pretty sure that Ricky needs to get out of the city and away from the connections to his drinking days."

"And she and Mary would go with him? What about her school?"

"She'd switch to a long distance program." Rachel waited for Susan's comeback. When no response came from the beach end of the conversation, she continued. "I don't know, Susan. Maybe it's not a bad idea. Listen, I promise I'll call you tomorrow as soon as I get an update. Good night. Love you."

She reached across John to hang up the receiver, and he pulled her down beside him. "What did she say?"

"Are you ready for this?"

"I don't know. Am I?"

"She said, and I quote, 'Well, I guess it's their lives,' end quote. I tell you, there's something going on down there at the beach."

John nuzzled her ear and pulled on the braid his wife had forgotten to unwind before bed. "How about we see if we can get something going on here. I've read enough for tonight. How about you?"

Rachel loosened her hair, tossed her book to the floor and turned out the light.

* * *

Rachel sat in front of her computer, her back to the door, when John entered the den the next morning. She didn't speak. He walked over to the desk and touched his wife's shoulder.

"Everything okay?"

"I got an email from George. You may want to sit down while I read it to you."

John walked across the room, sat on the sofa and waited.

"It's short," she said. "Dear Rachel." She cleared her throat. "I have found Phuong and her son, An, in the small village of Tam Ky. The search was simple. I found them where I saw them last. Imagine that. Some things in life really are simple. What may surprise you even more, however, is that I will not be coming back to the farm. Everything that matters to me most is here. I know you understand. Fondly, George"

Rachel turned and faced her husband.

"Do you understand?" John asked.

"Absolutely." Rachel shifted to the words on the screen. "There's more. In a postscript, he writes, 'I've been in touch with Simon and suggested that he ask Ricky if he wants to move his family out to the farm and take my place. He's a smart young man and needs some good country air to cure what ails him. It worked for me."

Rachel read the final line—silently, to herself—before she deleted the email.

"Worked like magic, Rachel," George wrote as one last good-bye. "Don't ever forget. I know I won't."

The End

Acknowledgments

Thanks to all the many readers of *It All Started with a Dog* and its sequel, *All Good Things.* Your love for Rachel and her friends provided the push necessary to create this final book in the trilogy.

You have waited a long time for the publication of *Black Dog Magic*, and I apologize. My travels down several paths took me off course, but truly, all good things come to those who wait.

Thank you for waiting.

Special thanks to Mike Simpson, publisher at Indigo Sea Press, for his patience as I traveled those other paths and for his professional and personal support. I admire him as he continues to do what so many others have let fall by the wayside—create the smell and feel of real books.

The reaction to the three books in the series that began with *It All Started with a Dog* prove one thing. We are all still hungry for a feel-good story and for the sense of community that Rachel and her world illustrates.

Without a doubt, a little black dog magic helps.

About the Author

Leigh Somerville is the author of *Long Time Coming: My Life and the Darryl Hunt Lesson, It All Started with a Dog* and *All Good Things*. She lives in Winston-Salem, NC, with her cat, Figaro, a very forgiving cat who doesn't seem to mind—at least, so far—that no cats play significant roles (or, for that matter, any roles) in the trilogy.

She lives in Winston-Salem, NC. Photo courtesy of Daniel Alvarez.

***Also from Leigh Somerville and
Indigo Sea Press:***

Ralph the dog is back, bringing with him the entire beautiful cast of characters from Leigh Somerville's inaugural novel *It All Started With a Dog*. Back is Dupont Circle neighbor Susan, downstairs tenants Belle and Mary, super-efficient legal assistant Georgia, George the aesthetic veteran, and a host of other memorable well-drawn individuals. Yet once again this wonderful continuation, *All Good Things*, is the story of young Ben Turner, his grandfather John and the love they feel for marvelous Rachel Springer. At 62, engaged to the man of her dreams, Rachel suddenly finds the idea of marriage to be absurd–until she makes the chance discovery of a secret bequest left to her by her grandmother.

"Leigh's books are somewhat reminiscent of Jan Karon's Mitford series in that we are given a marvelous set of characters we come to know and care about in short order. Where Leigh is surpassingly excellent, I think, is in the well-drawn themes she lures us readers into considering: the resilience of true love, second chances, changing culture and its burdens, and the price of commitment. As a huge fan of her work, I just had to find out if Rachel really made it to the altar."

–Laz Barnhill, author of Lacey *Took a Holiday* and *The Medicine People*

"If you're looking for a ripping good story about characters you can take to heart, *All Good Things* is it. At the core is Rachel, embracing a new life at age 62—marrying for the first time, opening her arms wide enough to take on a whole community of friends, complete with joys and tribulations, including hers. It's a fine tale well told, and that's about the best thing you can say about a book."

- Robert Inman, author of *Home Fires Burning* and *Dairy Queen Days*

"Leigh Somerville is a gifted writer with a flair for memorable characters and a keen insight into the human heart."

-Bill Milliken, author of *The Last Dropout* and *From the Rearview Mirror*

www.ingramcontent.com/pod-product-compliance
Lightning Source LLC
Chambersburg PA
CBHW060428180626
46817CB00007B/2711